THE INFINITE SUMMER

What Reviewers Say About Morgan Lee Miller's Work

All the Paths to You

"This book made me, a self-proclaimed hater of sports, care about sports. Even sporting events that were purely fictional. That in and of itself is impressive. ...My god, Kennedy and Quinn are such a cute couple, I love them!! I ship them so much it isn't even funny. Their chemistry is through the roof to be honest."—*Day Dreaming and Book Reading*

"*All the Paths to You* is the kind of romance that makes your heart ache in all the right places."—*Hsinju's Lit Log*

"This book had a lot of feel-good moments and I still have a big smile on my face. ...This was the feel-good and even a little inspirational book that I needed right now."—*Lez Review Books*

"I can strongly say that this is one of my new favourite books (and series) and is definitely a contender for my favourite book of the year so far. ...I'm so happy I had the chance to read it and I don't think I could ever recommend it enough!"—*Althea is Reading*

All the Worlds Between Us

"This book is really sweet and wholesome and also heartbreaking and uplifting. ...I would recommend this book to anyone looking for a cute contemporary."—*Tomes of Our Lives*

"[*All the Worlds Between Us*] deals with friendship, family, sexuality, self-realization, accepting yourself, the harsh reality of high school and the difference between getting to tell your own story and having your own story exposed. Each character plays a vital role...and tells the story of this book perfectly."—*Little Shell's Bookshelf*

"If you're looking for an easy, quick cute f|f read, you should give this a try. …This was a solid debut and I can't wait to see what else this author publishes in the future!"—*The Black Lit Queen*

"This book took me straight back to all of my gigantic teenage emotions and got right down to the heart of me. I'm not a swimmer and I wasn't out in high school, but I swear I was right there with Quinn as she navigated her life as a competitive athlete and a queer kid in high school. Experiencing love and betrayal and triumph through her story was bananas. Morgan Lee Miller, you ripped my heart right out with this brilliant book."—Melisa McCarthy, Librarian, Brooklyn Public Library

"I'm always up for fun books about cute girlfriends, and *All the Worlds Between Us* was certainly that: a super cute ex-friends to lovers book about a swimming champion and her ex-best-friend turned girlfriend. …*All the Worlds Between Us* is a great rom-com and definitely recommended for anyone who's a fan of romance."
—*Crowing About Books*

"[*All the Worlds Between Us*] has all the typical drama and typical characters you'd find in high school. It's a tough, yet wonderful journey and transformation. The writing is divine. …It's a complicated tale involving so much pain, fear, betrayal and humiliation. *All The Worlds Between Us* is a terrific tale of taking what you want."—*Amy's MM Romance Reviews*

"Morgan's novel reiterates the important fact which should be repeated over and over again that coming out should always be done on one's own terms, and how this isn't a thing that any other people, straight or queer, should decide."—*Beyond the Words*

"Finally, a sporty, tropey YA lesbian romance—I've honestly been dreaming about reading something like this for a very long time!"
—*Day Dreaming and Book Reading*

Hammers, Strings, and Beautiful Things

"There's more going on than first appears and I was impressed that Ms. Miller won me over with a well written book that deals with some more serious issues."—*C-Spot Reviews*

"*Hammers, Strings, and Beautiful Things* is an emotionally raw read with plenty of drama. The journey Reagan and Blair share is rough in places but there is a beauty that you won't want to miss out on."—*Lesbian Review*

Before. After. Always.

"Miller tackled the tough subject of grief in *Before. After. Always.* It didn't feel too painful reading, but all the emotions were there." —*Hsinju's Lit Log*

Visit us at www.boldstrokesbooks.com

By the Author

All the Worlds Between Us

Hammers, Strings, and Beautiful Things

All the Paths to You

Before. After. Always.

The Infinite Summer

THE INFINITE SUMMER

by
Morgan Lee Miller

2021

THE INFINITE SUMMER

ISBN 13: 978-1-63555-969-9

This Trade Paperback Original Is Published By
Bold Strokes Books, Inc.
P.O. Box 249
Valley Falls, NY 12185

First Edition: December 2021

CREDITS
EDITOR: BARBARA ANN WRIGHT
PRODUCTION DESIGN: SUSAN RAMUNDO
COVER DESIGN BY JEANINE HENNING

Acknowledgments

I have a soft spot for summer romances. There's just something magical about them that makes my heart so warm and happy. The first novel I wrote—by hand in a notebook…twice—was a young adult summer romance, although it was wildly dramatic. I was sixteen and wrote it during the peak of my obsession with "The OC" so angsty doesn't even begin to describe it. For obvious reasons, it will never be published.

When I retired that story in college, I decided to try again. I focused all my energy on my second unpublished novel: a summer romance about a musician falling for a pop star. I spent the next four summers pitching to literary agents, and all the rejection that followed sucked the fun out of writing. So I took a two-year writing break until it clicked that I could rewrite that story and make it queer. Even though the rewrite didn't include a summer romance, it morphed into *Hammers, Strings, and Beautiful Things*.

The Infinite Summer is about following your dreams until they're real, and I know the sixteen-year-old me, writing in my notebook late at night until my wrist cramped up, would be so proud to know that we would eventually publish a young adult summer romance, and it wouldn't have been possible without Rad, Sandy, and everyone else behind the scenes at BSB. Thank you for allowing me to write my summer romance and all my stories thus far. It's an honor to be part of Team BSB.

To my wonderful editor, Barbara Ann Wright, for being this story's biggest fan. Thank you for your kind words as well as all your hilarious comments during the editing process. I live for those comments now. Please keep them coming.

A special thank you to my BFF, Kris, the only person who I will pick up the phone for. Thank you for taking time during your lunch breaks to call me to instill words of wisdom, tough love, and pep talks when my anxiety started getting too much. You rock.

To Julie, Erica, and Sabrina for volunteering to beta read (and by that, I mean I adamantly persuaded them until they agreed to do it) and for always giving me honest feedback.

Researching space and the theory of time really sparks an existential crisis, so a special thank you to Julie, who helped me through that and was gracious enough to let me share everything I read online. I thoroughly enjoyed our deep talks about the meaning of life, alternate universes, and all the YouTube videos we watched about the block universe theory. I'm glad I had someone to nerd out with while writing this story.

And last but not least, an infinite thank you to the readers. Your support means everything, and I look forward to the day I can tell you in person how much you mean to me.

Dedication

They know who they are.

CHAPTER ONE

"They lost my telescope! I can't believe they lost my telescope."

The baggage claim carousel spun around luggage of all sizes from the next flight. Everyone from my Hartford flight had collected their luggage and had already carried on their way as I remained in the same spot with one bag down. One very important bag down.

"What? Honey, slow down. What's going on?" my mom said on the other end of the phone, significantly calmer than I was, but then again, she hadn't spent most of her graduation money on an awesome, portable telescope that was now lost somewhere between Hartford and Charleston.

"The airline lost my luggage, the one with my telescope. How do you lose a whole telescope?"

Anger boiled in me as I imagined my second suitcase chilling all by itself. I had watched the man behind the desk load my two suitcases on the conveyor belt, one after the other, at the Hartford airport. How did only one of them get lost? The most important one with the most expensive thing?

"My summer would start this way," I said and plopped in a seat.

"Remi, take a deep breath. Things get lost all the time," Mom said in a soothing voice. She was always my voice of reason when I panicked. "Go to the booth and file a missing luggage claim."

This had been my first solo flight. I barely had any idea how to navigate an airport, let alone file a missing luggage claim. I was lucky that I'd figured out my layover without missing my flight.

"Why did I come down here again?" I asked as I got up and followed signs to whatever booth my mom was talking about.

"To reconcile with your father." I rolled my eyes at how she said, "your father." How she said it then wasn't as harsh as all the other times, probably because she knew I was in crisis mode. They'd both had made it apparent that they didn't like each other. Fine. Understandable. But now wasn't the time. I'd lost my telescope, my baby, the thing I'd spent all my graduation money on and part of my savings for. There wasn't time for bitterness. Almost as if she caught herself, her voice softened when she continued. "Remi, open mind, remember? You're lucky that you have a father and one who wants to spend time with you."

I guess Mom was right. I was grateful for those things. I just wasn't grateful for everything that had come between our family over the last four years. A divorce that had turned ugly and greedy. I went from being both of their daughters to their messenger, and now, Dad had told me that if I didn't visit him for the summer, he wouldn't be paying anything toward college.

My dad was basically extorting me.

He'd told me this two weeks before I'd graduated high school, after I'd already decided on my out-of-state school, and the scholarship deadlines had already passed. Now, he'd made me choose between spending my last summer at home with my best friend Brie or in a city that I'd never been to with his super rich and super famous new wife that he'd married eight months after the divorce.

He knew how much college meant to me, he knew how excited I was for getting into my dream school, MIT, but I couldn't even enjoy all of that because my life and my dreams had become part of his divorce chess game, one last "fuck you" to my mom. He'd aimed the knife at her, but instead, it'd hit me.

It was icing on the cake that my summer of acquiescence started with one of my suitcases missing, the one that held my escape from all of this: my telescope. At least with it, I could leave the divorce and the anger on Earth and disappear into the sky. Just for a moment. One of many much-needed moments I knew I would need this summer.

Once I hung up with my mom and filed my first ever missing luggage claim, I wheeled my lone suitcase outside through the automatic doors to the arrivals area and halted in my tracks. It was the first time I'd met the thick, South Carolina humidity, and it was jarring, like an invisible wet flannel blanket draped from the sky. Not even a minute in, the humidity liquified into beads of sweat along my hairline and the back of my neck.

Did I land in hell?

I pulled my phone back out and saw I already had a text from my dad. When I slid open the message, my fingers left a trail of sweat on the screen: *Got stuck on a work call, but Serena has offered to pick you up. Will see you when you get home. Excited to see you! Love, Dad.*

I laughed because it was no shock to me that he wouldn't be able to pick me up. We hadn't made time for each other in the last year since his wedding, so what was another hour of waiting?

A white Range Rover pulled around the row of idling taxis and cars, then parked right in front of me. When the driver's door opened, a head of blond hair and elegance stepped out. Even with the square black Prada glasses hiding half of her face, I knew the woman in white jeans, a black tank top, and black wedge sandals. Serena DeLuca, darling of the Food Network. She'd started out on a reality show that followed a catering company and the high-profile events they cooked for, like the Met Gala and the Oscars, and the show had won a Daytime Emmy. Then she became the star judge on *Home Kitchen Masters*, where amateur chefs competed for a cash prize, and her newest show, *Chef Queens*, was on Hulu, where she traveled all over the world and met successful female chefs. Brie was obsessed with the show, and part of me really hated that.

On top of her TV appearances, she owned two high-end Italian restaurants in Manhattan and LA, both with Michelin-star status. And somehow, she was my stepmother.

I hadn't met her yet. While she and my dad had dated, I was too pissed off to meet her, and the few times I'd made it to Brooklyn to visit my dad, she'd been away filming in different African countries for season two of *Chef Queens*. The year before, they'd eloped in the Amalfi Coast in Italy, and a huge part of me was relieved that I wasn't expected to fake a smile at my dad's wedding.

"Is that Remi?" She said it in a way that showed she already knew the answer was yes. Her smile was wide and showcased pearly white teeth that she'd probably invested a lot of money in. "What a looker you are! Oh my God, it's so nice to meet you."

She opened her arms for a hug and took me in. She smelled like money, and the perfume wafting off her was probably worth more than my whole life.

"Hi, Serena. It's nice to meet you too," I said to be nice and respectful, not because I genuinely meant it.

As much as my dad had hurt me over the last four years since he and Mom had told me that they were separating, I still wanted to reconcile with him, and what came with that was learning to move on and accept his new wife. It wasn't really anything against her. Any woman he'd dated, then married, eight months after the divorce would have resulted in me having some sort of grudge against them. I didn't want to feel that way about someone I didn't know anything about, so I tried very hard to force out the pleasantries.

"How was your flight?" she asked while she took my suitcase and popped it in the back.

"It was fine," I said, biting back the fresh anger over my lost luggage. I knew Dad would ask the same question, and he would understand how upset I was when I told them the airline lost my telescope. That was one thing we still had in common: love for the stars. Nothing would take away Dad's love for space. He was the one who'd gotten me into it. He was the reason why I'd wanted to go to MIT, one of the best schools for aerospace engineering that would prepare me to go to space someday.

That was why it hurt a little more that he'd used my tuition against me.

But the summer needed to start with baby steps that would hopefully heal our broken relationship. I told myself I couldn't focus on the large cracks that had wedged us apart, like the divorce or the tuition. I needed to focus on the things that bonded us together, like telescopes and the stars. Honestly, I just really wanted my best friend back. Constantly running through the list of everything he did wrong was so draining and exhausting, I wanted it to be over. Swallowing my pride and the list of all of wrongs was like trying to swallow a watermelon, but it needed to happen. Maybe over the summer, that watermelon would turn into a seed. But the start of forgiving him started with me, and I couldn't start until I knew part of Old Dad was still in him.

"I bet you're hungry," Serena said. "Let's head back so you can get settled in, see your dad, and get some food in you."

I forced a smile. "That sounds great."

I'd never been to Gaslight Shores, South Carolina, but I'd seen countless pictures online. It was a small town on one of South Carolina's many sea islands that boomed during the summer. When we crossed over the bridge, a wooden sign with a palmetto hanging over a gaslit streetlamp read, "Welcome to Gaslight Shores. Incorporated 1936." It was roughly forty minutes outside of Charleston, but the small resort town mimicked the charm of the city. Once we drove through the low country, west end of the island, it became increasingly populated. Pastel-colored colonial, Georgian, and federal architecture trailed down Main Street, which pooled into the famous boardwalk adorned with a Ferris wheel at the end.

With that quick driving tour, the town piqued my interest. Serena told me that it was known as the Montauk of the South. I'd never been to Montauk either, but even with that reputation, an image popped into my head of a quaint, ritzy seaside town, and the actual sights of downtown Gaslight Shores lived up to it. A beautiful and lively oceanfront town that I was sure provided a beguiling backdrop for a quintessential summer. If only the circumstances were a little different, I'm sure I would have been open to seeing all of its beauty and not just the beauty that was apparent, like the buildings, palm trees, ocean glimmering in the sun, and the gas lamps that lined the boardwalk.

After the downtown tour, Serena drove to the southern part of the island, much quieter than the eastern part where the boardwalk and ocean were. Once we got off the main road, we turned onto a quiet one hidden under a boulevard of live oak trees dripping with Spanish moss, reflecting the image in my head ever since I'd agreed to this egregious plan. About a mile in, we approached a wrought iron gate that had a keypad on the left. Serena typed in a code, and the doors slowly opened.

I stopped my mouth from falling open, but in my head, I couldn't believe I was about to spend my summer in a gated community.

The live oaks continued to line the road that weaved around houses that grew larger the farther into the community we drove. The trees dispersed on the right, and bright green grass popped out of nowhere, an idyllic golf course in the midst of the surrounding marsh. A yellow crossing sign warned us on the right, and about a half mile later, we stopped for two carts full of middle-aged white men in polos. They waved, and so did Serena, and once they'd made it safely to the other side, we continued.

As gorgeous as the community was, I felt so out of place, and I wondered how Dad felt in it. We were middle-class and lived in a nice, comfortable, modest home outside of New Haven, Connecticut. Dad loved backyard barbeques and would find any excuse to grill out back. One time in the winter, it was surprisingly warm outside, and what did Dad do? He grilled steaks for us. He loved finding garage sales around our town, and if one was particularly good, he'd come home first to tell Mom so they could go together.

Somewhere in between those days and now, my dad had morphed into a guy I didn't recognize. A guy who married a woman twelve years younger than him, who lived in a rowhouse in the Upper West Side three out of the four seasons, and then traveled to his mansion in a gated community during the summers. Nothing about the Palms, its wrought iron gate, and its enormous golf course was Dad, and though the community's beauty was apparent and right in your face, it wasn't strong enough to prevent me from feeling more of my dad slip further away into his new life.

Serena made a left onto Palmetto Bluffs Way, where the richest people in the development seemed to live. The houses doubled in size. In the back of a cul-de-sac, Serena pulled into the half-circle driveway, and one look at the house I'd be staying in literally had my mouth parting in awe.

Serena's house looked like it belonged to a famous chef with three TV shows and two Michelin-star restaurants. The house—more like estate—had three, two-story columns greeting us from in front of a brick patio with a porch swing dangling on the left side. To the right of the house stood a detached, three-car garage with three windows above it, and I wondered if there was an apartment on the second level.

Inside the open garage doors, a golf cart was plugged into the wall next to a dark blue Jaguar coupe convertible and a dark gray Aston Martin Vantage convertible. My mouth fell again. A freaking Aston Martin. It had been my dad's dream car ever since he was a little kid because James Bond drove one. He and Mom had fantasized about what they would do when they retired and how they would spend their money, and he'd hoped to have enough for an Aston Martin one day.

Turns out, he'd finally gotten it.

"Holy hell," I muttered as I opened my door. I was reacquainted with the thick air and a cacophony of hums and chirps from the woods to the left. And then a massive brown thing the size of a cockroach flew right in front of me. I shrieked and swatted my arms everywhere. Serena chuckled. When the flying cockroach was out of sight, a potent shudder snaked down my spine.

"Aw, you had a little palmetto bug saying hello to you," Serena said.

"A what? And that wasn't little. That was a flying cockroach."

She tilted her head and looked at me sympathetically. "Honey, in the south, cockroaches fly. The cicadas make that loud sound all day. Also, watch out for the gators."

Suddenly, my disgust for the flying cockroach disappeared, and fear took over. "Gators?"

There was no way I'd survive this summer in one piece.

"There's my favorite daughter," Dad said, walking out of the double front doors on the other side of the columns, his arms open wide.

He'd always said this to me growing up. When I was a kid, I'd always laughed because I was his only child. Now it felt like a slap in the face, knowing everything he'd done in the last four years to contradict this statement. It felt like I was anything but his favorite daughter.

He scooped me up for a hug, and as bitter as I was that I was in an inferno with flying cockroaches and ferocious gators lurking in the swamps instead of being at home—with the daddy longlegs as the scariest bug in the state—I hugged him back. Starting the summer refusing to hug my dad did no one any favors, and I really had missed him: the dad from my childhood. Not the petty, divorced one with the Aston Martin.

"Hi, Dad," I said and swallowed my grudge, trying to sound happy.

"How was the flight?"

I grunted. "Awful. The airlines lost my telescope."

"They what?" Serena said.

"They lost my other suitcase, the one with my new telescope in it. I filed a claim, but I'm still pissed."

He patted my shoulder. "Oh geez, I'm so sorry, kiddo. That's not a good way to start the summer, huh?"

Kiddo. I hadn't heard him call me that since pre-divorce. I wasn't sure if I liked it or hated it, but I went along with it.

"No, it's not. I was really looking forward to using it down here."

"I'm sure it will turn up. Give it a day or so, and if they haven't reached out by then, we'll call, all right? In the meantime, Serena and I have a few things for you that might cheer you up. Want to see them?"

"Sure. Anything to get my mind off my telescope."

"Follow me."

Dad smiled the same smile I remembered him flashing whenever I was feeling down, and he would then surprise me with a trip to Dairy Queen or pizza. With this new Dad living a lavish style, I expected the Dairy Queen and local pizza to morph into something beyond my comprehension.

Dad went inside the garage and squeezed between the golf cart and the Aston Martin.

"Nice Aston Martin," I said flatly.

He perked up from the back of the garage, a smile wide on his face, as if he didn't hear my sarcasm. "Isn't she beautiful?"

"It was a little anniversary gift," Serena said as she stood next to me.

A little anniversary gift?

Serena worked hard for her money, she'd earned it, and she had a right to spend it as she pleased. But while Dad seemed to benefit from the divorce, Mom had to refurnish half the house to make up for the items Dad had taken when they'd split the assets, she had to take out a second mortgage, and already had to plan to retire later than she could have to make sure she could recuperate the money she'd lost from assembling her life back together post-divorce. I couldn't help but be so mad that Dad seemed to have gained everything from every perspective, while Mom hadn't gained anything except more bills.

Dad rolled out a teal bike from the garage, kicked the foot stand, and showcased it with his hands like the models on *The Price is Right*.

"Bikes are popular down here," he said. "Bike paths on the roads, lots of trails. The town is pretty small, so it's the preferred mode of transportation. We figured you would need one so you can go out and do your own things without having to worry about parking. It can get pretty hectic near the boardwalk."

"You mean, I can't have the car?" I joked.

He laughed. "Sorry, hon. But hey, let's take a drive around town sometime, all right?"

"That sounds good," I said and scoped out the bike. It actually was really nice, and a part of me was relieved I had my own mode of transportation that wasn't an exorbitantly expensive car. Too much room for error that I wasn't comfortable with. The bike was perfect, and after seeing the scenery of the town, I already knew I'd get some good rides in.

"Thank you both. I really like it," I said and meant it.

"Do you?" Serena asked with clasped hands in front of her chest.

"I rode my bike to school when it was nice out. I love it. Thank you."

Dad squeezed Serena's shoulder. "See? I told you she would love it. Now, want to see the other surprise?"

He led me to a door off to the left side of the garage and upstairs. He opened another door and said they'd recently finished the studio apartment specifically for me. The new paint and wood still smelled fresh. I had my own queen-size bed, a couch, and a smart TV, my own bathroom, and even a little kitchenette with a full-size fridge, sink, microwave, and toaster oven. There was even a framed poster of a Europa illustration above the bed. It was such a dad move, and it made me smile.

"Wow, this is so cool," I said as I wandered around and took in every nook and cranny. "This is amazing."

"Really? You like it?" Serena said.

I laughed at how she seemed shocked. The apartment was amazing, modern, probably the size of a real apartment that would be at least five grand in Manhattan. "I mean, yeah. I was expecting a spare bedroom."

"Oh no, honey. You're eighteen and deserve your own space, but the rest of the house is yours too, so no need to stay in here the whole time. You're welcome in the main house whenever. The key is right here." She showed off two silver keys on the kitchenette counters. "One for this apartment, and one for the house."

"Thank you both. Really."

"You hungry, kiddo?" Dad asked. "We have plenty of food in the kitchen waiting for you."

"And Laura just made a new batch of sweet tea if you're thirsty," Serena added.

I raised an eyebrow. "Laura?"

"The housekeeper. She's lovely. Stocked up the fridge, freezer, and pantry for you. Your dad has been eyeing the junk food. I'd get to it before he does."

Of course they had a housekeeper, and of course she was brought up so casually, as if everyone had one.

Inside the main house was exactly what I'd imagined: natural light streaming from the floor-to-ceiling windows, the smell of organic cleaner and wood. A chandelier hung in the two-story foyer, and the sun reflecting off the crystal made it glimmer rainbows against the white walls. She had a chef's kitchen the size of my garage apartment, and the backyard was beautiful, with a pool and a little in-ground hot tub. Tucked in the back was a view of the marshy river.

I pulled out my phone to text Brie an update: *Omg this house.*

Brie was a TV junkie and loved *Home Kitchen Masters*, claiming it had taught her how to cook, and *Chef Queens* made it her mission to go to India after college to taste all the delicious food she'd learned about from an episode of the first season. Needless to say, she was a big Serena DeLuca fan and was thrilled that not only was she my stepmother, but I got to live in her house and eat her food for free.

Brie: *OMG give me a tour please.*

Me: *Her kitchen is everything you would expect it to be.*

Brie: *Has she cooked you food yet? You know how lucky you are to eat her food? Most people have to pay like 40 a plate.*

Me: *No, but I'm drinking sweet tea that her housekeeper made. Does that count?*

"I was thinking of cooking a big meal tomorrow," Serena said, leaning onto the kitchen island across from where I sat trying my first real sweet tea. After dealing with the heat for only a few minutes, the temperature was bad enough for me to devour the tea in a few gulps. Serena filled my second glass and slid it over like a bartender. "Is that okay? Theo is coming back with some sandwiches from the shop."

"The shop?"

"Serena opened a new restaurant a few years ago," Dad said proudly, the way he used to brag about Mom to family or friends. "It's right on the boardwalk. Actually, speaking of which, Serena has been nice enough to offer you a job for some summer spending money."

"Only if you want to," Serena added.

"No. She's eighteen, a high school grad. She's old enough to start working for her own money."

He was acting like I was throwing a fit the second the topic was brought up. I'd been working all throughout high school. Summer jobs were nothing new to me, and he was acting like I was the laziest kid. It made my blood start to boil again when I got an unsolicited lecture about earning my own money, yet he benefited from his wife's culinary empire. Not once had I expected my parents to buy me things. I had no idea where his tone even came from.

"I worked at the science museum for the last three years," I said. "I know how money works. That's how I bought my telescope." I suppressed the eye roll and smiled at Serena. "But yes, it sounds good, Serena. Thank you."

A few minutes later, I heard the front doors open, and someone whistling made their way down the hallways and into the kitchen with two bags. I assumed it was Serena's son. He had the same light brown eyes, and his sandy blond hair was a few shades darker than hers but probably because she dyed. He wore coral chino shorts, Sperrys, and a light blue, short-sleeved oxford button-down that hugged his toned torso, not too built, but it was apparent that he worked out regularly. He looked like he could have been on the cover of Southern Frat Magazine, but with Serena DeLuca as his mom, I expected nothing less.

"You must be my new sis," he said as he placed the bags on the island.

"Remi, this is Theo," Serena said and slung an arm around his shoulder. He looked a few years older than me, fresh out of college. Definitely in his early twenties. "My one and only kid. Just like you, he's staying with me for the summer, but he's upstairs. Theo, this is Remi."

He opened one of the bags and slid me a sandwich wrapped in purple and yellow-checkered paper. "Yeah, consider yourself lucky that you got that apartment."

"Theo," Serena said.

He only said one sentence, and it was enough to validate the strange presence I'd felt him bring into the kitchen. He had a wide smirk that told me I couldn't trust him, and how he dressed made me wonder if he'd ever had to work for anything in his life. I was grateful for that apartment above the garage. I hoped that would limit my time around him.

The sandwich was fried popcorn chicken on toasted French bread, topped with shredded lettuce, white onion, mayo, mustard, and pickles. It looked and smelled amazing. When I took a bite, I wasn't disappointed. I hadn't had anything except an airport muffin, and the sandwich hit the spot.

"Theo, Remi agreed to work at Envie this summer," Serena said. "I'm hoping you can take her under your wing?"

I lowered my sandwich, guessing it was wishful thinking that we could limit our interactions, and if I had to work with him, I hoped he was just cranky and not actually an asshole like how his presence screamed.

He smiled at me. "Sure, wanna start Monday?"

"Sounds good to me."

"Ten a.m. sharp. Don't disappoint your boss." He cackled.

I cringed. There was something off about him I couldn't pinpoint. I told myself to stop judging based on all the ridiculous materialistic things that surrounded me.

After I spent the rest of the afternoon unpacking and chilling after a chaotic first half of the day, Dad texted me to come to the backyard in the evening. I decided to cling to the one thing that we'd still held on to despite all the things that had changed in the last four years: our love for space. Even though I was mad at him for a multitude of reasons, I was still grateful for the stars. As long as they colored the night sky, my dad and I would always share something.

A scattering of clouds prevented many stars from showing, but the ones that weren't covered by clouds were bold, bright, and plentiful, more so than back home, where the lights of New Haven dimmed them, even in the suburbs.

"Stars are nice here, huh?" Dad said. He stood on the porch with a craft beer bottle in one hand and a can of Sprite in the other. The fact that he still remembered my favorite soda made something settle in my chest.

"Yeah, they are," I said and took a sip.

After a few silent moments, I noticed the awkwardness pull up next to us. I didn't know what to talk about. Ever since Mom and Dad had separated the summer after eighth grade, we'd lost more topics as each year progressed. He had always been the cool parent, the person I'd turned to when Mom was in a bad mood. He would hide in the basement with me and play PlayStation, or we would take a walk in the park, get ice cream, or lie out in the backyard and look through his telescope. He hardly ever got mad; he was never one to hold a grudge or hate anyone. He was my favorite person and my best friend.

But then he got his new CFO job at a new startup company in Manhattan, and something about him just changed. I overheard Mom talking to her sister one night, and Mom said she swore it was his younger and single colleagues influencing him, the "boys' club mindset of Wall Street," as she said. Apparently, Mom had been feeling their relationship grow further apart for a few years. I didn't hear more of the conversation because I thought ignorance was bliss. They'd separated the summer before my freshman year, he'd started dating Serena eight months later, and the divorce wasn't finalized until the fall of my sophomore year. By then, Dad had turned into a selfish vulture when it came to splitting the assets and had even tried to take the house from Mom. She'd ended up keeping the house, had paid him half the price, and then had to take out another mortgage. Then Dad had cherry-picked everything he wanted like an entitled brat at one of his beloved garage sales, wanting things that he'd never even used before but hey, why not put up a fight for the run-down living room chair because he could?

I think he spent so much time being petty and bitter against my mom because she'd initiated the divorce he didn't want. In return, like a typical guy, he didn't think how his antics would deeply strain our relationship.

Now we only had stars to talk about, and even though part of me would always be grateful for that, I had to get to know my dad all over again. That was what the summer was about, and I had to leave Gaslight Shores with something more than the stars to share with him, or I had no idea if I'd ever get our relationship back.

"Serena has a boat," he said, breaking the silence. "Sometime this summer, after the airline finds your telescope, we should take it out at night and stargaze there. Then you'll really see the sky. I've always wanted to do that. South Carolina has some pretty good stargazing spots, and we should take advantage of it."

Of course Serena had a boat. It was another thing Dad had always wanted but never had. Any time the three of us went to New Haven, we'd walk around Pardee Seawall Park, following the nineteenth century summer cottages that made up the Morris Cove neighborhood on one side of the street and New Haven Harbor on the other. Mom would admire the charm of the cottages and said if she ever won the lottery, she would love to buy one overlooking the water. Dad had added to that, saying he would get the boat he'd always wanted and enjoy a day on the water. Then I'd chimed in with my fantasy. While Mom and Dad spent their retired life at their Morris Cove cottage, I'd fly in to visit them from my training at the Johnson Space Center in Houston, and the three of us would sit on the front porch that overlooked the harbor. Or another fantasy: I'd be on the International Space Station, looking down at Earth and searching for North America so I could "see" my parents while wondering what they were doing in their waterfront home.

Kids had all these different ideas of what their lives would be when they were older, and now that I was older with my parents' divorce weighing on me like a rock, I suddenly realized how stupid and naive I was to think that my parents' second home in Morris Cove would ever be my life—that it would ever be *our* life. It made me wonder what other stupid fantasies I had that wouldn't ever come true. Like going to space. Was naivety controlling my future? I wouldn't know until it was too late.

"What do you say?" Dad said. "A night boat excursion? I bet out there, it feels as close as you get on Earth to being in outer space."

"Did you bring the Celestron down here?" I asked. "We could bring it out. It would be better than my little portable one."

Dad's Celestron telescope was the very one that introduced me to space and the stars and made me fall in love. It had sat in our living room, pointing out the window. During summer nights, Dad would hoist it out to the backyard to enjoy the warmer weather. He was a hobbyist and then shared his love with me when I was old enough to appreciate what I saw on the other end. We'd spent so many nights in the backyard gazing through it. It was even better when I was learning about the solar system, and I'd seen the planets, a much better perspective than my science textbook. Dad teaching me about our solar system was a million times more interesting than how Mrs. Yates taught it, and I remembered bragging to my classmates about how I'd actually seen Jupiter in my backyard.

For many kids, a swing set or treehouse was the coolest part of their backyard, but I didn't have any of those. I did, however, have Dad's Celestron, and I felt so cool and honored when he shared his favorite toy with me. But on Splitting the Assets Day, Dad had come over to the house with his best friend, who had a hitch on his Jeep, and Dad and his friend had loaded all the things he'd "won" in the asset negotiation. One of the things was the Celestron, ultimately because it was his. As I'd watched him take it out of the living room, making it so much emptier, I couldn't help but wonder how the hell he would use the telescope in the city. It was as if Dad had forgotten the fact that a telescope in Brooklyn got as much use as a winter coat in Hawaii.

His smile thinned, and he pulled another drink. "No, it's not here."

"What? Why have it in New York when you could actually see something here?"

"It's not in New York. I don't have it anymore."

I lowered my Sprite. "Wait. What?"

"I'm sorry, kiddo. There was no point having it in the city."

My jaw clenched. I couldn't believe it. If the sticky outside temperature wasn't already warming up my body, anger would have taken care of it. After all the back and forth, all the drama that had ensued on Splitting the Assets Day, he didn't even have it anymore? Why put up such a fuss to bring it to the maroon-colored sky of Brooklyn only to get rid of it?

"Then why insist on having it in the first place?"

He chuckled. "Remi, it was my telescope. Surely, I wasn't going to leave it behind—"

"You had to have known that it wouldn't have gotten any use in the city. I could have used it. And I *would have* used it—"

"I know you loved that telescope, but it was something I bought. When you're an adult and you start making your own money, you'll understand. Like the telescope you got yourself."

"If I had no use for my telescope and knew someone else loved it as much as I did and would use it almost every day, I would rather give it to them than just throw it out and waste it."

"I didn't throw it out. I sold it."

"You...you sold it?" I slammed my empty can on the wicker table next to me.

"Remi, it was an expensive telescope. I'm entitled to take the things that I purchased."

I'm entitled to take the things that I purchased, the same exact line he'd used on Mom on Splitting the Assets Day. A perfect opening to the elephant in the room.

"Yeah, well, when you take things that you never planned on using, like the living room armchair, the basement coffee table, the dining room china, it's hard to tell what's yours and what you're using to hurt someone."

"Okay, I don't know what your mother told you—"

"She didn't tell me anything. I could hear you two bickering like toddlers from my room."

It was never Mom or Dad, anymore. It was always "your mother" or "your father," said with a bitter inflection, like they needed to clearly draw the line where one family ended and the new family started. It was me and Dad, and then me and Mom. Two sides. Not one entity. And every time they had to acknowledge each other's existence, they made sure that the bitter taste remained.

Honestly, they were better off not even referring to each other at all.

I grabbed my Sprite and got up. "I'm going to bed."

"Remi, stop."

But I didn't listen. As Serena came out with mosquito spray, I marched through the mansion and into my garage apartment. I vented to Brie in texts and told myself I would never tell Mom what I found out about the telescope, the boat, or the Aston Martin.

Somehow, just like that, the stars weren't ours anymore. If Dad couldn't share his telescope with me, I definitely wouldn't share mine. He might have gotten so many things from the divorce, but the stars were going to be all mine, and they would be the only things guiding me through this forced summer.

CHAPTER TWO

There was a white paper bag sitting on the kitchen table Monday morning. When Dad saw me standing in the entryway, his smile widened.

"Hey, kiddo. How did you sleep? Everything comfy over there?"

It was two days after our telescope argument. I'd spent the day before riding my bike around the neighborhood to marvel at all the sumptuous mansions, and then surviving a home-cooked dinner with Dad, Serena, and Theo. I was still too upset to force myself to be around Dad longer than an hour, and I'd spent the rest of the night alternating between reading the first two chapters of *A Brief History of Time* by Stephen Hawking and watching random TikTok videos.

"Yeah, everything is fine," I said, skeptical of his extra perky voice. It sounded like he was trying to drown out the awkward tension with chipperness.

Dad was never *that* perky.

"What's in the bag?" I said.

"A treat to start your first day on the job off right."

I furrowed my brows and looked inside. I smelled sugar and toasted coconut from the four doughnuts inside. The smell instantly took me back to being a kid, when Dad would buy us coconut doughnuts every Saturday from the bakery. It was always the best part of the weekend. It'd been so long, I'd forgotten that it was our thing, and the sweet scent helped untangle my morning crankiness.

"I haven't had one of these in a long time," I said, pulling one out and taking a seat.

I bit into it, and the toasted coconut flakes fell onto the plate. I closed my eyes and remembered how much I loved them.

Dad grabbed one for himself. "Neither have I. I've been really into bagels lately, and I never really considered myself a bagel guy."

"I guess that's what New York City does to a person."

He laughed. "I guess so." He took a bite. "Okay, coconut doughnuts are much better than everything bagels. Don't tell anyone."

"Your secret is safe with me as long as you don't tell anyone I won't even give bagels the chance to compete with doughnuts."

"I won't say anything."

Dad offered to drive me to the boardwalk, but I declined, not because I was still mad at him, but because I actually wanted to enjoy the bike ride. It was only five miles away, and I wanted the fresh summer morning air to fill up my lungs. There was something therapeutic about it, and when I locked my bike behind Envie, I smelled frying oil mixing with the briny air. I took a deep inhale of the wonderful smell of summer and stared at the expanse of the glimmering ocean, and something opened up in me too. I needed to give this town a chance. I needed to give Dad, Serena, and Theo a chance. Once I felt the ball of petulance in my chest loosen, I exhaled and went inside.

"It's my new stepsister," Theo said when I walked through the front door.

There was only one other person behind the assembly line counter, a boy who looked a little older than me but not old enough to be a college grad. Both of them wore purple T-shirts that said "Envie" in gold lettering with a neon green outline.

It wasn't even ten in the morning, and Theo had successfully made me cringe by referring to me, yet again, as his sister. We were far from there yet.

"Aren't you excited for all this bonding we're going to have this summer?" Theo asked as he slung an arm around me.

I peeled his heavy arm off my shoulder. "Sure."

"Cool. Well, I got you a shirt." He pulled a purple shirt from one of the counters underneath the cash register. "Back room is in the kitchen to the right. Pick a cubby, throw on the shirt, bathroom's back there, and come back out. We'll teach you how to make the best sammies on the boardwalk."

Did Theo have whatever Dad drank this morning? Or was it something about the ocean air that made everyone happy? It was probably the latter because the beautiful day and the smell of the salt and fried treats on the boardwalk did enough to fill me with a modicum of happiness. Maybe in the next few days, I'd adjust and become a morning person.

When I dropped my stuff in the back room and waved to the kitchen staff, Theo breezed through how to make one of the sandwiches. The menu was extensive, with every single kind of thing imaginable. For the protein, customers could choose roast beef, fried shrimp, fried fish, fried catfish, fried oysters, crab, fried chicken, skirt steak, hot sausage, and fried tofu. For the toppings: lettuce, tomato, raw onion, fried onion, pickles, sauteed peppers, bacon bits, coleslaw, jalapenos, avocado, fried egg, and french fries. Yes, french fries on a sandwich. I didn't understand, but Theo's eyes lit up when he showed me the fries as a possible topping. Maybe I was the one missing something. For the sauces: Cajun mayo, house Carolina BBQ sauce, remoulade, horseradish, chipotle sauce, lemon garlic butter, roast beef gravy, and herbed aioli.

"Whatever the customer wants, the customer gets," Theo said and then moved to the cash register. "You clock in on here. Follow the instructions. It's all self-explanatory. You can take lunch after the crowd dies down. Eat in the back or at one of the tables. Any questions?"

I thought for a moment. "No."

"Cool. You and Aaron will work with the kitchen to maintain the food. Make sure you fill the bins when there's a quarter left and put the older food on top. Don't wait until it's already empty. Lunch rush starts at eleven."

And then he disappeared into the back.

"Don't expect him to do much," the other guy, Aaron, said once I exhaled from all the information I'd gathered in five minutes.

"What do you mean?"

He rolled his dark brown eyes before leaning in. "He doesn't do anything," he said in a whisper. "Just likes to bark orders and chill in the back. Tracy says he has no idea what he's doing. She's always on his case."

"Tracy?"

"The executive manager. Our boss. She'll be in soon."

"Oh. Serena DeLuca isn't the boss?"

He laughed. "No. She's just the brand, the owner. Tracy reports to her. I've worked here since it opened two years ago, and I've only seen Serena DeLuca once. Seems sweet. But her son definitely didn't inherit it." He smiled. "But anyway, if you have any questions, feel free to ask me."

"Okay, thank you. I'm Remi, by the way."

He held out his hand covered in a plastic glove. "Aaron."

Aaron gave me a better rundown about how Envie worked and our duties. He was right; Theo occasionally popped out from the back room to check on the ingredients in their assembly line buckets, and if one was low, he told us to get it refilled, and then disappeared. Aaron said that Theo had this odd complex about low buckets. I made a mental note to have at least one empty bucket to watch Theo squirm. For my own entertainment.

The lunch rush started at eleven thirty and quickly progressed into a line that formed out the doors and onto the boardwalk. By that time, Tracy had arrived and had introduced herself to me before taking the initiative, herding hungry sunburned customers into a line that didn't disrupt the flow of the boardwalk.

We didn't catch a break until two o'clock, when the first lull of the day quieted the restaurant. By then, I'd made over fifty sandwiches, and my stomach was over the toasted coconut doughnuts and screamed for sustenance. All the ingredients I'd once thought were overwhelming made me eager to eat some.

"And now we eat," Aaron said with a smile, pulling out a French loaf and cutting it in half. He slid one half to me. "Fifty percent off for us."

He fixed up his sandwich and slid down the assembly line. I followed him. After making a variety of sandwiches for the last three and a half hours, I already knew what I wanted: fried chicken, lettuce, tomato, onion, peppers, pickles, and drizzled Cajun mayo and the chipotle sauce to finish it.

The sandwich was good and hit the spot, but I wouldn't necessarily wait in a line that extended out the front doors for it. It was like people waited to taste something made by Serena DeLuca rather than because they enjoyed the taste, like people who spent the hundred and fifty dollars for Ray Bans when the knock-off fifteen-dollar ones worked just fine.

"So," Aaron asked, leaning into the booth table. "How do you like it?"

I took another bite to gather up all my evidence. I went through every taste, mostly for dramatic effect, which worked because Aaron laughed, and he had a nice smile that I wanted to see more of. "It's good. It will satisfy my hunger, but I don't think I'd wait in that line for one."

Tracy had told us that the line had wrapped around the corner. For a sandwich. I would have packed my own sandwich if I was going to the beach or would have waited until at least one thirty to grab one. I couldn't think of any food that was worth that long of a wait while the prime sun beat down on me and with that damn humidity.

"Yeah, I know, it's a bit much, isn't it?" Aaron said with a laugh. "A huge difference from the Acadian."

"The Acadian?"

"Yeah. The other sandwich shop on the boardwalk. Right by the arcade and Sully's Fries. It's been here for years, decades actually. My family has been coming down here every summer since I was a kid, and we would always get Acadian po'boys. Now there's, like, this little restaurant rivalry going on between the Acadian and Envie, though it's not much of a rivalry."

"What do you mean?"

He shrugged. "I don't see a lot of people getting the Acadian now. They all come here. It's kind of sad, really. They remind me of summers here."

"If you love it so much, why work at Envie?"

He thought about that for a moment. "Good point, but Envie pays pretty well. I'm trying to save up to go to Europe with my buddies next summer after we graduate college, and working here... well...you get more than minimum wage, which makes sense because it's Serena DeLuca. I'm sure the Acadian would pay well if they had the means, but I don't think they do."

I thought about his words for a moment. Back home in New Haven, there was a pizza rivalry between Pepe's and Sally's. Mom, Dad, and I tried both restaurants plenty of times. Mom loved Pepe's, Dad loved Sally's, and I loved eating any kind of pizza. But the thing about the New Haven pizza rivalry was that it was friendly. Both businesses were doing fine. It wasn't much of a friendly rivalry when one was falling by the wayside.

"Which one do you like better?" I asked.

"Honestly?" he whispered and leaned in. "The Acadian is better. It's a true po'boy. Their signature sauce is amazing. So are their hush puppies. Envie is basically a fancy Subway with a famous name tacked on to it. Don't get me wrong, I like these sandwiches. I get why people love them but...I'm Team Acadian all the way. I just really need the money to travel, you know?"

"Y'all need to hurry up and refill the buckets," Theo said when he emerged from the back. He picked up an empty bucket and let it fall for dramatic effect, and the noise echoed throughout the dining room. I glanced over Aaron's shoulder at Theo, who was standing next to the assembly line and surveying the food with knitted eyebrows. "Sometime today?"

"He's such a dick," Aaron muttered after a quick eye roll.

The hardest part about the job was the lunch rush and dealing with Theo on his power trip. After that, it was smooth sailing until five when Aaron and I got to clock out right as the dinner rush started. We shared laughs and eyerolls whenever Theo would come out front and be a supercilious prick and then snickered harder when Tracy put Theo in his place and told him to do his job.

When I was free for the rest of the evening, I thought about going home to the weird tension with Dad and the weird tension with Serena that had less to do with her personally and more because I'd just met her. I wasn't in the mood to bond or socialize. I really wasn't a social person. I liked coming home from school, getting my homework out of the way so I could read, and getting lost in the universe through books. Brie called me a nerd and was occasionally able to lure me out of my bedroom and over to her house to hang out. We actually had plans this summer, ones that involved less reading about space and more hanging out and fully enjoying our last summer in our hometown. She was going to take me to my first party, I was going to taste beer for the first time, and ever since I came out as bi in the fall, Brie had her heart set on finding me a cute girl to make out with. I was so excited to have her as my wingwoman.

But then, Dad decided to pull this extortion stunt, I had to give up all of that, and I was still sad for all the things Brie and I had planned to do and all the things we wouldn't be able to accomplish.

I had no idea how I would survive the summer without any sort of friend. Part of me thought to try becoming friends with Aaron, but then I second-guessed myself. He was three years older than me and probably had a group of friends to hang out with if he'd been coming here since he was a kid. Plus, he was old enough to drink and probably couldn't be bothered to hang out with an eighteen-year-old. So instead of woman-ing up and trying to have a social life, I decided to go to the beach by myself.

I'd packed my summer read, *A Brief History of Time*, in my bookbag, already thinking about checking out the beach before I'd left in the morning. It was beautiful out. Only a few thin clouds were in the sky. It was hot but manageable. I found an empty spot on the sand and watched people play in the tide; some boogie boarded in the waves, others lay around and enjoyed the dying sun. There was a light blue shack about a block away with stacks of rainbow umbrellas next to it, and those same umbrellas lined the beach. Three guys my age stopped in front of me with boogie boards underneath their armpits, waiting for one of their friends to take off his shirt and sandals. One had shaggy brown hair that shone in the sun, and my eyes remained firm on him as he took off his shirt and tossed it away. All three were definitely cute enough to steal my attention. Then two girls walked through the sand to my right, talking to each other and looking amazing in bikinis. They had to have been in college, and they seized my attention from the boys. Both were brunettes, and over the last year of coming to terms with my sexuality, I'd also realized I loved brunettes. It didn't matter the gender.

It was a good thing I'd discovered my bisexuality a year ago because the three boys and two girls did a really good job of affirming it. The boys looked up as the college girls walked by with their hair blowing back from the soft wind. They seemed to have no idea that three boys and a lone girl with a Stephen Hawking book on her lap were checking them out.

I wished I was the type of girl to snag someone's attention. It probably would have helped if I'd ditched Stephen Hawking. That would be a good start.

❖

My third day at Envie, I caved and decided to be adventurous. Since I'd made so many sandwiches with french fries as a topping, I decided to add a handful to my skirt steak sandwich.

"What's the verdict?" Aaron asked, watching me as I tasted my creation.

"I might have been a hater of it at first," I said. "But it's not too bad. Steak is marinated perfectly, the gravy is flavorful, and the fries add a pleasantly odd taste."

I took another bite, and the gravy dripped down my hand while the fries pushed all the ingredients out through the bottom of the roll.

"I want to try the Acadian," I said.

Aaron widened his eyes. "Shh! You can't say stuff like that."

"Why? It's literally a sandwich."

"Theo is oddly invested in the restaurant rivalry. He makes snide comments at least once a day."

"I want to see what the fuss is about. I'm feeling adventurous today. Fries on this sandwich, and the next should be from the Acadian. How can I have a true Gaslight Shores experience without a say in this sandwich rivalry?"

"Okay but...just don't let Theo know. I made the mistake of telling him I used to go there all the time as a kid, and he hasn't stopped making fun of me."

I waved him off. "I'm not afraid of Theo."

"That's because he's your stepbrother."

I winced at the title. Nope, having a step anything was going to take more than a few days of getting used to. "I met him, like, five days ago. You know him more than I do. You want to come with me? Taste the nostalgia?"

Aaron seemed to weigh his options, and I hoped that he accepted because maybe then I was closer to developing some kind of friendship. "That does sound intriguing," he said. "But we can't wear these." He pinched his purple Envie shirt. "We need to be prepared for this. Bring a change of clothes tomorrow, and I'm down."

"You can tell me everything that's important for me to carefully consider my pick."

"Okay, but don't expect a similar menu. The Acadian has had the same menu since, like, they opened. They only have four options."

"Well, that's...underwhelming."

Aaron laughed. He had a nice laugh and a cute smile. "Probably why it's not competing well."

Something as simple as a risky adventure to the rival restaurant had me looking forward to the next day. It would pull me away from my summer reading and make me feel like I had a semblance of the exciting summer I'd thought I would have.

The next day, I made sure to shove a spare shirt in my bookbag, and Aaron showed off his change of clothes during our lunch break. We'd both packed a lunch so our stomachs didn't get overwhelmed by two sandwiches.

Once we clocked out at five, we changed, and I followed Aaron, taking a right down the boardwalk. We passed the giant blue Sully's sign at the corner of Main Street, and Aaron said Sully's was the place for the best fries in town. I believed him because the oil I'd been smelling since Monday permeated the air around the building, and anytime people with a cup or bucket of fries walked past, I could smell the oil, fried potatoes, and salt that had my stomach rumbling at ten a.m.

Right next door was the Acadian. A red, white, and blue striped awning hung above two windows that looked into the dining room. When we walked through the dark red front door, a bell jingled. A cool blast of air-conditioning welcomed us. I was surprised by how empty it was. When I'd left Envie, the line was at least ten people deep. Inside the Acadian, there was only one other couple.

A menu hung over the deserted assembly line, and like Aaron warned, there were only four options squeezed on to one menu, unlike Envie's, that spanned over three signs. The Acadian's four options were The Chicken, The Porky, The Shrimp, and The Original.

"Oh, crap, I'm so sorry," a startled voice said, and then a girl stepped out of the kitchen. What startled me was how pretty she was. Her brown eyes popped against her sun-kissed skin, and her brown hair was pulled back into a ponytail.

"Can I help you?" she asked with a bright white smile, and I noticed the cute freckles on her nose.

"I know what I want," Aaron said to me. "Do you?"

"No, what should I get?"

"Do you need help with the menu?" the girl asked. "Have you been here before?"

"This is her first time," Aaron said.

The girl smiled as she put plastic gloves on. Her face brightened. "Oh, really?"

Was the air-conditioning even on? Because it didn't feel like it. The Acadian became as overwhelming as Envie, and all it took was a beautiful girl to smile at me. How the hell did I need help with a menu with only four options?

"We've been here since 1948," the girl explained, a slight southern accent framing her words. "It's a family-run business passed through four generations. The man who opened this store had some of the very first po'boys in New Orleans in the twenties. Also, our Debris Sauce and our hush puppies are *everything*."

"Debris Sauce?"

"She's right," Aaron added. "It's amazing. Get extra. That's what I always do."

The girl smiled. "It's won tons of sauce competitions throughout the years," she said. "It's a secret family recipe. It's so secret that the cooks don't even know what's in it. Only three people who work here make the batch, and it's been that way since opening day."

"What does it taste like?" I asked.

"If remoulade and a creamy Cajun sauce had a baby. Boom. The Acadian's famous Debris Sauce."

"You're like an encyclopedia of all things Acadian."

She smiled as she straightened her back. "I am. I'm also trying to sell you. Is it working?"

"A little bit. I'm intrigued by this sauce. And the hush puppies."

"My suggestion is to dip the hush puppies in ketchup and then in the sauce, the perfect combination. It's what I do, and it makes my stomach so happy."

I turned to Aaron, and I could feel my doe-eyed expression. "What do you usually get?"

"The Original with extra sauce and a side of hush puppies."

I looked back at the menu. All of the po'boys included lettuce, mayo, pickle, and sauce; the only difference was the meat. It really was the most simplistic menu, and I had no idea if that was a good thing or a bad thing.

"The Original is a great choice," the girl said. "Actually, all of them are pretty great, but if you've never had a po'boy, which I'm guessing you've never had because you sound like a northerner, I recommend The Original. It's the proper introduction."

I frowned. "Wait, how do you know I'm a northerner?"

When those brown eyes met mine again, another wave of warmth washed over me. Her lips tugged upward in amusement. "Would you like whatever that machine dispenses?" She pointed to the soda machine.

"Um…sure," I responded.

"Which is what? What does that dispense?"

I looked over at the machine, reading the different sodas it offered: Coke, Diet Coke, Sprite, Barq's, and Fanta. Then I looked between Aaron and the girl, hoping one of them would help me out because I knew I was being quizzed, and I didn't want to fail. I never got anything lower than a B-plus in my life, and I wanted to keep it that way.

"Go on," Aaron said, giving me the same entertained grin as the girl. "Answer the question."

"Soda?"

The girl laughed, and she was even prettier when she smiled. It caused pinpricks of pleasure to pop up on my neck. "I was right. You can grab your *Coke* cup at the other end. I have you down for The Original, which has roast beef. Is that okay?"

My cheeks turned warm, still having no idea what I answered incorrectly. "Yes."

"Two Originals, both with hush puppies and extra sauce?"

"Sounds good," Aaron said.

"Great. I'll be right out with that, Yankee."

She winked at me before heading to the start of the assembly line, leaving me to stand there confused. Was that flirting? Was the cute girl flirting with me? How did people know what was flirting and what was being nice?

Once I filled my cup with Sprite and took a seat at an empty table, Aaron laughed and leaned in. "You're bright red."

I ran my hands down my face, and unfortunately, it didn't help me cool down. "Wonderful."

He glanced over his shoulder to check on the girl, and I followed his gaze. She glanced over as she sprinkled shredded lettuce on both of our sandwiches, and when our eyes locked, we both flitted our gazes away. My face filled with more heat than the blast of the air-conditioning could cool down despite the goose bumps on my legs.

"She's cute," Aaron said, and then studied me for a moment. He cocked an eyebrow. "Is that why you're red?"

I paused and studied him as hard as I felt him studying me. Did he already have me figured out? Even though I was out to my parents and my friends back home, I wasn't in Connecticut anymore. I was living in a state that recently took down the Confederate Flag from their state Capitol and that consistently voted for Lindsey Graham for the last twenty years. My sexuality wasn't information I'd freely toss around like Mardi Gras beads unless I was asking to be scorned by strangers down here.

But by his raised eyebrows and his intrigued grin, I didn't sense his question was out of judgment at all.

I leaned into the table. "I'm bi."

"No shit! Well, that's cool."

I shrugged. "No one has ever called me cool before, but I'll take it."

"I think she was flirting with you."

I didn't think my face could get any warmer, but there was still so much I had to learn. Being valedictorian, having a four-point four GPA, and getting into MIT literally meant nothing in the real world. I should have taught myself how to pick up on flirting cues or at least tell the difference between being nice and funny and flirting instead of learning about astrophysics in my free time.

"Really? You think?"

Aaron had three years on me, and he was really cute. I'm sure those two things together gave him some experience, and he could enlighten me on what he knew about the dating world. It had to be more than what Brie knew, and she was my only window.

I looked down at the receipt, wondering if it included the girl's name like some restaurant receipts. That was when I noticed that she'd circled "Cokes" in red pen and scribbled "not soda" next to the price.

I slid the receipt to Aaron to show him more evidence. He laughed again and gave it back. "So that's called flirting, my friend. Go do something about it."

"What? No." I paused for a moment and watched the girl wrap the sandwiches in paper. "Okay, how?"

I didn't know anything about girls. Nothing. Zip. It was either advice from a straight boy or advice from a straight girl, and none of them seemed like perfect solutions.

When I glanced back at the counter, the girl was walking over with two red trays. Somehow, goose bumps covered the tops of my thighs, but the other side of my legs stuck to the booth.

"I hope you enjoy," she said as she placed the trays in front of us and walked back to the counter.

I deflated, wondering if I missed my chance to do something. What that something was, I had no idea.

My stomach growled in response to the wonderful aromas floating into my nostrils. The roast beef and toasted bread seeped through the sandwich paper. I took one bite of the sandwich, followed by a hush puppy drenched in sauce, and I sunk in my seat. The cute girl was right. The batter and the sauce really sealed the deal. Envie might have had all the options to create a very unique and customized sandwich, but they didn't make me feel glued to my seat while hearing my stomach sing symphonies of praise like we were in church. Who could have thought something as simple as roast beef, gravy, lettuce, tomato, sliced pickles, and a mystery sauce would create one of the most magical things I'd ever tasted on a perfectly toasted French baguette? It wasn't until I took a bite of this iconic Gaslight Shores staple that I truly found the beauty in simplicity.

As I ate my sandwich and daydreamed about heaven being in my mouth and stomach, the Acadian got a few customers who were quick to order, as if they'd been coming here for years. The girl didn't have to sell them on sandwiches or hush puppies. She kept her communication short, plugged their order into the cash register, and brought their trays over when the food was ready.

"Go back to the counter and ask her something like, what is there to do over here," Aaron said after swallowing a bite.

I made a face. "That's it? That's your grand plan?" I said and popped another hush puppy into my mouth.

"Hey, it's something. She knows you're a Yankee, so go capitalize on that and ask her what to do."

Just as I finished my last hush puppy, dipping it conservatively in ketchup before dousing it in the last bit of sauce, the girl came from the back with a spray bottle and washcloth, spritzing one of the tables and scrubbing it of crumbs and stains. Aaron shot me a look, and I felt his shoe press into my legs. It made me cough while swallowing a bite, and of course, the cute girl looked over. I quickly reached for a soothing sip of Sprite and met her gaze. She still had a small smile, and the heat snaked through me once again.

"So, um, question," I said right as another cough tickled my throat. I relieved it again with another drink. Aaron pressed his lips together as if he was totally entertained by all of this, and the girl's smile never wavered. I had to power through this super lame question. It was either that or I walked out of here with nothing but that one short conversation at the front of the store. "What's there to do around here? I mean, I've never been here before. The town, that is." *Great, smooth. You're such a charmer. Keep making yourself sound like an idiot.* "What do people our age do for fun?"

Finally, I was done with that question that seemed like it took a million years to ask.

"Besides the beach and ocean?" the girl asked.

The heat crawled to the tops of my ears now. "Well…yes… the beach and ocean are a given. There has to be a variety of other things."

She relaxed her right leg and looked up at the ceiling. "Well, if you're already over the beach and ocean, the boardwalk is the best spot. There's a cool arcade two spots over to the right, if that's your thing. Then there's the Ferris wheel at the very end of the boardwalk. We have a mini golf place about a half a mile from here. And actual golf courses, if you haven't noticed those yet. Everywhere. Golf courses everywhere. Oh, and Reagan Moore has a summer house here."

"As in, Reagan Moore the singer?"

She nodded. "But she lives in one of the ritzy gated communities, so seeing her is like a unicorn sighting. Sometimes she makes an appearance around town, but I unfortunately haven't seen her yet. Oh, farther inland, there're some canals you can kayak and paddleboard. It's beautiful and peaceful out there. It's one of my favorite things to do. But, yeah, that's really it. We kind of thrive off the boardwalk and the beach, so that's really our claim to fame."

"And these sandwiches," I said.

The girl raised her hand. "Whoa, whoa, whoa. They're *po'boys*. Not sandwiches. Po. Boys."

"But it's like the same—"

"Ah! Stop. No, it's not the same thing. If you want a sandwich, go get some bologna and American cheese or go to Envie and put a bunch of french fries on it. This is a *po'boy*, a staple of Louisianan cuisine. My great grandparents would murder you if you called it a sandwich."

"Oh, you're part of the family?" Aaron asked.

She smiled and pointed to something behind us on the wall, a black and white photo of a man who looked to be close to thirty and I assumed his wife, standing outside the Acadian. A caption underneath the photo read, "Abel and Manón Hebert, Opening Day May 31, 1948."

"My great grandparents, Abel and Manón Hebert," she said, pronouncing her last name as "e-bear." "They moved here from Louisiana after the war and started this restaurant." She looked down at my empty tray. "I take it you liked the food?"

"It was delicious," I said. "I think I need to come back and try the other ones."

"Well, if that's the case, let me give you something."

As she headed over to the cash register, Aaron gave me a double thumbs-up. I looked back at the girl and watched her punch eight holes into what I assumed to be a rewards card before coming back over to give it to me. The card read, "Buy 10 of our famous po'boys, enjoy one for free."

She gave one to me. Not Aaron. *Me*, and that made my armpits sweat.

"Come back sometime before your vacation is over, and I'll give you a free one," the girl said with a smile.

"Wow, thank you. But I haven't had eight sand—I mean, po'boys."

"I know. Consider it a 'Welcome to Gaslight Shores' treat."

"I'm actually here all summer, so I'll definitely come back. I'm eyeing The Chicken next."

The bell from the front door jingled with a couple in their twenties strolling in, holding shopping bags and staring at the menu like it was foreign.

"Oh, tourists," the girl whispered. "That's my cue. Thanks for stopping by. Hope you both come back soon." And back to the counter she went.

I left the nameless girl to attend to her newest customers. I felt victorious with the rewards card in my hand but defeated that she became too busy for me to find out what her name was.

Aaron and I stepped back outside into the thick humidity. I glanced at the rewards card and the unpunched ninth and tenth circles. It was an incentive to come back, a tiny promise all for me, and knowing that made my heart erratically judder.

Aaron patted my shoulder. "You did it. This is basically like her phone number."

"Holy shit, I think I need to go jump in the ocean. I'm so sweaty." I slid the card in my back shorts pocket, and we started toward Envie. "Okay, but honestly, how lame did I sound?"

"Not lame at all. You sounded awkwardly endearing."

I rolled my eyes. "Great."

He nudged my side. "She didn't seem to mind. She was smiling the whole time. That has to mean something, right?"

Who the hell even knew? Smiling was a good sign. I knew that in the pit of my stomach. I just found it hard to believe that a cute girl would smile because she found me charming. Super weird and awkward? Totally. Those two words were synonymous with Remi Brenner. If I asked anyone who went to school with me, they would agree.

But maybe Aaron was right. When I got back home and texted Brie the entire story, she told me in all caps that it meant something. I let out the longest sigh from the pit of my stomach and stared up at the fan rotating on the ceiling. Cute Girl gave me an invitation to come back, and that within itself held so many possibilities.

My summer in Gaslight Shores unexpectedly got more interesting.

CHAPTER THREE

I shrieked when I came home from work to find my lost luggage sitting right outside my apartment door. My baby finally came. A week separating us, and Celeste was finally here, in perfect condition, without a scratch.

I actually hugged her. I'd missed her so much.

"You got your telescope back, kiddo?" Dad asked when I went to the fridge for a glass of water for dinner.

Serena smiled from the stove, whipping up something that smelled delicious and looked like some saucy Italian pasta dish. Her kitchen was always redolent with whatever delicious meal she was creating, and no two smells had been the same since arriving.

"Finally," I said, pushing the glass into the fridge's water dispenser. "Not a single scratch. Still won't be flying that airline ever again, but at least I got Celeste back."

"How about we take it to the backyard tonight? You can tell me what's new in the sky?"

It'd been six days since our argument, and I was long overdue for some time with my dad. I knew I had to swallow the anger about the Celestron. It wasn't personal. He was just a clueless guy, and my telescope was finally in my hands. All was sort of right with the world. So I agreed.

When the colors of the sunset had faded into a navy blue, with only a streak of sunlight left, Dad and I set a blanket on the edge of the backyard in a clearing. Since there was a marshy river at the edge of the property, both Dad and Serena made sure we bathed in bug spray because apparently, the mosquitos were vicious. My skin felt caked in an uncomfortable gloss, and the finish was the thick layer of constant sweat that came from the unrelenting humidity. But a cold can of Sprite somewhat eased my discomfort. Dad sipped his Bud Light while I set up the telescope and fixed it on the silvery-white dot that was Jupiter, one of the brightest bodies in the summer sky. Jupiter was a bit blurry through the lens, but the bands were still visible, and so were its moons, four speckles next to the planet. Jupiter had seventy-nine moons, but only the four Galilean moons were large enough to see through my telescope: Io, Ganymede, Callisto, and Dad's favorite, Europa.

When it was ready, Dad looked through the lens as I drank my soda and enjoyed the loud sounds of the night. Despite the gross temperature, at least the bright stars, the thin layer of clouds, and the sounds of the frogs croaking and crickets chirping made up for it.

Dad pulled away with a wide smile, one that I knew was generated from the stars. "That's a neat telescope you got there," he said. It wasn't as great as his Celestron, but I was still pretty excited to have Celeste as my own. It was good enough until I could afford my own Celestron. "Europa is looking good tonight."

Europa was Dad's favorite part of our solar system because it was utterly fascinating, and hardly anyone knew about it, which baffled the two of us. It had a cracked, icy surface, and those cracks hinted at a possible ocean underneath. The Hubble Telescope had even found water plumes jetting from it, further indicating that it had an ocean. When I was a kid, Dad had told me that Europa likely contained three times the amount of water than all of Earth's oceans. Where there was water, there was a strong possibility of life, and that meant that there was a huge possibility there was life within our own solar system, just chilling next to Jupiter this whole time.

"Are you still Europa's number one fan?" I asked. "I think yes, given the art in the apartment."

"I am. I'm even more into it now that NASA's going to send a spacecraft, most likely in 2024. Can you believe that?"

"Wait. Really?"

"Really. NASA's going to send the Europa Clipper to fly around it a dozen times to find the water plumes Hubble saw. And then the ESA is sending another to find molecules that will indicate if there *is* life or if there *was* life. Two different missions in the next ten years. I swear, if they find something…well, I don't know exactly what I would do, but I would be ecstatic. That's groundbreaking news. Other life in our solar system?"

"It would be wild. I have goose bumps thinking about it."

"Hey, maybe it will be one of your first NASA missions."

"Maybe. Though I would want to go to the moon first. Then we can check out Europa. Maybe I'll organize the mission that sends a submarine down there. I'll name the spacecraft Dennis."

He patted my knee. "That's my girl. Do it for your ol' dad."

I put my eye in the eyepiece and looked for the Big Dipper's handle and the galaxy that sat underneath it, the Whirlpool Galaxy. It always brought a smile to my face whenever I looked at it. The fact that we could actually see other galaxies from Earth still amazed me, and it always made my heart twitch whenever I saw the little spiral shape through the lens.

"Tell me what Stephen Hawking is talking about," Dad asked. "You seem pretty interested in the book."

"Besides the boring first chapter, it's actually really fascinating," I said. "You should read it."

He smiled and took a sip of beer. "I don't know, kiddo. I'm just an enthusiast. I'm not sure I'm able to understand everything he's saying like you."

"Yes, you can. Start with the second chapter. It's all about space and time. Reading it makes me feel like I'm one of the only kids on this planet who finds Einstein's general theory of relativity utterly fascinating."

Dad laughed. "See, you're speaking another language than me. Dumb it down for your old man."

"Okay," I said and crossed my legs. "Basically, Einstein says that time is an illusion. Can you believe that?"

Dad stared at me blankly for a moment, as if he needed to process what I said. "How is it an illusion?"

I straightened my back, ready to blow his mind. "Well, you know that time is relative. It changes depending on where you are, even on Earth."

"I do know that. That's why I have this watch."

He wiggled his right wrist to show off a silver watch. Of course he had a watch that screamed thousands of dollars. But I brushed it aside. I had more important things to focus on, like blowing my dad's mind and telling him all about the hoax that was time as humans defined it.

"What do you mean?" I asked.

"It's a quartz watch. You know what's so special about them?" I shook my head. "They use a little piece of quartz crystal to keep time because when you run electricity through quartz, it vibrates at a precise frequency. Pendulum clocks and regular clocks, you have to remember to wind them. If you forget, they stop. They also use gravity, and that varies where you are on Earth. Time runs faster on mountains than at sea level because there's less gravity there. Even the temperature affects pendulums. They expand on warm days and contract on cold days. But a quartz watch erases all those factors because of its precise frequency. This is the most accurate calculation of time we have, and it's all because of a tiny piece of quartz."

Suddenly, his watch became much more interesting. I had no idea. It made me realize that so many people in the world ran on different clocks. The clock I used on my iPhone wasn't as accurate as Dad's watch. Neither was the digital clock in my apartment or the analog clock in the living room. With each different kind of clock, it was like we hopped on different time trajectories like a game of hopscotch. No one was in sync.

"I want one of those now," I said.

"I'll keep that in mind. Maybe for Christmas? Now, tell me more about time being an illusion."

"Okay, so in Einstein's theory of relativity, spacetime adds a fourth dimension to the universe, and it creates something called a block universe. Think of a block made of cement with a line through it that represents the speed of light. Everything around the line is spacetime, and the line is the past, present, *and* future. The line exists in the entire block, so that means the past, present, and future exist simultaneously, and the distinction between them is an illusion because they exist together. If that's all true, it means that the future exists as much as right now, and that everything is predetermined. And get this, most physicists believe in the block universe because it's predicted by general relativity." I formed a fist with both of my hands and made an explosion sound as my fingers flexed. Every time I reminded myself about this theory, my mind was blown all over again.

Dad rubbed his forehead as if what I'd told him hurt his brain. It hurt my brain too when I'd first read it a couple days ago, and then it caused me to stare at the Europa poster for a long time, lost in my own thoughts.

Maybe it was what brought me down here for the summer. I still clung to the hope that the Old Dad was buried somewhere in him because according to Einstein, he still existed. He was still here despite the fact I hadn't seen him since before freshman year. I desperately needed to find him before the summer ended.

"But if the past, present, and future coexist, doesn't that prevent free will?" Dad asked. "Do we really make our own decisions if everything is already decided? Can we really enjoy the now, or is that already programmed into the timeline?"

"Well, according to Einstein's theory, no, we don't have free will. I read online that if we could actually time travel, we would only be able to travel into the future because that's the only direction the speed of light travels. But let's just say we somehow did figure out how to travel back in time to change something, events would readjust. Time is like a rubber band. You can stretch it and try to change it, but it will snap back into place."

"Wow, just…" Dad stopped for a moment, thought, and shook his head as if trying to get his thoughts out. He eased his confusion with a gulp of beer. "Wow. My mind has been blown."

These were the kind of conversations Dad and I used to have when looking through the telescope in our backyard. When I was a kid, he'd prompted me to think outside of my world that was only a few blocks wide. Back when I'd believed monsters lived under my bed, Dad had asked me thought-provoking questions that had debunked my belief. If monsters lived under the bed, how did they eat and drink? When I said a trap door, Dad had said right below my room was the downstairs kitchen. He even went into the kitchen and hit the ceiling with a Swiffer so I could hear and feel the vibrations. My monster theory was debunked after that. Then it came time for me to question the existence of the Tooth Fairy, the Easter Bunny, and Santa. Dad had already created a monster with the telescope and had asked me these thought-provoking questions, but then I'd wanted the answers to every life question. I had always known the Tooth Fairy was bullshit, but if I'd told my parents that, then they wouldn't have given me the five bucks I'd rightfully earned by losing a tooth, so I'd kept my knowledge a secret for as long as I could until they'd told me I was too old. And then I'd told them that I'd been questioning it since I'd lost my first tooth when I was six.

Santa had been the hardest. I'd always wanted to believe in him but knew that it wasn't scientifically possible to visit every kid in the world in a single day. Plus, why the hell would he ride around in his sleigh when he could stay in the comfort of his home and order from Amazon? They offered gift receipts and two-day shipping. If Santa was real, Amazon would have bought him out years ago.

"I thought showing you my telescope when you were little would make you interested in the moon," Dad said. "I didn't expect you to reconstruct my whole way of thinking about life and the universe."

I sat up straighter. The fact that I could get Dad to rethink everything he'd ever thought about in his fifty-five years on Earth was a badge of honor I'd proudly wear.

"There's much more to the universe than our galaxy," I said. "The Milky Way isn't even a blip on the universe's radar, and that really puts things into perspective. How big are our problems if our galaxy doesn't even affect the entire universe?"

"You're thinking at the astronomical level. What about at the 'quantum level,'" Dad said in air quotes. "Just because we're not a blip in the universe doesn't mean our problems aren't real. What if we're the only planet in the universe with life? Our importance is then massively significant."

"But if there's life on other planets, which is highly likely, then we're insignificant."

And if humans are insignificant, inanimate objects used to win a divorce were so tiny that they didn't even exist anymore.

"Why can't we think about the planet we live on? We're alive. We live on Earth. Our feelings and problems aren't any less real because they don't make a difference to the universe. We should care about the things that happen in our bubble."

I thought for a moment. "Yeah, that's true, but if that's the case, I think it's important to remember what's astronomical to our lives. There are some little things that we dwell on that aren't important. Relationships, yes. Materialistic things? No."

Astronomical things that impacted our lives: our jobs, our relationship with our family, and the people we fell in love with. Those were things that I worried about and things I wouldn't write off just because our galaxy wasn't even a blip to the universe. Quantum things that "impacted" our lives: what things you could win in a divorce. Dad needed to understand that. His relationship with his daughter was more important than winning the living room chair and the basement coffee table only to spite Mom.

"I agree," Dad said, even though what I was trying to imply seemed to go in one ear and out the other. "That's why I'm glad you decided to spend the summer with me." He patted my shoulder. "You're obviously the most astronomical thing in my life, kiddo."

I didn't have a choice, I said to myself. The thought danced on the tip of my tongue, wanting so badly to expose itself so he'd know this whole summer situation was pretty fucked-up. But I swallowed my words. I wanted to continue enjoying the moment with him and our deep conversations about the universe that I used to love so much. If I tried with Dad, maybe I could get the person he used to be to take over and get rid of the person he'd become.

"I guess what all of this means is that time as we know it isn't real, and the only truth we have is this present moment," I said. "I'm trying to enjoy moments more. It's my new life approach."

"Wise," he said. "Many people focus too much on the past and future. When you do that, you lose sight of the now, and it isn't until now becomes a memory do you realize you never really enjoyed that moment as much as you could have."

His words hit me like a brick wall. I had always kept my eyes on the future because the future meant going to space, and that was a million times more interesting than Earth. I had no comprehension when I was younger that the things around me then would be the things I'd long for now. Lying out in the backyard with the Celestron, with Mom only a few steps away inside the house. The three of us walking around Morris Cove. Saturday mornings getting warm, toasted coconut doughnuts. In all those memories, my mind had been in the future, willing for time to speed up.

Now I sat in Gaslight Shores, South Carolina with Dad's new wife a few steps away in the house, the Celestron sold to a family who I knew for a fact wouldn't love it as much as Dad and I did. Morris Cove was a failed pipe dream, and toasted coconuts were now used as an apology.

If I could get my dad back—even if it was for just one summer—I'd give up Celeste and the Celestron just so I could acquire new memories that were fully and truly appreciated.

I looked up at the sky and noticed that the thin clouds had started multiplying. "Is there anything in your life you regret not living in the moment for?"

"So many."

I looked back with a furrowed brow. *I wasn't the only one?* "Like what?"

"Well, for one, being young. You spend your whole childhood wanting to be an adult, and then when it happens, it's…well…not as fun. Don't get me wrong, there are plenty of perks to being an adult. Freedom, money—"

"Buying alcohol whenever you want?"

"Hey, alcohol shouldn't be on your radar," he said not too seriously, nudging my arm. We shared a laugh. "Yes, that's nice, but it's also nice to have a sense of invincibility and naivety that you don't truly appreciate until it's gone. I kind of miss being naive about all the things going on in the world. Enjoy these years, especially college. You have the best four years ahead of you."

A part of me did wish I was younger, in a time when I didn't have to worry about my parents using me as their liaison and therapist or worry about money or good grades. I knew that even my "issues" now wouldn't compare to the issues Mom and Dad had grown into like oversized T-shirts made for adults: mortgages, divorce lawyers, and saving enough money for retirement. For a moment, Dad made me pause, think, and slow down.

I was eighteen, and even though I wanted to get this summer over with, to finally be at college, to finally go to space, I knew deep down that it was a really good age. There was something magical about being a teenager. We saw the world differently, and whatever magical thing it was, kids couldn't see it, and adults had long forgotten it. If the past and future existed as much as now, then that meant life was made up of a myriad of nows. My current now was filled with some kind of magic that would disappear over time. Dad knew it too. He'd just warned me about it and told me to clasp it before it faded. I knew I had to take advantage of it and live in this moment. My mind had been so fixated on the past that it didn't provide any room to focus on what was in front of me. I had a whole summer with my dad, a dad who wanted to have a relationship with his daughter. He was trying, and I had to too.

"You spend so many years wishing for things to be different," Dad said. "And once they are, it's nothing like you imagined. Life hits you hard, kiddo, and once it takes its first punch, it doesn't really seem to stop."

He pulled another sip of beer before looking into my telescope, leaving me with the enigmatic undertones of his lecture. When did life take its first punch at him? How old was he when he realized it was too late?

It felt like life had just taken its first punch at me. Did that mean it was too late?

As the question ran through my mind, the patio door slid open. Serena came out with a deet candle, a lighter under her arm, and bug spray in her other hand.

"How are the bugs?" she asked.

"Bugs are okay," Dad answered. "Wanna join us, hon? Look through the telescope with us?"

Hearing him say "hon" was like a fork screeching against a plate. I stretched my neck to shake out the awful sound and decided then I should take the bug spray and reapply to protect from mosquitoes *and* their PDA.

As I stood and sprayed, I stole a glance at Dad and Serena. They were lost in a gaze, smiling at each other like newlyweds. Dad kissed her cheek and whispered something in her ear, and whatever he said, it made her smile glow through the darkness.

I'd never seen Dad make someone smile like that before.

He acted totally different around Serena than Mom. He smiled at her whenever she walked in the room. He even kissed her every time he left the house. Not some forced kiss that was quicker than a blink, like I'd witnessed countless times with Mom. But like a sweet, lingering peck on the lips, like Dad and Serena were two magnets meant to be fused together, and Dad and Mom had been two magnets trying to connect despite a mysterious force repelling them. There had to have been something about Serena that was more than the allure of a famous, super rich, gorgeous woman twelve years younger than him. It had to have been more than all the superficial things that made up so much of his new life. What was in that force that welded them together?

When I was little, Dad had told me that Mom's love for science was what first drew him in. Of course, part of it was because she was beautiful, but they'd shared an interest in science. Mom loved the world underneath the water and rambled about dolphins, turtles, and fish—it was what drove her to be a high school biology teacher. And Dad rambled about everything above the Earth. Two science nerds who loved each other, Mom had once told me.

I wondered what happened to people to make them fall out of love. How did you love someone for twenty years and then leave them?

How the hell did the CFO of a new and unknown startup meet a celebrity chef? Did I even care to know that story? What common interests did they have? I'd been in Gaslight Shores for a week and still had no idea. All I knew was that the way he acted around Serena paled the memories of my parents' marriage. They'd never had that. They were basically two people who'd raised a kid. They tolerated each other. Shared laughs. Had the forced good-bye pecks. A large king bed with enough space so they could forget the other was sleeping on the opposite side.

It made me wonder if Dad had ever been in love with Mom at all. From all the evidence I'd gathered in my eighteen years of research, my hypothesis was no. As long as I could remember, everything had been forced or tolerated. Everything with Serena seemed to flow as smoothly as a relaxing river current.

"What am I looking at?" Serena asked from the eyepiece. Her voice was higher, like a giddy schoolgirl talking to her crush.

"Europa," Dad said, snuggled close to her. "The coolest speck in the sky."

"That's arguable," I said and plopped back in my spot. "If Betelgeuse was out right now, it would totally be that."

Dad smiled, and Serena looked at us completely clueless. He told her all about Europa, and I could tell she tried her best to show enthusiasm. The second there was a lull in the conversation, she asked to see Saturn and then the moon. I hardly got a word in because I felt the two wrap themselves up in a love bubble. It felt so foreign to me. It showed a different side of my dad that I didn't know existed, and although I was glad he was happy, it came at the expense of our family.

I told them I needed to go to the bathroom, but I never returned. It was too much all at once, and maybe one day, I'd be more comfortable with the two of them. But right now, it was still too much, and I felt like I was intruding on their moment.

The feeling that the family I once had would never be again rotted inside my stomach, another thing I didn't fully enjoy until it was too late. This was my new normal. Watching Dad kiss Serena like he was always meant to, hearing Mom and Dad refer to each other as if saying their names tasted repugnant, and me, feeling like the rope Mom and Dad used to win whatever battle for that day.

That was my new now in a myriad of nows.

CHAPTER FOUR

After having a true po'boy at the Acadian, all the concoctions I made at Envie made as much sense as quantum physics to someone like Theo. Tofu with lettuce, tomato, coleslaw, bacon, fried egg, and horseradish. I'd never thought that tofu and bacon would ever be on the same plate, but there I was, whipping one up for a girl typing rapidly on her cell phone with Airpods in her ears. Then there was a guy who looked like Santa Claus on summer vacation: a bright red face from sunburn, trimmed white beard, and a blob of chewing tobacco stuffed in his bottom lip, who ordered a fried oyster with lettuce, tomato, fried onion, avocado, Cajun mayo, and roast beef gravy. And just when that had me close to gagging, this tall college kid with a farmer's tan cutting off right on his shoulders ordered the grossest combination of all: half skirt steak and fried catfish, lettuce, pickles, french fries, lemon garlic butter, roast beef gravy, and Carolina barbeque sauce.

Seeing all the gross combinations made me appreciate the simplicity of the Acadian's menu, and it gave me more of a reason to get closer to the tenth hole punch of my rewards card. It'd been three days since my first visit, and I'd been craving another po'boy as much as I was craving seeing the cute girl again.

"How soon is too soon to go back to the Acadian?" I whispered to Aaron when Theo was doing nothing in the back room. Probably harassing poor innocent girls on Tinder.

Aaron looked skyward and thought. "I don't know. They say you need to wait three days before texting someone after a first date."

I made a face. That wasn't seriously still a rule, like how you had to wait three dates before sleeping with someone. Was it? "Isn't that a bit archaic? Do you seriously wait three days to text a poor girl back?"

Aaron stared at me blankly. I laughed. "What? That's what everyone does," he said defensively. "If you think it's lame, then what do *you* do? Enlighten me on the new rules."

"I'm eighteen. I don't know the rules. That's why I'm asking you."

"You've never texted a girl after a date?"

I'd never been on a date with a girl. Never kissed one. Never slept with one either. Well, I'd never slept with anyone. My experience was dating Owen Gardner for two months last fall, going to a couple movies and sneaking in quick make-outs in the back of the theater and going to a pizzeria once. That was the extent of my dating life. But I didn't want to show Aaron all my cards or have him question if I was really bi since I'd never kissed a girl. He didn't seem like the type who would, but then, Owen hadn't either, but a few months after we broke up, he'd asked me how I could be sure I was bi if I'd never been with a girl.

"No," was all I said.

I decided to wipe the assembly line counter instead of looking him in the eye, fearing that he would make fun of me. But he didn't. He let out a nice chuckle and patted my shoulder. "I think you'd be fine going in tonight if that's what you wanted me to say."

I blew out a breath. "Really? It wouldn't be...aggressive?"

"She gave you a rewards card and punched eight of the ten holes. Clearly, she wants you to come back at the very minimum. How is coming in for another po'boy three days after the fact aggressive?"

Maybe because it isn't.

At four fifty nine, I clocked out, changed out of my Envie shirt, shoved it to the bottom of my bookbag, and went straight to the Acadian. I stopped for a moment to collect my breath right in front of Sully's, not only because I sped walked over, but because I was actually that nervous. What the hell did I say to Cute Girl? What happened if I finally got to my tenth hole punch and I hadn't woman-uped and tried to talk to her beyond giving her my order. What if I never found out her name?

I exhaled a deep breath and dabbed the sweat off my forehead with the back of my hand. The damn heat probably made me look like a wet dog. Damn it, was I too sweaty for a po'boy? I checked my face on my phone. On a normal day with normal temperature, my medium brown hair fell in natural waves to my collarbone. Add one-hundred-percent humidity, and bam, it was like I'd slept in curlers. I ruffled a hand through my hair to fix it, re-parted it, and tried to make it less chaotic, but the South Carolina humidity was the second strongest force on Earth behind gravity. The only thing I had going for me was that the sunlight made the green flecks in my hazel eyes pop out.

After wiping my hands against my jeans, I pulled open the door, and the bell jingled above me with the welcome blast of air-conditioning. My chest swelled with happiness when I saw Cute Girl behind the counter fixing two sandwiches for a middle-aged couple, the only customers. I hoped that while she finished those two sandwiches, the cold air-conditioning would dry up my sweat and defrizz my hair.

She rang up the couple and then spotted me at the other end. She rewarded me with a smile that warmed me all over again. "You craving a po'boy today?" she asked while trotting to the other side.

"I haven't stopped thinking about it."

She laughed, and my chest inflated. Yup, the air-conditioning wasn't going to work. "You'll be my last of the day," she said, grabbing a loaf of French bread from under the counter.

I wondered if she'd eat with me if I asked or if she had better things to do like run off with her friends or her boyfriend or girlfriend. I had approximately seven seconds until she cut the loaf in half and then sliced it open to muster enough confidence to ask. When she looked at me to tell her what to do, the question lodged in the back of my throat. "I'll have…um…The Chicken."

"With all the fixings?"

I nodded.

I followed her down the assembly line as nerves swirled and mixed with the hunger pangs to create an actual stomachache.

What the hell was I doing?

Finally at the cash register, she looked at me again, and those beautiful brown eyes did it for me. I'd come back for a reason: I wanted to talk to her, look at her, find out her name. If I came back in two days, it would be too suspicious. I had to do something.

"Could I have extra sauce?"

"It'll cost you an extra five dollars." She said it so seriously, I believed it for a second before she let her smile grow. "I'm joking." She squirted more sauce into the plastic cups. "Hush puppies and a Coke?"

"Yes, please."

"For here or to-go?"

"For here," I said and fished for a twenty out of my purse. She pulled a red tray from below and loaded it with the wrapped-up sandwich, medium hush puppies, a soda cup, and two sides of sauce.

Oh God, this is the moment. Once you take the tray from her, it's over. Say something now.

"You want to join me?"

My question hung between us like morning fog. I asked, and my heart raced as if I just did a sprint down the boardwalk. I couldn't even look her in the eye. Instead, I looked at Andrew Jackson, and that was definitely a huge downgrade for my eyes.

"Yeah, sure."

That pulled my gaze. She flashed me a smile as she reached for another red tray and set it by mine. "Wait, really?"

Her grin evoked both frivolity and confidence. "Yes…do you not want me to anymore?"

"No, I just…" I nervously scratched the back of my head as if searching for a response from the nest that was my hair. "I figured you'd be busy."

"I'm not. How about you go grab a seat. You have a wide range of options."

She gestured to all the empty seats behind me, and the fun in the air diffused a little bit when I noticed how empty it was for five o'clock. When I'd left Envie, the line was almost out the front door, and Tracy was getting ready to herd them around the block.

A few moments later, Cute Girl came over with her tray and a smile still tacked on. "You know, this is the first time I'm eating with someone whose name I don't even know," she said as she slid into the booth.

"I'm Remi."

"Remi the Yankee?"

"Yes. Remi the Yankee from Connecticut. So, like, I'm *really* a Yankee."

She laughed. "I'm Harper the Southerner but don't worry. My worldly views are very Yankee."

Harper. I repeated it a couple times in my head and savored how it sounded. I liked the name.

"Well, that's a relief," I said.

We shared a laugh. I reached for a hush puppy that spilled from the container and drenched it in sauce. I felt her watching me, and when I glanced up, her eyes flitted to her roast beef po'boy.

"You're here for the summer?" she asked before taking a bite.

I nodded. "I'm visiting my dad and his new wife. She has a place down here."

"You sound thrilled."

I shrugged. "It's whatever. It's an adjustment I'm still getting used to. But yeah, I'm here until August."

"Have you found anything to do? Checked out the arcade? The Ferris wheel? Mini golfed?"

"No, I've been working, doing some summer reading for school, but those are all on my list."

"Where do you go?"

"I'm about to be a freshman at MIT."

She choked on her bite and eased it with a large sip of soda. I didn't let out a relaxed breath until she spoke again, and I knew she wasn't going to choke in front of me. "Sorry. I guess that excited me," she said with a small laugh.

"It excites me too."

"Damn. MIT? You're a genius?"

I waved her off but was unsuccessful in waving off the warmth on my face. A cute girl thought I was a genius. I was as proud of that as getting into MIT. "Not a genius. Just someone who spends all her free time studying and reading. I actually have to try to be smart. It doesn't come naturally."

"I doubt that's the case. What are you going to study? This is when I expect you to say something really intellectual like math or biomedical engineering."

"Close. Aerospace engineering."

Her eyebrows rose. "As in...outer space?"

I nodded and took a bite to hide my grin. It was a breath of fresh air that someone my age actually found my degree intriguing. When I'd told some of my classmates, their eyes had glossed over, probably thinking how typical it was for Remi Brenner, the nerd who gave up any sort of social life to study and read Neil deGrasse Tyson and Stephen Hawking for fun. My AP physics partner, Jay Blankenship, had asked me if I'd ever heard of *Harry Potter* or *The Hunger Games* like a normal kid, and then he and three other kids had laughed.

Fuck Jay Blankenship.

"Yes, outer space. I want to be an astronaut."

Harper's eyes widened. "That's *so* cool. I didn't know people actually became astronauts, which is stupid because of course people do. But, like, I've never met anyone who studied it."

"I guess that makes me so unique," I said teasingly.

She smiled. "I guess so."

Once we finished eating, we stepped back outside, and the muggy, briny air greeted us. We both hesitated for a moment. If her pause was like mine, she was probably wondering what the hell to do now. Call it a night or find something else to do? I definitely didn't want to call it a night.

"What do you say about going on a tour of the boardwalk?" Harper asked.

My chest inflated. She didn't want to call it a night either. "I'm all for this. I haven't really explored it yet."

"Well, follow my lead, and I'll tell you everything there is to know. Now, if you turn around, ma'am, you will see our first stop, an iconic staple on the Gaslight Shores Boardwalk." We turned, and Harper gestured to the Acadian. She altered her voice to mimic a tour guide, and I loved how a twang of a Southern accent skirted her words. "No one really knows the official story about the po'boy. But the most well-known is the one about the Martin Brothers. They used to work as streetcar conductors in New Orleans, then opened up a restaurant in the early twenties. In 1929, the streetcar workers went on strike, so the brothers gave away sandwiches with roast beef, gravy, and fried potatoes on French bread. Anytime a striking worker came into their restaurant, one of the brothers told the other, 'Here comes another poor boy.' Other restaurants started serving the sandwiches, and they became popular during the Great Depression."

"What made your great grandpa get into the business?"

"Well, his dad was one of the striking streetcar workers. He would pick up sandwiches to feed the family, and my great grandpa loved them. When he went to fight in the war, he told all his Army friends about them. After the war, he and my great grandma moved to Gaslight Shores, which had just been built to attract tourists to South Carolina. He decided to open a restaurant to sell his favorite food. He was only twenty-seven when he opened the Acadian, can you believe that? My dad said The Original was my great grandpa's favorite because it was the closest thing to the original po'boys from the Martin Brothers."

"Wow, that's really cool," I said, genuinely impressed. "Especially the fact that your great grandpa had a po'boy from the inventors."

"Alleged inventors, but for the sake of the authenticity of the Acadian, let's go with it. And that's why I had you start off with The Original. It was the only proper introduction."

"It was a very wise choice and is what really brought me back for a second."

She was the other reason, but I'd keep that to myself.

She winked, and my cheeks flushed. "Okay, follow me."

We turned the corner, and she gestured to Sully's Boardwalk Fries. The smell emanating from the walk-up booth was intoxicating. Pools of peanut oil commingled with the thick air and the smell of salt from the ocean. A line formed, and customers walked away with blue and white-striped cups of thin-cut fries.

"This is the best place in town for fries," Harper said. "They're the second oldest business on the boardwalk. Started in 1949. This is a must for you to try this summer. Add it to your list."

"Could I have an Acadian po'boy, hush puppies, and Sully's fries?"

"I think that's a genius idea and one only a future MIT astronaut would think of."

Thank God she veered to the left down Main Street because I could feel the blush blossoming on my cheeks again.

Next to Sully's was Mia's Lemonade Stand, with the best lemonade and frozen lemonade, much better than a ballpark, Harper said. Next to Mia's was Grandpop's for homemade popcorn with twenty different flavors to choose from.

On the other corner of Main Street was the Gaslight Shores Chocolate Factory, the third oldest restaurant on the boardwalk, built in 1951. I peered through the window and noticed that the whole right wall was made up of a variety of chocolate candy that customers could scoop into plastic bags. On the left side was a variety of non-chocolate candies: jelly beans, gummy worms and bears, and jawbreakers. Lining the middle to the cash register in the back were barrels of saltwater taffy. Harper told me that they made the taffy in the back, and in the glass display under the cash register were some chocolates they also made by hand.

As we walked, the smell of cheese and pepperoni pizza wafted from Basil, and customers enjoyed large slices on greasy paper plates. Next to Basil was the Purple Cactus, known for their amazing tacos and margaritas. Then a souvenir shop, a boutique clothing store, and South Pole Treats for soft-serve ice cream, snow cones, and an old-fashioned soda fountain. A fancy steakhouse sat at the end of that block next to South Pole Treats, and we crossed Front Street, which had a seafood restaurant on the corner.

That was when we discovered the line pooling out the familiar purple door of Envie and wrapping around the corner of the seafood restaurant.

"Ah, and there's the bane of my family's existence," Harper said and shook her head. Any sort of blush and rumble of nerves in my gut came to a halt. "This is Envie, the place stealing all our customers, as you can see from this line. You know that famous chef, Serena DeLuca?"

I tried to swallow the lump in my throat. "Um…I've heard of her."

What the hell was I supposed to say? *Oh yeah, she's my stepmom*, after Harper said that Envie was the bane of her family's existence? My brain froze, and it produced meaningless words to fill in the space.

"She's a judge on *Home Kitchen Masters* and now has this new show on Hulu, *Chef Queens*?"

"I've watched a few episodes of *Home Kitchen Masters*."

"Well, this is her restaurant. She opened it two years ago, and ever since then, all the tourists are flocking to it. I've never had one for obvious reasons, but my two friends went in to investigate. I guess the Serena DeLuca brand is really its selling point."

I scratched the back of my head and realized how much sweat had collected in my thick hair during that short walk. "So…um… does it have any history?"

She let out a laugh with no humor in it. "Hell no. Serena DeLuca is from Long Island, went to school in Manhattan and Italy. No ties to anything in New Orleans. They brand themselves as a sandwich shop, but funny how the word 'Envie' means 'desire' or 'longing hunger' in Cajun French. So it's like a riff on the Acadian, which is named after the descendants of the French who settled in Acadia, aka, my ancestors. Sorry," she said and ran a quick hand through her straight, chestnut brown hair. It fell perfectly back into place, a little past her collarbone. "I don't want to be a Debbie Downer. Envie is a sore subject right now."

"You're totally fine. Let it all out."

"It sucks that my family's restaurant has been around for seventy years and used to be the staple of the boardwalk. Hell, it's still the longest-running restaurant on the boardwalk and the only restaurant that's rapidly dying, all because of this place. We probably won't survive next summer."

"Are you serious?"

She pressed her lips together and nodded, a look of sadness coating her eyes. "Yeah. My parents told me a couple of months ago. I really wanted to go to culinary school somewhere outside of South Carolina. You know, the chance to 'spread my wings' and see the world. My parents tried making it work, but they worry about the cost of going somewhere out of state, and the Acadian, it's not..." She let out a heavy sigh. "It's living on borrowed time."

My throat started to dry up as the guilt weighed heavily on me when hearing about all the ways Serena and Envie had shaken up her life. I wondered if telling her Serena DeLuca was my stepmom would repel her from being my friend for the summer. We'd just met, but I could already feel us becoming friends.

"I'm sure there's a college nearby you could go to."

"South Carolina doesn't have the good culinary schools. The big cities do, like LA and New York. Plus, even if the Acadian survives this, my parents expect me to take over."

"And you don't want to?"

"No, I don't." She turned and looked at the beach. "Wanna go sit in the sand?"

I followed her. She kicked off her flip-flops when we reached the sand, which was still warm from collecting sun the whole day. We sat and watched the waves crashing onto the shore.

"Why don't you want to take over the Acadian."

She offered me the thinnest smile, but it didn't reach her eyes. "Don't get me wrong, I love it, but it's not what I want to do. I've been working there since I was thirteen. It made me realize that I have this passion for food and cooking, and it's helped me gain so much knowledge about running a restaurant, but I'm not interested in po'boys or a fast-food shop that only gets business one season out of the year. But I feel bad leaving my parents to clean up the pieces of their dreams while mine take off."

"You shouldn't feel guilty for wanting something different. You're your own person. You have a right to do whatever you want to do."

"What about the Acadian? What about my family's legacy? What happens if I want to start my own restaurant?"

I didn't have that answer. I didn't know how the restaurant industry worked. I wished I had something better for her. She was eighteen like me, the age when the future should have excited and inspired us. We were finally given the blank slate we'd been wanting since we were kids, able to find out who we were and what we were destined to do. Our dreams weren't supposed to be demolished yet.

"Okay, enough doom and gloom," Harper said, correcting her tone as if she needed to do damage control. I didn't think she had anything to apologize for, but I let her steer us back to lighter conversation. "You must try Sully's fries, saltwater taffy from the Chocolate Factory, and a snow cone from South Pole Treats. If you're taking suggestions, the sour black cherry snow cone...or slushie, if you'd rather drink your dessert. Oh, and try one of their old-fashioned ice cream sodas. My favorite is chocolate."

"I'm taking all the suggestions. I want my stomach to be satisfied by the time I leave."

"I promise that you'll be satisfied." She picked up a fistful of sand and observed it seeping through her fingers. I glanced back at the beach and watched a few kids boogie board into the shore, a few groups packing up their umbrellas and towels, probably after a full day in the sun. Harper told me that sometimes after she closed, she brought a blanket to lie out on the beach to read and watch the sunset.

"You ever stay long enough to stargaze?" I asked.

"I usually pack up before it gets dark. You would think I would have more stargazing-on-the-beach-experience since I've lived here my whole life."

"It's my favorite thing to do. When I was little, my dad and I would camp in our backyard in the summer, and he would bring his telescope. I actually brought my portable telescope down with me. I took it out the other night, and it was amazing. I bet they're even better here on the beach."

"You have a telescope? I've never looked through one before."

My throat became arid. I looked at the sand and scooped a large handful. "I can bring it out," I said, my throat rapidly closing around my words. I eased the discomfort by letting the silky sand fall through my fingers. "It's pretty cool."

"That would be awesome. I want to see the moon and Mars and Saturn."

"You can see all those things."

"Okay, well, next clear night, I think we should do it. Can I see your phone?"

The question sent my heart into a sprint, and when she plugged in her number, excitement inflated my lungs, and I thought I was going to float away. Cute Girl gave me her number, and I sure as hell wasn't going to wait three days to text her.

"Now you can let me know when the stargazing festivities can happen," Harper said when she handed me my phone. It felt significantly more valuable now that her number was in there. "Or, you know, next time you want a po'boy. You are only one punch away from the free one."

"I might be back in soon. I have to try the whole menu."

"You're going to help us stay in business, huh?" She nudged my arm. "My two friends and I are going to go paddleboarding on Wednesday if you want something to do. I figured I could give you a tour of the hidden gems too…since, you know, you were asking about what there is to do."

At first, I thought I was imagining it, but when I found her peeling her gaze away from me and down at the sand too, the shyness in her voice was as pronounced as the waves curling into the shore. It lasted for only a moment, as if a riptide of insecurity zipped through her and dissipated.

"I've never been paddleboarding before, but I do want to see the hidden gems."

"Then come with us."

"Consider it done. You show me the hidden gems in Gaslight Shores, and I'll show you the hidden gems of the sky."

She looked over and smiled. "We'll show each other the best of our worlds."

Time really was relative. My four-hour shift at Envie felt like twelve hours, and then, I spontaneously hung out with Harper, got a tour of the boardwalk, and talked to her on the beach, and we left right as the gas lamps lining the boardwalk flicked on, and the sun started its descent toward the horizon. Those three hours with her seemed like three minutes.

When I rode my bike home, an unfurling grin took over, the kind of grin reserved for people I thought were really cute. It was the same kind of grin and feeling when Owen Gardner first messaged me on Snapchat to ask me to the movies.

Except there was something about Harper that was more alluring than Owen. I wasn't quite sure what it was yet, but I was eager to find out.

CHAPTER FIVE

D o you know how to paddleboard?" I asked Brie on FaceTime.

"Do you think I know how to paddleboard?" Brie said with her dark eyebrows furrowed. "Ever since we went tubing that one time—and I tubed right into a giant spiderweb on a fallen tree in said river—I've shunned things in rivers and lakes. I stick to chlorinated pools. Very minimal bugs."

I rolled my eyes for dramatic effect, even though I missed her dramatic self. "You could have said no."

"No, I haven't gone paddleboarding, and I don't plan on it. I'm not really into activities that are working out disguised as pleasure. But I'm open to a boat. Less effort for me."

"I can't ever have a normal conversation with you. What if a cute guy asks you to go paddleboarding as a date? Like, a jock with abs and a V. Like Brayden Whitmer."

Brie groaned. "I guess I would do it for Brayden Whitmer, but I wouldn't be happy. He could woo me in so many other ways, like food. Or a boat." She paused for a moment. "I take it you're going paddleboarding?"

I flopped on my bed and lay on my stomach. "Cute Girl asked me if I wanted to go with her friends. Oh, I also got her number and spent like three hours with her the other day."

Brie leaned forward. "What? Are you serious?"

"Dead serious."

"Aren't the waters in South Carolina infested with much more terrifying things than spiders? Like alligators?"

I watched my playful smirk wash away on my phone screen. "I forgot about alligators."

"Yeah, dude. What if you fall and get attacked? I don't think it's romantic to have a cute girl trying to stop blood gushing from your leg."

"Damn it. I don't know how to paddleboard, and I probably don't even have the core to do it, which means I'll totally fall in and be gator food. Should I tell her I can't go?"

Brie directed a sharp eye through the camera. "No. Cute Girl is going to teach you how to paddleboard, and that will involve a lot of touching in bathing suits. And if you fall and a gator snaps at you, I'm sure Cute Girl will at least *try* to save you. It's the right thing to do."

"And what if she's straight? All that touching will get me excited for nothing."

"Aren't you supposed to fall in love with a straight girl some time in your life? Isn't that a thing all queer women have to do in order to initiate themselves in the LGBTQ+ community?"

I shrugged. "I don't know how it works."

"I'm pretty sure that's how it works. I see it all the time on Tumblr and TikTok."

"So what you're saying is, if Cute Girl is straight, and my crush intensifies from the touching, at least I'm finally initiated into the queer community?"

Brie smiled and pointed at the phone screen. "Yes, that's exactly it."

I grunted. "Thanks, Brie."

"Hey, if she's straight, you could go back to talking to Cute Restaurant Boy. Plus, he's in college, and hey, maybe you'll fall in love by the time he goes to Europe, and you can be his date. I look forward to the updates. In the meantime, enjoy paddleboarding with Cute Girl and don't get eaten by an alligator. I need you in my life."

"I'll try to live for you."

Harper texted me and offered to pick me up on the way to the boat ramp, and since I wasn't about to bike seven miles to the other side of the island, I agreed to it. But after all the talk about how much Envie and Serena had negatively impacted her family's life, the last thing I wanted to do was have her pull up in the driveway and recognize Serena or her house.

I don't know how the gate works, so I'll just meet you outside of it, I texted, which was one-hundred-percent true. Dad was on a call in his office, and Serena was out somewhere, so I had no resources to figure the gate out.

She pulled up to the gate in a red Toyota Corolla and eyed me carefully from the driver's seat. I opened the door, and once I got in, I noticed her rounded eyes looking at something behind me.

"What?" I asked as I strapped myself into the passenger's seat.

"You live in the *Palms*?"

I looked back at the sign to the left of the gate. "I don't live there, but my stepmom's summer home is in there. Yes."

Her mouth fell. "You know you live in the most expensive development on this island, right?"

An embarrassed warmth crawled across my face. I didn't want to be associated with that label. My stepmom might be loaded, but I wasn't. My mom wasn't. My dad did well and was loaded by association, but that didn't mean that my upbringing was as extravagant as my stepmom's life was.

"What the hell does your stepmom do?"

It took me a moment to scramble. "Um...she's a...a business owner."

The fabrication felt like a wad of hair on my tongue. I hated how those words tasted, and I couldn't pull them back in. But even if I could, I had no idea if I would. I didn't want something out of my control—like Serena as my stepmom—to scare away a possible friend.

Harper started driving away from the gate, and I focused on how the sun flickered between holes in the mossy canopy dangling over us instead of focusing on the guilt pressing on my sternum.

"Okay, so there are really three kinds of people in this town. You have the golfies." She gestured to her left at the golf course. "They're the locals who live in the golf course neighborhoods. Almost all of them are on the north part of the island on the river. Most of these people are old money, and the kids are most likely going to Rice University, Vanderbilt, and University of Virginia. You don't see them on the boardwalk because their subdivisions have their own private beaches, and many of them have their own pools. And they can't be bothered being around tourists. I used to have a friend who was a golfie. Kinda sucks when your family relies on the tourists, and golfies don't think it's a cool thing to do during the summer."

"But the boardwalk is so cool."

"Yeah, I know, but it's not high-end enough, and the beaches are too crowded. Why go to a crowded beach with tourists when you have your own private beach with more space? I always thought that was bullshit because the chummers practically built this town and keep it alive. We're the reason why people flock here in the summer."

I raised an eyebrow. "The chummers?"

"Yeah, you know, like chumming. Leftover parts of a fish that you use to bait the larger ones. These families are blue-collar workers like fishermen, construction, the small businesses that really only make money during the summer. Plus, with all the golfies, we have a lot of cleaning services in the area, so that includes housekeepers as well. We live in the middle or in the western part of the island, right next to the bridge that takes you inland. We live in spots less scenic than the northern and southern parts."

"So…you're a chummer?"

She smiled. "Correct. I mean, my family used to do okay, good enough to help send me to culinary school. I had more privilege than a lot of chummers, but with Envie and everything, we're not as lucky anymore." She turned onto the main artery of Gaslight Shores, Route 7, that took us into town and the boardwalk. "And then last but not least, you have the slocals, the summer locals, like yourself. They're mostly all on the eastern part of the island where their families have second homes as close to the boardwalk as possible. The difference between the golfies and the slocals—besides the fact that the golfies live here all year—is that the slocals can appreciate the boardwalk and the town's small businesses. They have the attitude and money of the golfies but an appreciation for the town like the chummers. The fanciest slocals live in the Palms if they're *really* rich, like Serena DeLuca and Reagan Moore."

I perked up at that. I had no idea the most famous singer in the world had a house practically around the corner from me. All those times I'd hopped online exactly when her tour tickets went on sale just to wait in the queue to get stuck with overpriced nosebleed seats, and all I had to do was ride my bike around the neighborhood in the hope of running into her. Or better yet, Serena probably knew where she lived. Celebrities stuck together, right?

"You said she lived in a gated community, but I had no idea she lived in the Palms."

Harper smiled. "Yeah. Your neighbor is the biggest pop star in the world."

"I've only been to one concert. The summer right before sophomore year, my best friend Brie and I saw her at Madison Square Garden, when Blair Bennett's band opened up for her. It was such a great show."

"I've never been to one. I'm so close to seeing her in the flesh. She and Blair Bennett sometimes make it around town. This one kid I went to high school with works at the seafood restaurant and said they came in last summer. I was so jealous. I would probably die if they came in." She shook her head and laughed. "I can't believe you're staying in a mansion. Maggie and Vera are going to flip when I tell them."

"Do we have to?" I asked, hearing desperation accidentally spilling into my voice. "It's...well...it's not really me. That's all my stepmom, and I don't want people to think that I'm super rich or snooty or spoiled. That isn't a reflection of my life growing up. It's just a place I'm staying for the summer. I literally met her almost two weeks ago. I'm barely even associated with her."

Harper looked at me sympathetically and gave me a small smile. "Okay, that makes sense. I won't tell them."

If it ever came to me telling her that Serena DeLuca was my stepmom, hopefully, she would be able to separate us. Serena wasn't my family. She wasn't a confidant or a friend. But I guess I could be considered guilty by association. My dad had been with her for four years, married to her for a year, though the only impact she'd had on my life was in the form of a home for the summer. Hopefully, Harper saw that after getting to know me and realizing that I was far different from Serena and her culinary empire. I wanted Harper to see me for me, not for my stepmom, who was a mere acquaintance at best.

When we arrived at the boat ramp, she pulled into the gravel parking lot, and rocks clanged against the side as she parked next to a black Jetta. She waved to her two friends, Vera and Maggie, who stood at the trunk of the Jetta as if waiting for us to hop out. After she introduced us, Harper pulled a bottle of SPF 30 out of her bookbag. She took off her pants and shirt and carelessly tossed them on the ground as she squirted lotion in her hands. The thought of getting attacked by an alligator disappeared when I saw Harper in a black bikini. Vera and Maggie also wore bikinis, but my eyes went to Harper and her magenta belly button piercing and her toned stomach that clued me in that she probably paddleboarded frequently.

I forced my stare away. As much as I could feel my eyes wanting to steal another glance, I had to control myself. The last thing I wanted was for Harper to notice.

I had no idea how I was supposed to learn how to paddleboard when she looked that good.

All three of them had skin that hinted that they spent a lot of time in the sun. Harper was a few shades tanner than Maggie, whose natural red hair was pulled into a ponytail. She had freckles dotting her face, and her shoulders were a few shades darker than the translucent bikini lines that told me she'd already had a few good days in the sun...or one decent burn that had faded into some color. Vera had dark brown skin, a few shades darker than Brie's, but I still noticed bathing suit lines on her shoulders. Both Vera and

Maggie glimmered in the sun, letting us know they'd already put on sunscreen. And then there was me, my skin hinting at a long, cold, dark New England winter, glowing with paleness compared to the rest of them.

I was destined to get fried this summer, especially if the default sunscreen was SPF 30. At least my sunburn would be worth spending a day with Harper in a black bikini.

Once everyone was lotioned up, Harper turned to me and slapped her oily hands together. "Are we ready to give Remi here her first paddleboard lesson?"

I snapped my gaze to her eyes. *Yes, her beautiful brown eyes. Ignore the belly button ring and the sexy stomach.* But when I followed my own rule of ignoring the rest of her body, I was reminded of the cute freckles peppering her nose and the smile that had the power to make my body feel like it was set on fire.

"Um…yes. I'm ready," I said and drank the rest of my water until the plastic bottle crinkled, then smashed the crumpled bottle in my bookbag.

"All right, let's go get these paddleboards," she said.

We paid to rent the paddleboards at the small shack and carried them a couple feet down to the boat ramp. That was when I learned the hard way how heavy paddleboards were. The three of them made it look so easy. I traipsed behind, dragging the board along the ground like I'd never lifted anything over ten pounds in my life.

Once Harper plopped hers on the dirt, she turned and laughed at what was probably the hilarious sight of me awkwardly attempting to carry it.

"You need help?" Harper said and picked up the end of the board.

"This weighs as much as Earth. I'm sure of it."

Right as we dropped my board next to hers, Vera and Maggie waded through the water, crawled on their boards, and popped up on their feet.

"Wait," I said. "We're swimming in the water?"

"Oh, I'm sorry. I should have asked if you wanted to paddleboard on land. How rude of me."

Vera and Maggie giggled, only encouraging Harper's smile to grow.

"Are you making fun of me?"

Her lips curved upward. "Maybe."

"You have gators in the water. Getting attacked by one was not part of my Gaslight Shores bucket list."

"You're adorable," she said through her laugh, and her words halted all my worries about getting eaten, leaving my brain to center on the fact that she thought I was adorable. A cute girl called me adorable. Hell, no one had ever called me cute or adorable except my parents, but obviously, they didn't count.

I wished I could have recorded what she'd said so I could replay the sound over and over again.

"The creek is saltwater. Gators live in freshwater," Vera said. "Most of the time. They can tolerate saltwater but only for a few hours."

"So there *is* a probability of being attacked by one," I said.

"It's extremely rare to see one in saltwater," Maggie said.

"They're really not that aggressive," Harper said. "If you leave them alone, they'll leave you alone. Trust me. I've been doing this for years. Think about all the fish and birds you'll see."

"I saw a bald eagle a month ago," Maggie added. "We might even see some dolphins. Focus on that."

"If a gator chews on my leg, I'm not going to be very happy," I said not too seriously and pushed my board into the water.

It took me a couple minutes to figure out how to balance. Anytime I fell off, my life flashed before my eyes as I wondered if a gator saw my flopping legs as a nice appetizer. Harper, Vera, and Maggie couldn't stop laughing at my flailing limbs, but after a few tries, I got the hang of it. Once I steadied myself, I cautiously followed their lead.

By the time the boat dock was out of sight, the quietness and serenity of the marshy river took over, calming me down and helping me get my groove. Paddling through the calm water gave us a front row view of the low country. Walls of marsh grass poked through the surface, creating a playground for the herons and ospreys to swoop through. I kept my eyes peeled for more wildlife, especially dolphins, bald eagles, and that alleged rare gator. Vera and Maggie were a few feet in front of us, and Harper stayed next to me. I wondered if it was to keep to my pace. When I looked back at her, the sun glistened against the thin layer of sweat on her midsection. As if she could feel my stare, she glanced over and caught me in the middle of checking her out. I averted my gaze to the tiny ripples lapping against my board in front of me.

"How are you liking it?" she asked. "You got the hang of it pretty quickly."

"Being gator food was good motivation to balance." She laughed, and my stomach did a somersault knowing that I could make her laugh. "You do this a lot, I take it?"

"All the time. It's what I do to relax. I come out here and listen to the silence, watch the birds, get some sun. It's my Zen."

Yeah, your body definitely shows it.

"It helps that it's absolutely beautiful out here," I said.

"Isn't it? With all of this restaurant stress, I've been doing it a lot lately, like once a week."

Every time she mentioned the restaurant, I felt guilty, like it was my fault. Obviously, it wasn't, but living with and working for her enemy really helped the guilt swell inside me. It made me feel pinned against a wall, and I had no idea what to do. Not say anything or tell her that Serena was my stepmom, and both options were so uncomfortable.

"I'm sorry," I said. "But hey, I have some good news for you."

"What's that?"

"If you need something to distract you tomorrow night, we could check out my telescope. Tomorrow night is supposed to be clear, so I'm definitely heading to the beach to stargaze. If you want to join."

Harper perked up. "Really? Awesome. I close at nine tomorrow, but you could meet me at the Acadian. Hey!" she said and used her paddle to send a small wave over to me. I flinched as the wave splashed, then wobbled on my board and recovered like a true CEO of paddleboarding. Maybe I was a quick learner. "I could save us some po'boys?"

"Yes! And we can get a bucket of Sully's fries?"

"And a box of saltwater taffy for dessert."

"I think you might be the genius now."

"Oh my God, y'all, look!" Maggie said and pointed her paddle to something on our right.

I clutched mine at the sudden yelling, prepared for her to tell us it was an alligator snapping through the surface of the water. But instead of that, I noticed two black, triangular figures. My first thought based on the shape was a shark. My heart raced when the two figures bobbed through the surface again, but this time, their backs breached, and I realized they were dolphins swimming about twenty feet in front of us.

"Oh my God," I said through my clenched jaw, holding back my excitement so I didn't scare them. "Oh my God. Are those dolphins?"

The two dolphins breached again, and Harper gasped, quick to cover her mouth. I stood there in awe, my heart pounding as I waited for their dorsal fins to pop out again.

"There're three of them," Harper whispered loudly, and that was when I found a third dorsal fin racing to catch up to the other two.

"How cool is this?" Vera said softly.

The four of us quietly and gently paddled, trying to remain as calm as possible so we didn't scare them off. And it worked because the three swam over. One dolphin swam to me and turned on its side. I froze when our eyes met. Right in front of me, I saw the bottlenose dolphin's smile and its black eyes looking up at me. The fact that I got to see one in the wild and not in a tank made me smile so wide. I almost felt like crying because I was so ecstatic that I was this close to a beautiful wild animal. The dolphin circled my board, and the two others did the same to Harper. We exchanged mouth-dropping grins and then turned to Vera and Maggie, who did the same. Seeing them react like that told me that this wasn't normal down here.

After a few minutes, the dolphins regrouped and continued down the river, but it took the four of us the whole way back to the boat dock for our smiles to dwindle just a little.

"I can't believe how close they got," Vera exclaimed as we paddled back. "I've seen a few dolphins here once or twice, but they never came over to me. They were right there!"

"I've never been that close to a wild animal," I said, my pulse still twitching from the thrill of it, even an hour later. "That was, like, the coolest thing I've ever seen."

"They must have come out to give you a proper Gaslight Shores greeting," Harper said, and the wink she gave me made me hyperaware of the sunburn forming on my face.

It should have been illegal for a cute girl with a belly button ring in a bikini to wink at a bisexual girl. She made my thoughts spin like an out-of-control carousel, and the fluttering in my stomach didn't stop until Harper jumped into the water. Vera and Maggie followed, and I stood there trying to balance from the small waves lapping at my board. When Harper emerged, she wiped the water from her face and said, "Remi, get in."

"Hell no," I said. "I'm not taking any risks, thank you."

Maggie sprawled on her back. "But it feels so good."

"Come on, you have to be warm," Harper said, treading in place.

She was right. After being out for over an hour in prime sun, nothing sounded more pleasant than jumping in the water to cool off. I wasn't even worried about the gators anymore.

I set my paddle on my board and jumped in. The water was the perfect amount of cold to feel refreshing on my sweaty body but not cold enough that I wanted to jump back out. I floated on my back, spread my arms, closed my eyes, and enjoyed the sun on my face even though I knew it would turn into a sunburn once I took a shower.

The fluttering resumed in my stomach when we got back to Harper's car, and she put her clothes back on. Her shirt absorbed the water from her bikini and left marks under her breasts. I realized then how dehydrated I was. As she tossed me a towel, I swear her gaze slipped from my eyes and down to my stomach. It was only for a moment before she turned to put her things in the trunk as if trying to hide what she knew I'd caught.

I hoped that meant something. I told myself it meant something. The sunburn was totally worth all of it.

❖

As dusk started to fall on the town the next night, I rode my bike to the boardwalk and locked it at the rack right outside of Sully's and Mia's. I wore my bookbag and had my telescope inside with its hard case wrapped in a blanket. The frying oil from Sully's was more potent than usual, probably because of the crowd waiting for their bucket of fries. When I got to the Acadian, Harper emerged from the back with her purse slung around her.

"I'll see you Monday, Andrew," she said, waving good-bye to a kid behind the counter. And then she met my gaze for a moment before it fell to my legs. She quickly pulled her eyes back to mine and smiled. The glance over slammed my cheeks with a warm blush that not even the blast of the air-conditioning could put out.

She raised a plastic bag holding two wrapped-up po'boys. "I got our dinner ready. How do you feel about trying The Shrimp tonight?"

"Does it pair perfectly with a bucket of Sully's fries?"

"It pairs perfectly with everything…and lemonade from Mia's."

"Perfect. Let's do this. My stomach is about to be so happy."

We bought a large bucket of fries and got two large lemonades at Mia's. Then we picked up a variety box of taffy from the Chocolate Factory. Harper said it was important to have both salty and sweet snacks, and I agreed. With full arms of the town's best treats, we followed the flickering lamps along the boardwalk until the path spilled onto a dark beach, a more secluded area with minimal light pollution from the shops.

I pulled out the blanket when we found our spot, and Harper helped spread it across the sand. We used our flip-flops to weigh the corners down. I plucked a pink taffy from the box while I set up the telescope. Harper drank her lemonade, and my stomach tugged as she watched me intently. Once the telescope was put together, I rewarded myself with a fry. They were still warm and fresh, and the salt and oil with a splash of malt vinegar stuck to my fingers. One taste and I was in love. Honestly, all the things Harper made me try didn't disappoint. I loved the lemonade and po'boys, and Sully's fries tasted as good as they smelled, and I knew my teeth would hurt later from enjoying too much taffy.

"Do you have a favorite star?" Harper asked while unwrapping her po'boy. "I'm guessing that you probably do."

"Of course I do," I said and grabbed a handful of fries. "It's Betelgeuse." Pronounced like Beetlejuice, which added to my love for the red supergiant.

"Why is it your favorite?"

"Many reasons. One, the name. Find me a star with a better name. It's not possible. Two, it's one of the closest stars to the sun, and it's enormous. Like, it would engulf Mercury, Venus, Earth, Mars, *and* the asteroid belt. That's fucking massive. And that's not even the best part. It's one of the brightest stars in the sky. Well...it used to be the tenth brightest star in the sky."

"It used to be?"

I nodded. "It's acting weird. It recently dimmed to a third of its usual brightness, and you can visibly see the change on Earth."

She put the bucket of fries in between her legs. "Whoa," she said and shoved a few fries in her mouth, her stare rounding with intrigue. "Why is it doing that? What's wrong with Betelgeuse?"

Luckily, the gas lamps didn't provide too much light on the beach. There was enough darkness to cloak my insecurities and trick me into thinking that I didn't have any because a cute girl asked me about the stars. It helped me be more confident in all my space knowledge, like I hadn't bored my peers countless times growing up. I finally met someone other than my dad who encouraged it.

"This is the best part," I said, eager to tell her one of the most exciting facts about space. "It's the most important reason why I love it. Are you ready?"

She leaned forward as if I was about to spill some tea. "I'm totally ready."

"It's dying."

I beamed at the same time Harper frowned. She lowered her handful of fries. "Wait, what? It's dying?"

I nodded in excitement. "Yeah, it's dying. In the next one hundred thousand years, which is basically, like, any day now in an astronomical sense, it will use up all its fuel, collapse under its own weight, and explode into a supernova. When it explodes, it will be as bright as a full moon in broad daylight, and it could stay that bright for a year or even more."

"Whoa," Harper said in a long drawl. "That's…intense and fascinating."

"I know, right? Basically, Orion's left shoulder is a ticking time bomb, and no one knows about it except for a few star geeks."

"Will it destroy Earth when it blows up?"

"No, we're too far away. Plus, we'll all be dead by the time it happens."

"Well, damn. I want to see this ticking time bomb in the sky." She moved the bucket aside as if she didn't care about all the deliciousness. "Can you show me?"

I stole the bucket and ate a few fries. "Orion isn't out right now. We have to wait until winter to see it, but I can show you Saturn and Jupiter and other cool things."

"Do they have cool stories like Betelgeuse?"

"Uh, for sure. There could be life on one of Jupiter's moons, and I can show you that one."

"Wait, seriously?"

I nodded and looked into the telescope to find Jupiter and the four specks right next to it. "This is my dad's favorite thing in the sky. This moon is what got me into space and stars and everything. Here, look." I presented the telescope and continued eating while she looked. "It's one of those four dots next to Jupiter. Europa has a frozen crust with cracks all over it. That's why every space person is freaking out about it because if there are cracks, that indicates that there's water that refroze, and water means life. Basically, long story short, it's the best chance of finding life in our solar system."

Harper pulled away and observed me intently, as if I was giving her the juicy gossip of the universe. "Wow. That was really Jupiter." She pointed to the telescope.

"Yup. And there might be life on one of those tiny dots. Neat huh?"

"More than neat. This is fucking awesome." She put her eye back on the telescope, and I sat there with my po'boy with my heart ready to take off like a rocket. I never thought I'd impress any cute person with my space facts and enthusiasm. And then entered Harper Hebert, who made all the boring things on Earth fascinating. "Are we ever going to know if there's life on Europa?"

"Funny you ask. Europa's number one fan, my dad, said that NASA's planning to send something out there soon. And Europe's NASA equivalent, the ESA, has plans also. Both within the next ten years."

She pulled away and looked back. "And then we'll be able to tell if there's other life in our solar system?"

"Exactly!"

Excitement bubbled in my chest at how intrigued she seemed to be. The only person who looked at me with wide eyes and intense curiosity about the sky was my dad, and for the last four years, I hadn't really had anyone. Sure, Mom and Brie enjoyed the occasional stargazing, Mom more than Brie, but that was because she wanted me to be happy. But for people not obsessed with space, there were only so many times you could look at a planet before growing bored.

I wondered if Harper would ever get bored.

"Can I see Saturn?"

I smiled. Already, she showed more enthusiasm than anyone else, and I'd only covered Betelgeuse and Europa. "Sure. Let me find it for you."

I pointed the telescope in the direction of Saturn and focused to get the best view of the planet and all of its rings. It was a perfect shot, and even though I'd seen the planet countless times, it never got old.

Harper gasped when she put her eye on the lens. I unwrapped a taffy and popped it into my mouth as my smile grew from watching her.

"Oh my God, this is amazing," she said and then glanced over. I caught a wave of her fruity shampoo. Of course she'd smell amazing. "You can see the whole universe."

"Telescopes are severely underrated," I said, chewing on my watermelon taffy.

After Saturn, I showed her the moon, saving the best for last. Looking at the moon through the telescope felt like you were actually on it. The craters were so detailed, and watching Harper take it in for the first time reminded me of when I was eight, and Dad had showed off his Celestron for the first time. That first night, we sat outside and spent hours looking through it. He'd showed me the moon and then Europa, unveiling all the juicy details about it. That was the night I'd fallen in love with the night sky.

We took turns using the telescope and sitting back to enjoy the sky with just our eyes. The dinging of the arcade games on the boardwalk faded into silence, and the only thing filling in the space were the waves lightly crashing onto shore. To our left, in the distance, the lighthouse flickered, and to our right, the colorful lights of the Ferris wheel signaled the opposite end of the boardwalk. It was a perfect night.

"It's crazy how small we are compared to these things," Harper said, pulling away from the telescope and eating more fries. "Isn't it?"

I grinned. She'd thought about it too. Looking at a planet could really send you into an existential crisis. "I think about it all the time and how we dwell on all these issues here on Earth when they really don't matter."

Silence took a seat between us. As I looked skyward, from the corner of my eye, I could see Harper study me for a moment before doing the same.

"Even on the plane down here, I looked out the window and felt so removed from everything," I said and kept my gaze on the sliver crescent moon.

"Sometimes, I wish I could feel removed from everything. Maybe then I could get some clarity."

I turned to the colorful reds, blues, and purples of the Ferris wheel about a half mile away. "Have you ever been on the top of the wheel?" I asked.

"Hell no. I hate heights."

It had to be a little over a hundred feet tall, and when I was much closer, I'd noticed that the steel cabins were enclosed, preventing anyone from falling out. "You should try it. Remove yourself enough to breathe a little bit. Get that clarity you want. We could go together if you want?"

Harper looked at me like I'd proposed something wild. Her dark brown eyebrows stitched together. "Now? It's..." She checked her phone. "Almost ten," she said it as if she was disappointed.

"What time does it close?"

She hesitated. "Eleven."

"Plenty of time."

I jumped up and reached out. Her eyebrows arched as her eyes pleaded with me to let it go, but I wasn't going to take no for an answer unless she really put her foot down. I wanted her to see how significantly smaller things appeared when she looked at life from a different perspective.

I wiggled my fingers to speed her up. "We're going on an adventure."

"But I don't do heights—"

"And I don't swim with gators, but I did that. You're a lot stronger than you think, Harper Hebert. Come on."

"Ugh." She grunted and placed her hand in mine.

A jolt zapped through me at her touch. Her hand was so soft, and her grip was so gentle, I didn't want to let go once I pulled her up. But I had to in order to pack up the telescope and the blanket while forcing myself to act like an intense ripple hadn't fluttered through my chest a moment before.

My heart didn't stop hammering until we reached the Ferris wheel. The lights illuminated Harper's wide-eyed stare. "I can't believe I'm doing this," she said once we took our spot in line. There appeared to be about a ten-minute wait, which was the perfect amount of time for Harper to prepare. "Vera and Maggie have been trying to get me to do this for years."

"And you haven't?"

"Nope."

An overwhelming surge threaded through me at the newfound knowledge. For whatever reason, she'd decided to ride with me instead of her two best friends. I had no idea how long she'd known Vera and Maggie, but I'd say that being childhood friends was a safe guess. She'd met me ten days prior. I sucked in my bottom lip and looked away so she didn't have a front row view of my poorly suppressed grin.

Once we got into the cabin and the employee locked the steel door, Harper clutched the handgrip on the side of the cabin and closed her eyes.

"You know, we don't have to do this," I said. "I just thought that—"

"No, no, you're right. I need to master this," she said through a clenched jaw. "If I can't master some stupid Ferris wheel, how can I expect to master anything else?"

"You're sure?"

"Positive. I'm just going to close my eyes until we get to the top."

The cabin jerked forward, and Harper's whole body stiffened as we slowly rotated toward the sky. We went around two times before stopping halfway up. I stole a glance at Harper. She lifted an eyelid and looked down. Then her free hand snatched mine and squeezed it, and at the same time, a shudder snaked down my spine. I looked at her fingers curled around mine, and it seemed like all the air left my lungs. *Oh my God, she's squeezing my hand.* Was it only to relieve her anxiety, or did it actually count as holding hands? My whole body became as stiff as hers but for a completely different reason. I was too afraid to flinch in case that caused her to retrieve her hand. Instead, I held in the very little air in my lungs, clenched my jaw, and stared out while being hyper aware of every atom that made up my right hand. I couldn't even focus on the sights of the boardwalk below. All I could think about was the intensity of the thrumming in my chest.

"Oh my God," Harper muttered softly, hand still holding mine.

I found the courage to face her. Her eyes were open wide, back glued to the seat, and her body looked like a statue. But she soaked up the scene. I could tell by how steady her stare was. More than a hundred feet in the air, everything looked so small. The people, the buildings, the Acadian and Envie. It was almost like being in an airplane and so removed from life that the problems on land appeared so infinitesimal.

"Isn't it pretty?" I asked.

We had a beautiful view of the boardwalk and the stunning lamp flames flickering down its length.

"Pretty terrifying? Yes, yes, it is."

I laughed. "It's beautiful. Look at all the lamps and how small the people look. They look like little figurines."

Harper leaned over to get a better look below, and just as she did, the Ferris wheel lurched forward. She tightened her grip on my hand, my heart swelled, and the wheel did another rotation until it stopped us at the very top.

"They…" she said through a tightened jaw, and her throat moved along with a big gulp. "They do look like figurines."

"Doesn't it seem a little fake from up here? Don't you feel a little removed from all the things happening on the ground, or am I making things up?"

She didn't say anything at first. A light breeze wafted through the cabin, and her hair fluttered backward, giving me a better glimpse of her face. She retrieved her hand from mine and ran it through her hair, leaving my hand burning from the lingering touch. Her stare was still transfixed below. I was proud of her for agreeing to go on the wheel and actually opening her eyes. She seemed to really study the sights as if searching for any sort of new perspective.

"No, you're not making things up," she said softly, her gaze not flinching. "I feel it too."

"Like, for me, I feel more removed from the drama with my dad." For the first time since we were locked into the cabin, Harper turned to me with confusion crisscrossing her features. I grunted when I realized that I had to quickly explain myself. "My parents separated the summer after eighth grade. On Valentine's Day of my sophomore year, my dad called me, wished me a happy Valentine's Day. I don't know…we used to be so close that he always would give me a Valentine's Day card and Sweethearts candy."

"That's really cute, actually."

"I know, right? Sophomore year, he calls me to wish me a happy Valentine's Day and to ask if I got the card and the box of candy he'd mailed. I asked what he was doing, and that's when he told me he was going on a date. I have no idea if that was their first date or if they'd started dating before, but Valentine's Day is an intimate holiday, you know? It probably wasn't their first date."

Harper thinned her lips. "Yeah, it probably wasn't."

"Well, that woman is now my stepmom. Last summer, they eloped in Italy. And…I don't know…I'm just so mad at how quickly he moved on from my mom. They were married for twenty years, and he finds someone else to marry eight months after the divorce was finalized. He was such a dick during it too, and I don't understand how he gains this new lavish life with his multi-millionaire wife, and my mom is left paying a mortgage and lost half her furniture to him. The only reason I'm down here for the summer is because he told me he wouldn't help me with my college tuition if I didn't…the college tuition he'd been promising me my whole life. Paying for college isn't the problem. I'm fortunate enough to have parents who can help even a little bit. The problem is using it against me so he can get what he wants. That really hurts, and he knows that going to MIT has been my dream. I feel so betrayed by him."

Right as the anger started to snake through me, her soft gentle hand rested on top of mine and squeezed it for the briefest moment. "I'm so sorry. That sounds like…well…it sounds like a lot."

I glanced at our hands intertwined, and when I did, she pulled away. This time, I felt the thin layer of moisture on her palms, but it didn't gross me out. I didn't even care if her hands were a little clammy. Mine were too, not because of the height of the wheel but because she sat so close, and my whole body longed to touch her again. It was almost as if she was embarrassed that she'd held my hand. But what about the other moment when she'd clasped my hand all through the first rotation, the first stop, and the second rotation?

Had that just been a nervous reflex? Or was it something else?

"Yeah, it was a lot," I said, pulling my gaze away from her and back to the flames licking the inside of the lamps. "I told him last weekend when we were looking at my telescope that when you think about the whole universe, Earth isn't even a speck. We're not even detectable, so why do we care so much about things that don't really matter when the Earth's existence doesn't really matter? Why did he care so much about furniture when it really doesn't matter?" I blew out a heavy breath. "I don't know. I guess looking at Earth from a plane...or even this Ferris wheel...it makes me see my life differently. You see how small people are from here. People are just people up here. My dad is a human, and even though he's been a real asshole the last few years, he hasn't always been that way. Those four years of being an asshole were only a speck in comparison to the fourteen years when he'd done so much for me. I mean, he used to be my best friend. He was the coolest person I knew. Something as little as looking at the ground from a plane or a Ferris wheel helps me pull back a little bit and reminds me that I'm lucky I have a dad who loves me and wants to actually be my dad. Sometimes I forget that, and it's easy to forget when you're on the ground, and you have so many other things blocking your view."

We sat there for a moment watching people carry on with life and enjoying the mid-June night. I wondered what problems infiltrated the minds of the people on the ground and if they were able to somehow pull away to see the bigger picture, to not let the little things weigh them down the way the little things in the divorce had wedged a giant hole between me and my dad.

Dings from the arcade filled in the silence, but it wasn't an uncomfortable one. We spun around a couple more times, and I could feel Harper loosen up next to me, as if her mind was lost in something else so that it had forgotten about the height.

After we stepped out and walked down the steps onto the boardwalk, Harper turned back around and glanced up at the wheel. "I get it now," she said before facing me. The little curve of her lips told me that the fear that had weighed on her for the first few minutes had faded away like a low tide. I absorbed the sight of the faint, victorious smile and the Ferris wheel lights dancing on her beautiful face. "Something about being up there made everything down here seem smaller."

"Did you get any clarity?"

She looked skyward for a second. "Yeah, I think I did."

"And what is it?"

She let out a small laugh and watched the wheel spin around with its new riders. "How much I've grown out of Gaslight Shores."

I followed her stare back to the wheel. Harper, like so many people, had seemed fixated on a future that only consisted of a bunch of what-ifs and what-could-be, events that hadn't even happened, events that weren't yet real. She'd painted the world in only blacks and whites. There were no grays on her palette. I couldn't really blame her. She'd never left her hometown. She thought she was destined to forever live in a small town in conservative South Carolina. I wanted to show her all the grays and in-betweens that she was missing out on. The world was a much bigger place than what she'd thought, and there was plenty of room for her and her dreams.

"You mastered the Ferris wheel," I said. "I bet you can master anything else too."

She glanced over with a soft smile. My stomach spun like the wheel at the sight, and I knew I was witnessing an epiphany settle in her. "Maybe you're right."

I smiled because I knew she saw the same thing I saw at the top of the wheel: her horizon extended beyond Gaslight Shores, and she was strong enough to reach it.

CHAPTER SIX

I'd never been to a party.
Not counting the innocent sleepovers with pajamas, soda, snacks, and movies in middle school. But one thrown when parents—for whatever reason—trusted their teenage kids with their house and went somewhere for the night. An abandoned oasis for teenage hormones, one that straddled the line of the law with alcohol.

When Harper texted and asked if I wanted to go to a party with her, Vera, and Maggie, of course I agreed. Brie and I were supposed to go to one together, and I wanted to keep some semblance of the summer I had planned. When I texted Brie that Cute Girl invited me to a party, she FaceTimed me.

"Look cute," were her first words.

I loved how the two of us were so close, we skipped the greetings all together. "Do I usually not look cute?"

"I mean, you *are* cute, but don't wear your retro NASA shirt."

"Hey. That's my favorite shirt."

"But the goal is to kiss a girl…or a boy…or anyone in between. The plan is to get kissed."

"Harper actually finds all my space love intriguing, so my retro NASA shirt might work on her."

Brie face-palmed herself. "You're not wearing the NASA shirt."

I had two suitcases of clothes for the summer, so it only took Brie around twenty minutes to pick out black shorts, a dark green top that she said would amplify the green in my hazel eyes, and when I told her that Harper wasn't going to pick me up until eight thirty, and it would be too dark for anyone to notice the green flecks, Brie stood firm about me wearing the top. She gave me my very own makeup tutorial, as if she was a pro YouTube artist, since I only knew how to put on mascara.

"Oh my God, look at my Remi," Brie said and clapped once the simple makeup touches enhanced my facial features. "You're going to be in a little bi daze from all the attention you're going to get at this party. You're adorable."

I straightened my back. I'd gotten called adorable twice in a week. Brie's only half counted because she was my best friend. We didn't want to kiss each other, so based on that, it didn't hold as much weight as Harper's.

"Hopefully, Cute Girl thinks the same thing," I said. "She did call me adorable the other day."

"Ugh," Brie said. "She held your hand on the Ferris wheel, called you adorable, gave you a rewards card with eight out of the ten punches completed. This girl likes you, Remi."

"She could just be an affectionate person—"

"No. Stop it and do something about this, or I'm going to fly down there and kick your ass. Or better yet, I'll drag you over to Cute Girl and tell her that you like her and want to kiss her."

"Brie…"

She laughed. "Pick your poison. You do it yourself, or I do it."

I stood outside the front gate and waited for Harper to pick me up. I rested my back against the Palms sign and watched the lightning bugs speckle the falling dusk. The crickets and frogs were already out and harmonizing with the cicadas rattling in the live oak trees. With the sun falling, the heat dissipated, and even the humidity wanted to relax tonight, only coiling a few of my waves into curls.

Two headlights emerged from the street, and I smiled when I saw the red Corolla pull up and park in front of me.

"You ready to leave Kansas?" Harper asked when I hopped in her passenger seat. She had both of her front windows rolled down, and the smell of wonderful summer saturated the inside of her car.

"What do you mean?"

She paused for a moment as her stare moved from my face down my body, and when she looked back up, the corners of her lips rose the smallest degree, as if she was impressed with what she saw.

Was Harper checking me out?

"You ready for your first chummer party?" she said, and the Southern accent popped in her voice. I swallowed hard at how adorable it was. "Our friend Cody lives right by the bridge. Time for you to see the Gaslight Shores that they don't show you in the travel magazines."

My world in Gaslight Shores was the length of Serena's house in the Palms and extended five miles to the boardwalk. I hadn't traveled to the north side of the island where the golfie subdivisions and famous golf courses were. There was no reason for me to go anywhere that wasn't between the Palms and the boardwalk.

"I'm up for anything fun," I said.

"It will be fun. I promise."

The famous lamps that illuminated the boardwalk as well as Main and Front Street were no more as we drove inland. The dense trees helped the darkness become thicker, more lightning bugs flickered all around, and the splat of a bug hitting the windshield happened at least ten times on our drive, and it made us jump every time.

Harper turned onto a dirt driveway, and small pebbles hit the tires and the sides of the car until a long porch glowed through the dark. The white house was small, modest, with a front porch that spanned the entire length. A couple kids hung around in front of it, each holding a Solo cup or a beer bottle around the beer pong table in front of the porch steps. Country music played faintly, and as much as I hated country music, it did set the scene. A Southern summer night was probably the only time I'd tolerate Garth Brooks without a single complaint.

I followed Harper as most of the party greeted her with waves and hugs. It was my first glimpse at the kind of person she was in town and school. Not like it mattered to me, but it gave me more insight into who she was as a person. Given how many people said hi to her, she was popular. She introduced me to a few people, too many to remember. I was relieved when we finally found Vera and Maggie on the porch, two familiar faces I'd turn to if someone pulled Harper into a conversation.

"Wanna get a drink?" Harper asked.

This was my time to experience the party life, right? "Yeah, sure."

We went inside where a couple more kids hung around the kitchen. One guy hugged Harper as if they were good friends and handed her two cans of black cherry White Claw. She talked to him for only a moment and then leaned into me, "Come on, let's go back outside."

The hairs on the back of my neck rose when her words landed on my lips, and I got a whiff of her fruity shampoo and minty breath.

Yeah, I needed fresh air and something cool against the back of my throat after that.

Vera and Maggie flirted with two boys on one end of the porch, and we went to the other end and took a spot on the empty swing. I took a cautious sip of White Claw. The cold bubbles were exactly what my throat needed to unclasp the nerves hanging in the back.

"You like it?"

I smacked my lips together. "It's pretty good. I expected my first alcohol to taste like shit."

"This is your first drink? Oh my God, you're growing up." She shook my upper arm, and my whole body stiffened. "I'm honored to be a part of this moment."

I pulled another sip and was determined to have another can after I finished this one. "Yeah, this is my first drink. I was kind of a nerd in high school and never went to a party. Was too focused on studying, making sure I graduated with honors, became valedictorian, got into MIT—"

"Wait," she said and rested a hand on my arm. I froze again, and as long as her hand remained on me, I'd wait as long as she wanted. "You were valedictorian?"

I faltered and wondered if that made me more nerdy or more appealing. "Yes?" The insecurity only lasted a millisecond because Harper's smile expanded and made my chest dance along.

"So you *are* a genius! I knew it."

"If that's your definition of a genius, sure, but it came with a price. Minimal social life, hence now having my first alcoholic beverage."

She waved me off. "Don't compare yourself to others. It doesn't matter when you have your first drink or if you even want to drink it at all. Honestly, I didn't have my first drink until last summer, so really, this is, like, my third or fourth time."

"Okay, good. That makes me feel less lame."

She bumped her elbow into my arm. I wasn't sure why I was getting all these touches, but I loved it and hoped many more were in my future. "You're not lame at all, Remi Brenner. I promise."

Her light brown eyes were luminous, sparkling against the patio light that buzzed any time a bug ran into it. A kind of look like nothing I could do or say would make her look at me differently. I'd never considered myself an insecure person, but Harper had the ability to make me feel apprehensive while at the same time, flooding me with confidence.

Headlights pierced the darkness as rocks crumpled underneath tires. A few moments later, two girls got out of a car, and the patio lights revealed their faces.

"Oh, shit," Harper muttered and quickly turned her back to the brunette and strawberry blonde.

I glanced at the newest additions standing at the end of the table. Vera's and Maggie's giggling faded enough to pull my attention in their direction. The strawberry blonde glanced over and then snapped her attention to the table. Whatever the hell was going on, it was enough for Vera and Maggie to abandon their crushes to walk over, the patio creaking under their footsteps.

"Oh, geez," Vera said and rested a hand on Harper's shoulder. Harper rolled her eyes and took a longer sip of White Claw. "I had no idea that she was coming."

"Ignore her," Maggie said. "She won't even say anything. She hasn't in a year."

"I know but…" Harper trailed off and turned to steal a glance at one of the new girls before facing us again. "I want answers."

"You're never going to get them," Maggie said. "Unless you confront her tonight and demand them."

"But even then, she'll make excuses," Vera said. "She always made excuses for everything."

The two girls walked up the stairs, and the conversation died. Harper silenced herself by drinking, and Vera and Maggie sealed their lips shut and looked at the patio. I was the only one to watch them make their way inside. The strawberry blonde didn't look over, but it wasn't enough to clear the tension that hung over us. It was so palpable, it started sticking to my skin, the porch light reflecting a thin layer of sweat that I could feel on my face and that I could see on Harper, Vera, and Maggie.

"Who are we talking about?" I finally asked.

Harper rolled her eyes. "It's nothing." How dramatically the conversation had shifted once those two arrived said that was far from the truth.

"An ex-friend," Vera said.

"Can we not talk about it?" Harper said and then shook her empty can; only a splash clanged against the aluminum.

"Want me to get you another?" I asked.

Harper downed the last splash. "Yes, please."

"I'll go with you," Maggie said. "I want to make Autumn squirm. It's fun." She wiggled her auburn eyebrows at Harper and Vera before leading me back inside.

Maggie said hello to a few people standing around the kitchen island, and I looked for the two girls. With no knowledge of what was going on, I could tell the ex-friend was the strawberry blonde because after one quick glance at Maggie, she looked away and made conversation with a girl next to her. Maggie let out a quiet laugh, opened the fridge, and pulled out two mango White Claws.

Quick and painless—yet super awkward at the same time— Maggie and I went back outside and found Harper and Vera rocking on the patio swing, leaning close and whispering.

"She saw me and then started talking to Holly Anderson," Maggie said and laughed. "Funny, I didn't know they talked. She's definitely not going to say anything to any of us. She can't even look us in the eye. You're good, Harp."

Harper grunted. "This is going to be *so* awkward. We've managed to avoid each other so well until now."

Maggie waved the comment off and handed Harper a new can. "Nah, she's going to hide and avoid. She's good at it. Give her more credit."

Vera stood. "We're next in beer pong. Come over if you need to escape."

"Or let me know. I'll happily confront her," Maggie said with a mischievous smirk.

Harper met my gaze and let the smallest smile take over again. My chest flipped at the knowledge that somehow, by looking at me, her worries eased. "Remi and I will join in a few."

Vera and Maggie walked down the steps, and I took a spot next to Harper.

She steadied the rocking of the swing with her heels. I made sure to be on high alert and focused on the front door in case the strawberry blonde came back out and added palpable tension back into the air. But for now, the air was light like it had been before, just a little bit of moisture to dampen my skin but not dose me in disgusting sweat.

"So...who's the girl?" I asked. I had to ask, and I think the silent moment that squeezed between us when I came back from the kitchen warned Harper that I would.

She fiddled with the can tab. "Old friend, I guess." She ran a hand through her hair, and another wave of fruit washed over me. It was a simple but sexy gesture. "Okay, if I tell you something, you promise you won't judge or tell anyone?"

"Why would I judge? I nerded out to you for, like, two hours about space last weekend. I'm the last person to ever judge."

Fear seemed to round her eyes, and it pained me to see that whatever she was about to tell me really weighed on her mind, to the point where she thought others would judge her. I'd only known her for two weeks, but even then, she hadn't been anything other than welcoming and selfless. I wasn't sure how she could do anything worthy of judgment.

She gave a thin smile that didn't reach her eyes and glanced at her can. "I haven't even told Vera or Maggie."

"What? Why?" Now I was really curious. What was it about me that made her feel more comfortable going on a Ferris wheel or telling me something that not even her two best friends knew?

She shrugged. "I don't know. Maybe it's because we've all been friends since third grade, and it's harder to tell them because they know Autumn too. Also, it's not really fair for me to tell them."

"You don't have to tell me if you don't want to. It's really okay."

"No...I mean...ugh, I feel like I can tell you because you don't live here, and I kinda really need to talk to someone about it. It's been eating me alive for the last year, and you don't really seem like the type of person to judge."

"I'm not. I'm here if you need someone to listen. If you don't want to talk about it, then we can make fun of how bad the boys are at this game." I nodded to the beer pong and laughed at how Vera and Maggie were already crushing them.

"Okay...well...um," she began, her voice much softer than before, as if she didn't want the wind to carry her secret to other parts of the party. "Like I said, we'd been friends since third grade, and as we grew up, Vera and Maggie would always talk about boys. Like, nonstop, and we weren't as boy crazy as them, so...I don't know. I guess we formed this closer bond making fun of Vera and Maggie's boy obsession while we didn't care at all. Then, about a year and a half ago, everything started changing. I didn't really realize what was happening at the time, but I know what it was now."

"What was it?"

Autumn and her brunette friend stepped outside. Autumn stole a glance at us, and when we made eye contact, she averted her gaze and followed her friend down the steps and to the game, leaving Harper and I sitting in the discernible hostility that was as thick as the humidity. Harper kept her eyes on her sandals, her heels still rocking us back and forth. I looked over at the game. Vera and Maggie had defeated the two boys and were now playing the brunette friend and another guy. Autumn stood awkwardly off to the side, focusing only on her friend and the cups on the table.

"Okay, so anyway," Harper said, lowering her voice a couple of decibels from a moment earlier. She leaned in closer, and the heat of her body added another complex layer to the surrounding space. My heart stuttered at how close she was. I eased my tightening throat with another cold drink from my can. "We picked up this kind of banter that I thought was lighthearted and stupid. Like flirting, winking, holding hands. It was normal for us. It started out as a joke, something funny we did, something to pass the time while Vera and Maggie were on their boy rants. Last summer, we were at Vera's ex-boyfriend's party. We partnered up in beer pong, got tipsy, and then we went to the bathroom together, and that's when she kissed me. I was so taken aback by it at first, but the thing was, I wanted to kiss her. All that stupid fake banter and flirting turned into some actual feelings that I didn't even know I had until she kissed me."

My mouth wanted to fall open at the information, but I clenched my teeth to prevent it from happening. Inside, I jumped and danced that maybe—just maybe—all of this meant that Harper had flirted with me. Maybe Brie was right this whole time. Maybe all those little things she'd said and done that I'd brushed off as being friendly could have actually meant something.

"We made out for a long time until someone knocked and ruined the moment," she continued. "After the party, she kind of acted weird. Our usual flirting wasn't there. She could barely look me in the eyes. That is, until she had a party at her house a few weeks later. That's when she pulled me aside and whispered to me that she wanted to kiss me *again* and that she'd thought about it ever since the first time. We snuck off to her room a few times to make out, and I couldn't say that it was the drinking that made me want to kiss her like the first time because we weren't drinking. After everyone left, I stayed behind, and we made out for hours. She asked me to spend the night because she said she was afraid of sleeping by herself while her dad was out of town."

"So did you?"

She pressed her lips together and nodded. "At one point, we started taking each other's clothes off. Once I realized what was happening, I stopped it because I was scared of where it was going. I hadn't slept with anyone before, and she hadn't either, but she told me that she'd liked me for the whole school year, and that the flirting and hand-holding was real, and I believed her. I trusted her. I mean, as much as I was scared about our friendship becoming weird, I liked her. I thought because we'd been friends for so long and because it was both of our first times, it would mean something, that she wouldn't hurt me. Well, I was so fucking wrong."

I directed my stare back on the game and found Autumn's eyes on me. This was the second time our stares connected for a millisecond before she looked away again.

Jealousy and envy ran through me. Knowing that Harper liked girls started making my innocent crush rapidly bloom, but then finding out she'd already had sex made me feel inadequate, a wonderful reminder of my virginity and how I'd spent too much time studying to become valedictorian and getting into MIT, when I should have given myself time to put my love life into action. I knew it was silly to think that, but the regret came and went like waves, and hearing that Harper was on a different playing field than me made the regret wash over and roll me around in my own insecurities.

"The next morning, she was totally fine and kissed me good-bye," Harper continued. "And then after that, everything was different. She was so freaked out by it, she avoided me, only made plans with Vera and Maggie, until they asked her why she was avoiding me. Autumn told them that she didn't want to be friends with me anymore. Gave them no other reason other than that. I tried talking to her about it, but she never texted or called me back. School started, and she didn't sit with us at lunch anymore. Completely wrote us off. Still to this day, I never got closure with her. We never talked about it, and I spent a good portion of my senior year feeling so awful about it. Vera and Maggie keep asking what happened, but I can't out Autumn. I don't know how she identifies or if anyone else knows, but I can't tell anyone until she tells people."

"Do Vera and Maggie know how you identify?"

"They know I'm a lesbian. I told them last fall and said I slept with a slocal instead of telling them it was Autumn. It sucks that I can't really talk to anyone about it because it still hurts like hell."

"I'm sorry, Harper. You can talk to me."

Harper pulled a sip from her can, and vulnerability staggered in her stare, as if she'd laid her cards on the table and expected me to trump them with my hand. I squeezed her knee to comfort her, and something jolted in me at the contact. Harper must have felt it too because at the same time my insides lit up, she glanced at the connection. Feeling her eyes on me intensified everything coiling around my chest. The little crush I had started to unravel at rapid speed.

It was kind of like how I viewed the sky without the telescope. Sure, I saw the stars twinkling. They were nice to look at, but they were just specks. Fascinating specks. I couldn't see enough of them to fully understand how amazing they were. But when I saw them through a telescope, it opened up a whole universe. I could actually see them and their beauty that was more than a sparkling dot in the sky. Their beauty was so much more detailed, complex, and so unique to them. That was what it felt like knowing that Harper liked girls, only girls, for that matter. Before the knowledge, I knew she was beautiful. She had me looking, but I'd assumed she was straight, and I'd hated myself for defaulting to heteronormativity, but I couldn't help it. Knowing I liked girls and never experiencing anything with a girl made me hide behind heteronormativity with my insecurities. But the truth Harper revealed was the telescope that made me fully see her. She wasn't an untouchable dot. My feelings for her became more detailed, like how much I loved her smile or her eyes in the sunshine or the cute freckle on the nape of her neck and the ones that speckled the top of her nose. And maybe, just maybe, I had a chance.

I pulled my hand away before I got too lost in the feelings. "If it makes you feel any better, I don't think she likes that I'm sitting with you," I said.

The corner of her lips pulled upward. "Why do you say that?"

Somehow, the space between us had narrowed. I hadn't moved and neither had Harper. Maybe we'd both leaned our heads closer so the whispers didn't travel, but when those brown eyes stared into mine, my stomach flipped. I felt every sweat bead dripping down my neck and sticking to the fabric of my tank top. Harper staring at me like that, like I was the only thing in the world, made me feel each individual atom that made up my body.

I swallowed the nonexistent saliva in my arid throat. "I've caught her glaring at me multiple times," I said, softening my voice to match hers.

Harper laughed, but it didn't quite reach her eyes. "It was a stupid thing to do," she said, shaking her head. "I can't believe I let it happen. I knew every time we kissed, it was a dumb idea. That thought never went away. I knew it in my gut that it was a bad decision, or at least, *she* was a bad decision. I just…I thought she would respect me and appreciate me. I really thought my first time was going to be something special because it was with one of my best friends who I'd known for years, someone who I'd trusted for years."

The rattle in her voice came back, and her gaze pulled off me. I could feel the insecurities swaddling her. I hated how it made her act, how it made her speak, how it made her think of herself. And it pissed me off no end that someone who she'd trusted had done that to her.

I really wished I could comfort her. I had no idea what to say because I wanted the first person I slept with to treat me the way Harper wanted to be treated, how anyone wanted to be treated after such a big moment and their first dose of intimacy. And the fact that Harper didn't get that respect really bothered me. It was a good thing Autumn wasn't looking over now because I would have glared at her.

"It really does a number on you, you know?" Harper said.

"I bet. But some people need time. To come out, that is. Maybe when she's ready, you'll get some answers."

Coming out was a prime example of how time was relative. Being in the closet up until last year, my days had moved by so slow and heavy, like I had to trek up a mountain with a hundred-pound weight on my back. Even when I lived in a liberal state that voted for Clinton and Biden, and those blue anti-hate signs seemed to be on every front lawn, it still didn't make coming out any easier. It didn't take back all the homophobic and biphobic comments floating around on the internet, saying I was confused and really gay but hiding behind boys. I knew what I was. I was bisexual. I found some boys attractive, but I was a little more attracted to girls, but just because I was more attracted to girls didn't make me any less bi. Some people knew what they liked since they were five. Some people didn't know until they were twenty-five. Not every queer person realized they were part of the LGBTQ+ community by the time they graduated high school, and just because someone was fifty and realized that they might be a lesbian or trans or bisexual didn't mean they were confused at all. There was no statute of limitations for realizing gender or sexual identity. The time to figure out who we were was completely relative, and Autumn was on a different pace than Harper, and that was okay. I sympathized with her.

What wasn't okay was shredding years of trust and hurting Harper after such an intimate moment.

"Take me, for example," I said to break the silence. "I didn't come out until last year." I gathered from her rounded eyes and raised eyebrows that she was as shocked to hear my confession as I was to hear hers.

"You're...I mean...okay," she stammered. "I'm sorry. Go on."

"You're not the only girl who likes girls at this party, Harper." I nudged her side and got a little laugh out of her. "Sorry to steal some of your thunder."

"Wow, okay." She laughed and scratched the back of her head. "See, I kind of had a feeling."

"What? About me?" She nodded, and a smile wrapped around the bite of her bottom lip. "Wait, how?"

"I don't know. I just did. Maybe I mastered gaydar at a young age."

"Well, whatever it was, you were right. I mean, don't get me wrong, I like boys too. I even had a boyfriend at the beginning of senior year, but I've realized since that I also really like girls. Since my boyfriend, all my crushes have been girls."

"That's because girls are pretty great, aren't they?"

"They're wonderful and beautiful."

I didn't really know how wonderful they were. They were beautiful and intriguing, yes, but I hadn't kissed one yet, and I could only imagine what that felt like. Knowing that Harper had kissed a girl and liked girls, I couldn't help but drop my stare to her lips for the briefest moment. They were full, slick from her biting her bottom lip. They were also probably so soft and gentle, probably tasted like mango White Claw and whatever minty gum she'd chewed on the ride over. I bet the White Claw tasted so much better on her lips than it did in a can.

"I feel like we should be a part of this game," I said, desperate for something to take my mind off kissing Harper. "We should go join the fun. Who cares if she's there?"

"But...it's going to be so awkward."

"You're going to be next to me, Vera, and Maggie. She hasn't said anything yet. She's not going to say anything now. Plus, Maggie kind of scares me, so I feel safe next to her. Want to join in? Be my first ever beer pong partner?"

Harper considered this. "I would be honored to be your first ever beer pong partner."

"Only if you cut me some slack if I suck. I am a newb, after all."

She stood and grabbed my hand, and I wondered if she could feel my body quickly turn to stone. "Let's do this." She pulled me down the steps and over to Vera and Maggie. Right as we stood beside them, I expected Harper to retrieve her hand, but she didn't. Our hands remained loosely clamped together as we watched Maggie sink the last cup of the game. She tossed her arms victoriously in the air, then high-fived Vera.

I'd forgotten that I was the one to suggest that we play, but that was before Harper held my hand and continued holding my hand for the next minute or so. I glanced at our intertwined fingers and already loved the way our hands looked pieced together and how it lit up every part of my stomach.

If this was what it felt like holding a girl's hand, I couldn't even imagine what it was like to kiss one.

"Our turn," Harper said, finally letting go, and I didn't like how weightless it felt.

I'd never played beer bong before, and even though it showed because I only sunk one cup, it was still fun. Even better that the cups were filled with water, so I didn't have to drink shitty beer. Instead, because Harper was driving, anytime she had to drink, she passed her drink to someone else at the party, and no one gave her crap for not wanting it. Once I finished my second can, one of the guys got me another, and I shared it with Vera and Maggie.

After we lost miserably to Vera and Maggie, the majority of the party moved to the porch where the country music turned up louder through Bluetooth speakers. Vera and Maggie danced with the boys they'd flirted with earlier, and Harper pulled me by my hand over to them. I really hated dancing. I didn't feel coordinated enough to do it, but Harper made me feel a little more at ease.

A few songs later, I trailed Harper's gaze to Autumn, who stood outside the dance circle still glued to the beer pong table, eyes boring into us. I felt Autumn's jealousy shift Harper's mood as she struggled not to look. So to help her out, I grabbed her hand, spun her around, and pulled her closer. Our hips swayed together to the upbeat country song about some dude's tractor, and Harper gave me a relieved grin. She wrapped her arms around my neck, and I put mine on her waist. The smell of her hair wrapped me up in a daze as we danced like that for a few songs. I focused on her beautiful eyes and the connection that strung us together. My skin tingled where Harper's hands slid down my arms to the beat of the song and rested on my hips. I could feel her breathing on my mouth again, and her breath was like a ghost haunting my lips, and I so badly wanted to be haunted for the rest of the night.

Dancing with her made me forget all about Autumn, and given the fact that she danced into my body for the rest of the party, I got the sense that Harper forgot all about her too.

CHAPTER SEVEN

Gaslight Shores really went all out for the Fourth of July. For a state that once upon a time didn't want to be a part of the country, I found it very ironic that all the lamps lining Main and Front Street, as well as the boardwalk, had red, white, and blue ribbons wrapped around the posts. Several stores had the American flag perched on the flag stands all week leading up to the holiday. At any point in summer, if I'd forgotten what country I was in, I could thank Main and Front for reminding me with the flags taking up more real estate on the side of the road than the gas lamps.

Apparently, it was an even bigger event with Serena. While she only had an American flag on a post mounted to the front porch, inside, a concoction of smells imbued the house. When I walked into the kitchen, Serena was already dressed, messy bun up, black apron on, plastic gloves on like she meant serious business, and ingredients, bowls, spices, and appliances scattered over the counters. She and Laura zipped around like cartoon characters with a trail of dust behind them. Dad walked in to grab some coffee and kissed Serena on the cheek, and she acted like it didn't even happen and continued lathering up what looked to be two pork shoulders with some kind of spice rub.

Dad squeezed my shoulder. "Come on, kiddo. Let's leave the kitchen alone."

I followed him out to the front porch where we both took a seat on the patio chair. The sound of the cicadas rose to a crescendo before fading again like the sound of an ocean wave, growing louder and then pulling back. Dad sipped on his steaming coffee as if it didn't already feel like eighty degrees at ten a.m. Watching him nurse his hot coffee made the back of my knees sweat.

"Are you not going to help her?"

"No matter how hard I've tried, she wants me out of her office. This happened last year. She insisted on throwing her Fourth of July party a week after we got back from our honeymoon. I always tell her we don't need anything huge, but it's like the holiday of the season down here. She says it's what she enjoys, so I leave her be and always remind her I can help, but I don't think she wants me to."

"So…she enjoys stress?"

Dad laughed. "I think she would say it's high pressure."

"That's the professional way of saying 'stress.'"

He patted my shoulder. "You're wise beyond your years, kiddo."

I didn't see Serena catch a breath, even as all her guests started arriving the next evening. About thirty people filtered through the house and poured out to the backyard. That was when I discovered how seriously they took the Fourth, at least on the other side of the secured gates of the Palms. Everyone dressed in a variety of red and blue shades, as well as white. I was the only one in jean shorts and a nice black tank top while the other women wore summer dresses, and the men wore Vineyard Vines polos or button-down oxfords. I really felt out of place in the sea of rich people, those who flaunted their money with pearl necklaces, diamond jewelry, and Rolexes. It was clear that I deserved to be locked on the other side of the gate, and I was completely okay with that.

I wondered if Dad ever missed the simplicity of a Connecticut backyard barbeque. The ones where he could wear khaki shorts and a Boston Red Sox T-shirt while grilling Ball Park Franks and premade hamburger patties from Stop & Shop. He had more in common with all of our old neighbors than he did with the ones who filled up his new expansive backyard. Dad wasn't fancy by any means. He was laid-back and enjoyed quiet and peace. This was anything but, and now, he blended right in with his guests with a light blue, short-sleeve button-down and navy blue chino shorts. That was a new look.

The one plus of Serena's barbeque was how elevated the food was. I'd never seen so much food in my life. The whole downstairs smelled like a mixture of pork and sugar since she'd started getting everything ready the day before. Serena had marinated the pork shoulder overnight, and with the help of Theo, smoked it in the smoker in the backyard. The shredded pork was now on three large serving platters, one of many dishes on the buffet tables stretched across the length of the entire backyard patio with every other food imaginable: fried green tomatoes, deviled eggs, mac and cheese, squash casserole, corn on the cob, bourbon baked beans, banana pudding, and strawberry pretzel salad.

My eyes went wide, and my stomach sang in a loud rumble as I filled my plate with every single dish. I could only get through the first quarter of the buffet before I ran out of room on my plate, so obviously, I had to go back for seconds and thirds until I'd tasted everything. All the hard work Serena had exerted paid off; the bar for Fourth of July barbeques had been set excruciatingly high. The food was spectacular, and I wished time traveling to the past was possible so I could go back to twenty minutes before, when I had an empty stomach and could taste everything for the first time all over again.

While I sipped sweet tea and my food digested, I pulled out my phone to text Harper: *Save me from this party.*

She replied five minutes later with a skull emoji, followed by a second text that read, *No Reagan Moore or Blair Bennett?*

Dad had introduced me to a bunch of neighbors, and I'd hoped that eventually, I would spot a head of blond hair and an aura of glowing opulence standing next to a tall brunette with a sleeve tattoo. A surge of disappointment traveled through me whenever I didn't see them and met another unfamiliar face.

I responded, *If you see 15 texts in a row, then I've spotted them. But for now, it's a negative.*

Harper texted, *You still think you can sneak away for the fireworks?*

I'm not missing that show. We're still on.

Harper responded back, *Awesome. Meet us at the boardwalk at 8:15.*

Like hell I was going to miss a chance to watch the fireworks with Harper. When it was seven forty five, I told Dad I was meeting friends for the show. He raised an eyebrow like he was shocked I actually had plans that didn't involve him or Serena. But since he was too preoccupied playing host, I had a clear path to my bike with minimal explanation.

I raced to the boardwalk as if I was competing in Tour de France, but my pace slowed when I quickly ran into bumper-to-bumper traffic. Hugging the side of the road, I pedaled slowly and cautiously next to the cars trailing a path down Route 7 to Main and Front Street.

Right when I started to feel bad for all the cars that would eventually have to fight for parking, I discovered that finding space on a bike rack was just as difficult. My usual, and favorite, rack in front of Mia's Lemonade Stand was full, and I couldn't find a spot until I reached First Street, one block over from Envie. Once my bike was locked, I meandered through the slow-moving crowd down the boardwalk. Every restaurant had a line that snaked through the flow of traffic. The South Pole Treats line was backed up to the corner where the fancy steakhouse was, and that seemed like the one place without a line out the door. Instead, it had outside tables with guests enjoying the calm space blocked off by an iron fence around the patio.

When I found Harper, Vera, and Maggie in the South Pole Treats line, Harper waved as I walked over, and the smile she flashed me let me know it was just for me.

"There she is," she announced. "Right on time."

"Holy crap, this place is hopping," I said.

The three of them laughed. "The Fourth is the biggest holiday of the summer. It's like our Christmas. This is as wild as it gets. Now, you ready to check South Pole Treats off your list?"

I went with Harper's recommendation: a sour-black-cherry slushie. She got one also while Vera opted for a chocolate milkshake, and Maggie got a hot fudge sundae that she quickly regretted because the vanilla ice cream melted into a pool in her plastic cup by the time we found an empty spot on the beach.

It seemed like everyone in the town that weekend was on the beach, staking out their spots for the fireworks. Once we laid the blanket in the small patch of unoccupied sand, Harper was quick to sit and pat the space next to her. Of course, I didn't hesitate. She bumped my shoulder after I crossed my legs and took another sip of my delicious slushie that helped ease the warm night sticking to my skin.

"How was your party?" she asked, leaning into me. "Despite not getting a selfie with Reagan Moore."

She was so close that I felt the end of her words on my lips, and I had to suck in my bottom lip to fight against the rare charge that swaddled us into our own little moment.

"I ate everything," I said. "There was so much food, and it was the fanciest July Fourth party I've ever been to. I feel like I was judged for wearing this. But this is much more of my style. I'd rather be here."

I swear, through the falling darkness, I saw pink highlight her face. "Well, I'm glad you're here. You're in for a good show too. Serena DeLuca and Reagan Moore always donate some money, so the show is amazing and gets people coming here to visit. It never disappoints. I promise you that."

The first batch of fireworks launched into the sky a few minutes later. The whistling rocket made us both flinch, and we laughed at each other before directing our gaze to the explosions that lit up the beach in a kaleidoscope of lights. Each pop pounded in my throat as it took up what seemed to be half the sky. The crowd oohed and ahhed for all the varieties: the zig-zag ones, the raining ones, the whistling ones, and the firefly ones. I leaned back until I could reach past the blanket and dig in the sand for extra support, allowing me to get more relaxed. That was when I felt Harper's fingers on a graceful search through the cold, silky sand. A wave of nerves curled in my gut when her pinky finally rested on top of mine. She glanced over, and another wave tumbled when our eyes held for a moment before she looked skyward.

I gave myself three more fireworks until I gripped her back, and once our fingers were secured, it felt like fireworks went off in my chest. I glanced back at the sky; at least, I tried to make it seem like I was, but my periphery was working hard to watch Harper, and I got the sense by how tightly her pinky held on to mine that she was watching me too. If she was lost in the display, wouldn't her grip mindlessly loosen? It didn't waver once, and it made me feel so alive.

The finale lit up the beach like Pop Rocks on steroids for five minutes until everything went still and black, and the beach blended into the night. Everyone cheered and clapped as rocket smoke slowly billowed over the ocean and scented the air.

"Well, shall we?" Maggie said, getting up with the rest of the crowd.

Harper looked at me for a moment, and my chest flipped in protest when she followed Vera and Maggie instead of staying put. She took her pinky back, and I immediately felt the loss. The feeling of her finger wrapped around mine didn't go away even while we packed up the blanket and shuffled with the rest of the crowd to the boardwalk.

Since my bike was all the way on First Street, four blocks from where we were, Vera and Maggie said their good-byes before Harper and I turned in the opposite direction and headed toward First Street. As much as I liked them, being with Harper alone was always an exciting adventure. I offered to walk her home, trying to buy more time with her and hoping that maybe—just maybe—the pinky holding would evolve along the way.

"Let me go to the bathroom really quickly," I said.

"All right. I'll be here," Harper said and rested against the wooden railing.

Of course, there was a line for the bathroom, and I debated whether the slow pace I wanted would be kind to my bladder or not. To pass the time, I texted Brie an update since she had been begging for one, as if making sure I was on track to have my first girl kiss this summer.

If we can't spend our last summer together like we planned, you're sure as hell going to kiss a hot girl, she said in a Snapchat to me.

Pinky holding to kissing seems like a jump, but I'm trying, I wrote back.

It's not a jump. It's a sign she wants to kiss you. So DO IT.

When I emerged from the bathroom a few minutes later, a disturbed look contoured Harper's face, a stark contrast to the smirk she'd given me before I stood in the bathroom line. Three tall guys surrounded her, and a familiar face stood out from the crowd of strangers.

Theo.

It was easy to recognize the slicked back sandy blond hair and the stupid American flag shorts he'd apparently changed into after his mom's party. The smirk staining his face matched the Joker's, scarred with malice, and his brown eyes were saturated in a thick gloss one could only get from alcohol. He dangled a little dolphin keychain above Harper as if teasing a dog with a slice of lunch meat.

I pushed my way through the crowd. It felt like swimming against a riptide and struggling to get air, but the air would only come when the sharks swam away, and somehow, I had to get those three tall, muscular men away from Harper.

"How about you give it back and then grow the fuck up?" Harper said and tried to snatch the dolphin out of his hands, but he stretched his hand higher above his head.

"Uh…no. This is way more fun. Wanna know what's even funner?" Funner. Yeah, he was that much of a moron. "Watching people pass your sad little restaurant like it's the beggar of the boardwalk."

His friends rewarded him with laughs, and Theo patted one friend on the shoulder as if searching for a tip for his stupid joke.

Without giving myself a moment to think, I slapped his stomach with the back of my hand. That was when I learned that the asshole had a pretty solid core. He yelped at the same time I stifled the pain, and he dropped the dolphin keychain. While he keeled over, I picked it up and shoved it in my back pocket.

"Don't ruin this moment for them," Harper said to me. "This is the only way they can get attention from women."

"Shut the fuck up," Theo said and snapped back into my direction. "What the hell is wrong with you?"

When he lunged at me with furrowed, threatening eyebrows, it hit me like a pile of bricks that I wasn't supposed to know him. Harper didn't know Serena was my stepmom, and here I was, standing in front of Theo right after I'd smacked him in the gut. All it would take was for him to say my name.

I shouldn't have said anything. I should have just grabbed Harper's hand and whisked us away from them.

Right as I turned to face Harper to do exactly that, Theo's sweaty palms clutched my arms and spun me around. My body went limp in his strong grip. I was close enough to smell the expensive cologne mixing with the alcohol wafting off his breath, and when he breathed on me and his eyes darkened, I realized how stupid it was to smack him. This guy was at least six-three and clearly worked out every day. He held me like a ragdoll in his grip, and it hurt.

"Don't fucking touch me again, you hear me?"

"Let her go," Harper said, and a wave of her liquified black-cherry slushie doused Theo's shoulders and dripped down his biceps. He let go of me and surveyed the damage soaking into his white Vineyard Vines shirt. "There, now you look like a human snow cone. You'll definitely get attention from women now," Harper said.

She snatched my hand and bolted down the boardwalk. Because of all the pedestrian traffic, we were easily lost in the crowd.

We didn't look back until I unwrapped the lock around my bike handles and noticed that the guys hadn't chased us. Groups of families with young kids passed by, and I had a good feeling that the families with babies in strollers and toddlers walking unevenly while holding their parent's hand would say something. At least, I hoped.

I sucked in a breath of briny, fried oil air for a moment and then released it, finally letting out the anger. The weight of everything washed over me fast and hard. I swallowed the lump rapidly budding in my throat and willed the stinging in my eyes to go away. When I successfully pushed back the tears, I handed Harper the dolphin keychain and found her assessing me for damage. She observed my face and then my arms, and while she did so, I noticed her eyes sparkling in the glow of the lamps as if she too was fighting back tears.

"Are…are you okay?" she asked softly and grazed her fingertips on both of my arms.

When she touched me, yes, I was okay. Her hands were so soft and gentle that goose bumps broke against the lingering pain.

"I'm fine," I said through the lump in my throat.

What I really wanted to do was cry. I'd been picked on all throughout school for being different. The worst it got was when my bully carved "Remi Brenner sucks" into my desk. I'd cried for a whole week, Mom and Dad went to the principal, and then the principal went to every fifth-grade class to give an anti-bullying lecture. But even at the peak of being bullied, I'd never feared being physically hurt. Not until Theo had me in his tight grip with his drunken anger staring straight at me. We lived on the same property, he knew where I slept, we ate dinner together a few times a week, and we worked together. Avoiding him was almost impossible. If he didn't chase us then, it was only a matter of time before he did.

"Are you okay? What happened?" I said and kicked the bike stand up and started down Front Street toward Route 7. Harper followed silently.

"I don't know. I was looking at my phone, and they came out of nowhere. Probably from Envie, actually."

Once we crossed Route 7 and turned left, the only sounds were the crickets, frogs, and my bike wheels spinning along the sidewalk. The farther away we walked, the louder the night bugs were and the more lightning bugs speckled the darkness hanging over the tree silhouettes.

"That's Serena DeLuca's son, you know," Harper said low, as if he lurked behind us. "The one who grabbed you. Anytime he sees me, he likes to make comments."

I swallowed and directed my eyes on the sidewalk. I could feel my world starting to close in around me. The guilt of acting like I didn't know anything about Serena or Theo stacked on me like bricks. As much as I wanted to be honest with Harper—knowing how much Envie was ruining every aspect of her life to now knowing that Theo harassed her regularly—I was terrified that my very loose association to them would push her away.

I couldn't label him as my stepbrother now. Not after all that. Not when we were still calming our breath.

"What kind of comments?" I asked, nervously scratching the back of my head.

"Comments about the Acadian failing. One time, he saw me leaving work, and he was like, 'Hey, where are your customers?' But the comment he made tonight is the new winner. How he loves watching people pass the Acadian like it's a beggar."

A rich brat like Theo who didn't have to worry about anything would make some ignorant, tone-deaf comment like that. He was probably someone who had no ambition in life and was forced to go to college by his successful mother, who would pay for whatever degree he wanted. He was an asshole, entitled, and thought everyone was less than him. He'd probably never worked for anything in his life except trying to get women. He probably struggled at that a lot.

"Does Serena DeLuca do anything?"

Harper shrugged. "I don't know. I don't know a thing about Serena DeLuca other than Envie and that she lives in the Palms."

I wasn't sure what was better: Serena knowing that her only child was an asshole or being so far removed from him that she didn't know at all.

Silence found its way between us again as we walked into Harper's development. I had no idea what to say. Not to Harper. Not to Theo when I saw him next. Not to Serena. And not to my dad. I wanted to believe that my dad would do something if or when I told him about what had happened. But who really knew what my dad would do anymore? He seemed so far gone into Serena's world, I wondered if this summer would repair even a stitch of our broken relationship.

"He seriously makes this whole thing worse," Harper said. "It's one thing to lose business. It adds a whole other layer of anger and frustration and stress when you get bullied by the owner's son. I don't know why he does it."

"Because he has nothing else going for him." She looked up with a furrowed brow. "What? I mean, isn't that what bullies do? Their own lives are so miserable that they project it on others, easy targets. Envie is outdoing the Acadian, so he sees you as an easy target. I was an easy target for my bully too because when I was a kid, I was super shy and nerdy."

"You were bullied?"

"Harper, I can talk about Betelgeuse for, like, an hour straight. Of course I was bullied." I elbowed her arm and was glad that I was able to squeeze a small smile from her. "I had my wild curls, braces, I got amazing grades, and knew the answers to all the questions in class. The only time I talked was when I raised my hand to answer a question. People saw me as a know-it-all and a teacher's pet, so they weren't lining up to be my friends. Chris Murray was popular, and girls liked him. He made fun of me for being a nerd, having braces, and joked about things getting lost in my curly hair. He also got really shitty grades and acted out in class so he would always have recess detention, and one of those times, he carved 'Remi Brenner sucks' into my desk. Then in high school, he started doing drugs and disappeared. My friend Brie told me he dropped out before senior year started, so who knows what he's doing now. But he proves my point. Miserable people want to make others miserable."

"I'm sorry that happened to you."

"Hey, I'm fine. I was valedictorian and got into MIT, and one day, I'll be waving at Chris Murray from the moon."

Finally, we reached her house. In between two mossy live oaks was a three-story home, the first level being the garage and stairs that led up to the second. Her street was dark, and we had a front row view of all the lightning bugs. Lights emanated from the three-panel windows on the second floor, and I caught a glimpse of the top of a TV. It gave me some peace of mind that at least Harper was safe for the time being, and that she'd walk right into her house and be swaddled by safety.

"Thanks again for walking me home," she said.

Only a few short inches separated us, and when those beautiful eyes looked up, my heart broke into another sprint. I kicked my bike stand down to let it rest on its own because if Harper was going to stand this close to me, and my heart was going to pound this fast, I wasn't about to let my bike slip out of my clammy hands.

"It's not a problem," I said and tried to suppress the shaking in my voice. The silence around us made her seem even closer. "I just wanted to make sure you got home safe. You sure you're okay? Because I can stay until you are."

"No, it's fine. I'm okay. Unfortunately, I'm used to this."

"That doesn't mean you're okay. It's okay not to be okay, you know."

She gave me a small smile, but it didn't reach her eyes. "I know, but I am. You punching him in the gut helped." She let out a giggle that knocked over a couple of weights on my chest. I smiled at the relief. "You sure *you're* okay? He grabbed you."

She rubbed over the spots on my arms. I could still feel Theo's strong grip wrapped around them, but then Harper erased it. My breath hitched when her touch made my skin tingle, and right as the goose bumps broke out, she retrieved one hand to take something out of her back pocket.

She held out the dolphin keychain. "I won you this."

My breath caught and released. "Wait? What?"

"While we were waiting for you to leave your party, we killed some time at the arcade. It's the only thing I could buy with my tickets. I don't know. It's just a little something, a reminder of our paddleboard trip."

"I...I love it."

There went the rest of the weights. My chest felt like it was about to flutter away. The air around us still held the same kind of charge that seemed to always suffuse us, and if things felt different when we watched the fireworks, it shifted yet again. Everything was more electric, and I couldn't take my thoughts away from us holding hands longer than we should have at the party or how her pinky hooked around mine or how standing a few inches away from her now had every nerve ending on fire like the tip of a match.

"Thank you for getting him off me," I said softly, an attempt to ease the thrilling unsteadiness below me, like I was getting ready to experience a trapdoor waterslide.

I looked at her lips and wondered how they would feel against mine, how they would taste, how they would caress mine back. When I glanced up, I noticed her scanning my arms. There wasn't enough light to reveal any damage, but she went back to rubbing her fingertips along my biceps as if searching for evidence of his hands. I wished I could have controlled the goose bumps because there was no disguising their cause. And I knew Harper felt them because when they broke through my skin, she slowed down and instead felt them as if she was reading braille. Apparently, she was fluent because they only spelled out one sentence: lean in and kiss me. My heart was ready to climb out my throat as I felt her soft breath against my lips like before, only this time, instead of a ghost of a kiss, it actually came to life.

Holy hell, she kissed me, and everything went white. My heart misfired a couple of beats, and every nerve lit up and pulsated when she opened her mouth and welcomed more of mine. I had no idea what to do except follow her lead. It was such a simple, sweet kiss, like she wanted to erase the fear and pain Theo had caused. She did and then some. I couldn't believe I was kissing a girl, kissing Harper. My gut and chest worked together harmoniously, and I had the magical ability to feel bold colors inside me, starting in my stomach and spiraling up, things I didn't know I could feel from a sweet kiss like that.

It was such an unexpected way to end such an intense night.

When she pulled away, her eyes were still loosely closed for a moment longer, as if she was savoring me, and my whole world went still. "And so you know," she said when she opened her eyes. She reached out and felt a curly strand of my hair. "For what it's worth, I really like your curly hair."

I'd never once liked my hair. It was too wavy and thick, and it doubled in size in the humidity. Brie always told me how much she loved my hair because apparently, it had the right amount of curl in the waves. She said it wasn't too curly but just right. I always thought she was wrong, but that was before Harper ran her fingers through it with a salacious bite on her lower lip.

That was the moment I loved my curly hair because it made Harper look at me like that.

Chapter Eight

Waking up the next morning was bittersweet. My lips still buzzed thinking about Harper's kiss. I lay in bed for a good hour, letting the memory run wild and kissing her for the first time over and over again, and every time, my insides danced and flipped.

Then the wonderful memories smacked into a brick wall when I remembered that I had an afternoon shift with Theo after slapping him in the stomach. The anxiety of being near him and knowing what he was capable of squeezed my chest the same way he'd squeezed my arms. But then it hit me that I didn't owe him anything. I didn't need to show up for work. What was he going to do? Fire me? Cool. And when my dad and Serena questioned why, I would tell them he'd grabbed me, and I didn't feel safe. I didn't need the job at Envie. I had almost a thousand dollars saved up from the science museum job the last three years. Working at Envie was something to give me additional cash and something to do during my stay.

So I decided, fuck it and fuck Theo.

Instead, I lay out on a lawn chair in the backyard, enjoyed the beautiful day and the sun adding color to my skin, and attempted to read Stephen Hawking, but my brain kept defaulting to kissing Harper. I tried shaking the memory so I could get some reading done, but I absolutely didn't want to. Not when I could still feel her lips, which kept my stomach constantly tumbling. I was desperate to see her again, desperate to kiss her again. I wanted to text her, but

I had no idea what to say. Did I acknowledge the kiss? Did I ask if she wanted to stargaze soon? Was texting her now too soon after our kiss? How the hell did kissing and dating work?

I had no idea what to do.

While I read a boring chapter about the uncertainty principle, my phone chirped, and my gut plummeted as if I was on a roller coaster, thinking and hoping it was Harper. But all those fun emotions came to an abrupt halt when I saw it was Theo.

Where r u? Your shift started 30 min ago.

I ignored him.

I went back to reading and daydreaming, and a half hour later, my phone went off again. Right as the twirling flickered in anticipation of Harper's text, it was instantly killed yet again because of Theo.

So...ur not coming in, I take it? Because that's seriously so proffessional. *The line is out the door, and I'm down a sandwich maker. Really fucking great, Remy.*

He couldn't even spell my name or "professional" correctly; he was actually that dumb.

I'll tell my mom and ur dad u completely blew me off. Don't expect any tips this week.

I smiled reading his text messages. I didn't feel guilty one bit.

I survived reading the uncertainty principle chapter and rewarded the accomplishment with a dip in the pool. All I wanted to do was knock out the next two boring chapters so I could lock myself in my apartment, turn off my phone, and dive right into the chapter about black holes before the rest of the fascinating chapters I was eager to read: the fate of the universe, the arrow of time, and then wormholes and time travel. Half of me wanted to screw all the other boring chapters, but I decided to practice self-control. If my summer read was going to be *A Brief History of Time*, I was going to read every word.

Once I mentally prepared myself to knock out what I was hoping to be the last boring chapter, Dad stepped through the sliding patio door with furrowed eyebrows. "What are you doing here? Don't you have a shift right now?"

"I do," I said and continued to situate myself in the lawn chair. "Okay...so why are you out here?"

"Because Theo is an asshole." Dad laughed, but I shot him a glare over the brim of the book. "What's so funny?"

"Just because you don't get along with someone doesn't mean you can blow off work."

"I blew it off for very good reasons."

"Care to share? I'll be the judge of that."

I closed my book, making sure he heard the seriousness in the slam. "He harassed a teenage girl at the boardwalk last night. So I smacked him in the stomach, and then he grabbed me. Hard, I might add. So I don't feel safe working with him."

"He what?" Dad's voice rose. At least there was anger in his tone.

"Yeah, so fuck him."

"Remi...language," Dad said with an annoyed sigh, as if my foul language really didn't bother him, but he felt the need to parent me.

"I don't need to work at Envie. I spent all of high school working and saving up money so I can manage until school starts. I'm not going to work for an asshole who has no respect for anyone. If you have an issue with this, go talk to him. Apparently, he bullies this girl quite frequently—"

"Which girl?"

"She works at the Acadian."

Dad sighed and shook his head. "The Acadian?"

"That's what she told me. He was dangling something she won from the arcade above her head and mocked the restaurant. He had friends encouraging it. College kids harassing a teenager. Classy."

"Did the girl have brown hair? Your age?"

I frowned. *How did he know?* "Yes."

"Jesus," he muttered under his breath and then rubbed his temples. "Okay, I'll have to talk to Serena." He paused. "Are you okay? Is Harper Hebert okay?"

I lowered my book and gave Dad all of my attention. "How do you know her name?"

"It's a small town, kiddo," he said with a chuckle. "We know the Heberts."

I felt my face contort in confusion. How did he sound like it was a given? How did he know exactly what she looked like as if they'd met before?

"Yes, we're okay. Just shook up."

"I understand. I'm sorry you two had to deal with that. Theo's been going through some…well…issues. Not like that's an excuse at all."

"No shit."

"If you don't want to work there, I understand. I'll talk to Serena."

"Thank you."

Dad headed back inside. He paced with the phone to his ear, and I knew that he was complaining to Serena. After his call, he came back out and told me to get changed because he had a sweet tooth. I smiled at the little glimpse of my best friend resurfacing. The same guy who stormed into my elementary school to complain to the principal when Chris Murray carved his insult into my desk. Dad had bought a dozen toasted coconut doughnuts the next morning, and I'd woken up each morning with a doughnut for breakfast for the rest of the week, and something as little as that had helped me power through. Dad was always the first one to pick me up when I was a kid. Apparently, that hadn't changed.

"What do you say about taking the Aston Martin into town?" he asked in the driveway and dangled the keys.

"Wait, seriously?"

"Seriously. Let's ride in style."

And we did. Sitting in the Aston Martin made me feel like I was hovering an inch above the road from how low the seats were, but I still felt a million times cooler than I'd ever felt in my life. Every time he accelerated, the engine made a glorious rumble. As we hit stop signs and red lights, people walking on the streets, biking, or driving stopped next to us, did a double take, grins widening and fingers pointing, but Dad was too oblivious and too busy explaining to me how to drive a stick shift to notice. Him talking about how cars worked was like me talking to him about the Second Law of Thermodynamics. The only thing he said that stuck was that the car could reach a hundred and ninety-five miles an hour, and I was so confused. Where did you take your car to go that fast?

When we parked, a couple of people approached him and complimented his car. I could only imagine that any time he took it out, people flocked around it like bees hovering around sugar.

When the small crowd dispersed, we finally made it to South Pole Treats. He got his favorite dessert: a chocolate malt, and I decided to try something new and got a half banana split. We sat on a bench with the Aston Martin in close sight. We laughed anytime a guy stopped and observed it. I alternated glances between the car and Envie a short walk away from us, and I wanted so much to wave my middle finger at Theo through the window and then tell Aaron I was sorry for leaving him.

"So why is Theo a piece of shit?" I asked and scooped a vanilla-ice-cream-covered banana bite in my mouth.

Dad laughed. "When did you get a dirty mouth?"

"The second I turned eighteen."

"My precious little Remi Girl is gone now, isn't she?"

"She is," I said and shared a laugh with him before scooping another spoonful, this one covered in hot fudge.

"Serena's ex-husband is…well…he's something."

"What do you mean?"

I didn't know Serena DeLuca's whole story. I mean, I could have easily looked it up on her Wikipedia page, and I already knew I would that night just from the little teaser Dad gave.

He said that Serena had Theo when she was twenty-two, and shortly after he was born, she married his father, who she'd met in culinary school in New York. But she'd felt obligated to marry him because they had a baby, and they'd both thought it was the right thing to do. Serena put her culinary dreams on hold to raise Theo while her husband worked his way up in his culinary career. When Theo was a little older, she got a night job at a catering company. By then, her husband was an executive chef at a Brooklyn restaurant, but when the financial crisis hit, his restaurant closed. They were tight on money, and the husband became bitter and angry that her career had launched when his had tanked. A few months after he lost his job, the Food Network approached the catering company to create a reality show based on it. With a secured paycheck, Serena found a way out of the marriage and immediately left.

Ever since the divorce, her ex-husband had been trying to make her life more difficult, and as Theo grew up, he'd listened to his dad and started resenting his mom. At one point, Serena's ex-husband had made her believe that she was a horrible mom because all her successes had only been possible by putting Theo and motherhood on the backburner. It was something the ex-husband had actually told Serena, Dad said. She'd thought helping Theo through college and giving him some experience with Envie during the summers would help him find responsibility and would help them rekindle their broken relationship.

When Dad told me that, I wondered if it inspired him to do the same with me, but because I was already responsible and a good kid, he needed to find another incentive, and that was my college tuition. I couldn't shake the theory out of my head while he continued with Serena's story, ending it by saying her ex was too much of a bad influence on Theo with his alcoholism, anger, and immense grudge against Serena.

It all made sense as to why Theo was the way he was and affirmed everything I'd told Harper the night before: miserable people loved making others miserable. But even though the background humanized him in a way, it still didn't mean I had to like him, and it still didn't make him a good person.

"What he did wasn't okay, Remi," he said on our drive back to the house. "I know that, and Serena knows that."

"Dinners with him are going to be awkward now."

He shook his head. "Maybe, but he brought that on himself. Good thing he's always out with friends and hardly at the house. Hopefully, that makes you more at ease when you're home too. You better believe we're going to talk. Serena's had about enough of him."

Whatever that meant, I hoped it meant I got to see less of him, and the thought of that made me smile.

❖

I didn't get to see Harper until that Friday. She texted me the day after the Aston Martin ride to see if I wanted to come over to watch "a movie or something," which meant I overanalyzed what "or something" meant for the next three days, which also meant that it took me three extra days to read the boring elementary particles chapter because my mind kept glitching to Harper and our kiss and "or something."

I was never going to get to enjoy the black hole chapter. I was certain of it.

It's code for making out time. Get your lips ready and hydrated, Brie said in her text reply.

My heart didn't stop racing for the rest of the week. Once I propped my bike against the Hebert's porch steps, my heart thrummed in a steady staccato rhythm. My hands were already clammy, and I prayed to whatever thing in the sky that Harper wouldn't immediately try to hold my pinky like on the beach. The last thing I wanted to do was scare her away with my sweat.

After ringing the doorbell, Harper greeted me with a wide smile. "Hey," she said, a little breathlessly, and I wondered if seeing me again brought back the memory of our kiss like it did for me. "I feel like I haven't seen you in ages."

I smiled, so glad that I wasn't the only dramatic one. It felt like four trips around the sun since the Fourth.

"You need to stop working," I said jokingly.

"I wish. My parents wanted me to cover this one girl because she's sick, so I just did what they wanted. But hey, I got a little extra money now."

"That's always nice. That means we can go spend it on boardwalk food."

"Exactly. Now come in and help me beat my parents in Monopoly."

"Just to warn you, I'm not good at it. I've only played it once, so I don't know what I'm doing."

"Well, damn it. I was hoping for a lifeline."

"I've got nothing but emotional support."

"I could use that. In exchange, I can give you some homemade madeleines and Cheerwine."

I pretended like I knew what the hell madeleines and Cheerwine were and accepted.

The inside of her house was open and homey. She made a pit stop at the fridge and pulled out two bottles of Cheerwine, handing me a dark, cherry-colored drink in a glass bottle, and then scooted a plate of what I assumed to be madeleines across the kitchen island.

"I made these madeleines this afternoon," she said. "They're French butter cakes." I took a bite of a scalloped-shape sponge cake sprinkled with powdered sugar. My eyes went wide, and Harper smiled. "Did I do okay?"

"Are you a secret baker?"

She shrugged. "A recent hobby I've picked up, French desserts. Grab the plate and follow me."

She led me to the screened porch, and the sweet summer air blew through the three screened walls while the crickets and the frogs chirped the loudest I'd heard them.

"This is Remi," she told her parents. "She's the girl I met at the boardwalk a few weeks ago. She's visiting her dad for the summer from Connecticut."

Her parents smiled at me. "It's so nice to finally meet you, Remi," Mrs. Hebert said. "Harper has told us so much about her new friend."

Harper had already mentioned me to her parents, which meant she thought about me when we weren't together. I hoped my wide smile and the warmth of my cheeks didn't make my feelings too transparent.

"Hopefully, all good things," I said.

"All great things. Like how you're going to MIT in the fall?"

"Yeah. I'm pretty excited."

"And you want to be an astronaut?" Mr. Hebert asked.

"That's the pipe dream," I said while my face became increasingly hotter. "But that's not a big enough reason not to try for it."

"One day she'll be on the moon or Mars or in charge of the team that sends a rocket to Europa."

My heart inflated like a balloon at the mention of Europa. She stole a glance, and when our eyes locked, she flashed a small, private smile just for me. From my periphery, I noticed her parents giving us a confused look. One mention of Europa plucked us into a different world for the briefest moment, and despite having an audience, we were alone, and that moment was ours.

As if she remembered her parents, she snapped her gaze from me to her Cheerwine bottle. She twisted the cap off and held it up for a toast. I followed, clinked my bottle with hers, and said, "Cheers to getting Park Ave."

Mr. Hebert laughed. "She's not getting Park Ave. She's not good enough at this game."

"Thanks, Dad."

"I love you, sweet daughter of mine, but not enough to forgive your debts." He wiggled his fingers. "Pay up."

She acquiesced and handed him a handful of colorful money. When Mrs. Hebert passed Harper the dice, she closed her palm, kissed it, and unleashed them. She went up eight spaces and landed on Baltic Avenue. She tossed her hands in the air. "Monopoly!"

"It's about time," her dad joked.

On her next turn, she toggled the dice in between her palms and then turned to me. "Kiss for good luck?"

My body froze, surprised that she not only asked for a kiss, but she did so in front of her parents. I was desperate to touch her again. I wanted to kiss more than just her fist. I wanted to kiss her like we had the other night. I wanted those very hands holding my cheek, grazing down my back, and skimming under the hem of my shirt. I wanted our tongues to clash, and I wanted to taste the Cheerwine and madeleines on her lips as she pinned me against the wall.

But for now, I'd settle for kissing her fist. I kissed her knuckles, quickly backed away, and popped another madeleine in my mouth and washed it down with a gulp of Cheerwine to cool my burning cheeks. Her parents seemed too focused on her double sixes to notice what I could only imagine was my bright red face. Harper cheered as she moved her Scottie dog to States Avenue, blocking her dad from a monopoly.

Thirteen fist kisses later, I failed at being her good luck charm, and Harper declared bankruptcy. Despite her dad's playful mockery, Harper didn't seem that upset about it and was quick to tug my wrist out of my seat so I could follow her inside.

"So," she said, and her gaze dropped to my lips before flitting quickly back up. A dull heat curled low in my body as the temperature rose in her kitchen. "Want to watch a movie?"

Or something. She forgot to mention "or something."

This was what they called Netflix and chill, right? Watching a movie never meant watching a movie. Owen Gardner asked me to the movies on Snapchat. I thought I'd take advantage of seeing my first R-rated movie in theaters and the fact that the comedy had apparently five seconds of boobs, according to Owen. I really wanted to see the scene so I could celebrate being old enough to see a boob scene in a movie theater and also because it intrigued me, despite having no idea why it intrigued me at the time. However, Owen and I had the far-left corner to ourselves, so we'd spent at least a half hour making out and missed the boob scene.

My only example of how a movie didn't mean actually watching a movie, and Brie had at least five more examples backing that theory up.

"Does it involve more Cheerwine?" I asked, raising my empty bottle.

Really? That's how you respond to her encrypted message?

She took my empty glass and stepped inside the screened porch for a second. I rolled my eyes and rubbed my stupidity out of my forehead. College was the time for me to shine and grow into myself. I was going to find a bunch of people who were as big of a nerd as I was, and the chances of finding someone cute who would also indulge in my space fascination was quite high. Whatever Harper and I were doing or becoming, I at least hoped I left the summer with the bare minimum of how not to sound like an idiot in front of beautiful girls. If I wasn't impressed with me, how did I expect others to be?

Harper came back into the kitchen with Mr. Hebert behind her. "My dad is going to make us his awesome stovetop popcorn."

Mr. Hebert laughed. "It's not that grand. Just a little bit of coconut oil and a sprinkling of salt."

"Still," Harper said. "I tried to make it once when Vera and Maggie spent the night, and it wasn't the same."

"You're a great chef," Mr. Hebert said and ruffled the top of his daughter's head. Her cheeks instantly flashed red as she fixed the little messy hairs. I sucked in my grin at how adorable it was when she got embarrassed.

Once the popcorn was popped and salted, we scurried upstairs with the bowl, the plate of madeleines, and two new bottles of Cheerwine. Harper's room was surprisingly clean for an eighteen-year-old. Everything seemed to have a place, and her bed was made, unlike my room at Serena's where I found no point in making my bed and tossed things wherever seemed logical at that time. I got situated on her bed as Harper turned off the lights and turned on Netflix. She sat so close to me, our legs rested against each other. I froze, afraid one small twitch might falsely indicate I wanted her to scoot over.

"There's this new gay movie that I've been dying to watch," she said. "You down for it? Girls kiss in it." She waggled her eyebrows and tossed a kernel in her mouth.

With those beautiful eyes and her smile mere inches from me, I would have done anything she wanted to do, no questions asked. "Sounds great," I said.

She said she'd been waiting for the movie to come out since it was announced a year and a half ago. It was a film by Devon Gualtieri, an out queer director, writer, and producer who'd started her career creating documentaries about inspiring women and then recently started directing movies about queer women. I'd heard of her before but hadn't seen any of her movies.

"You should watch one of her documentaries," Harper said. "*Rainbow Power* is about the gay rights movement in San Francisco during the sixties, and wow, I learned more in that documentary than I ever did in history class. And then there's *Price of the Runaway* about models getting ready for fashion week in New York, Paris, and Madrid. I'll text you everything you should watch."

If watching those movies meant I would impress her, I would watch them all in one night.

Once she pressed play, every nerve was on high alert. I tried focusing all my attention on the movie because the premise intrigued me. A romantic comedy about two strangers, fresh out of college, who became roommates and navigated their post-college lives in New York City. But then Harper fetched a blanket and draped it over us, and that made it that much harder to watch. It was impossible with our legs still pressed together and how our fingers collided when digging for more popcorn, and then Harper gushed about how hot the two main actresses were. All those moments in a short amount of time had my brain on spin cycle. I hoped that watching a movie under a blanket with the lights off meant that there would be more kissing, but I worried that the movie progressing meant there was a ticking clock for when the "perfect opportunity" was to kiss her again.

The room shifted to a whole different playing field when the two main characters kissed for the first time, and it was incredibly hot. The characters were at a club, dancing together, just friendly, but we, the audience, had been watching their feelings manifest since the opening scene, and the forty minutes of buildup paid off when the main character pulled the love interest's necklace until she landed on her lips. Harper's room got significantly hotter when they dove into the kiss, and there was a millisecond where I saw the love interest's tongue slipping inside the main character's mouth. Then the main character combed her hands through the love interest's hair, and I felt the sexual tension jumping off the screen and curling in my gut and traveling lower. As I watched the scene unfold, I imagined that I was the main character doing all of those things to Harper. I stole a glance, and Harper's mouth hung open while her eyes were still glued to the TV.

After their first kiss was over, I decided to use that buffer time to go to the bathroom to process all the things I felt. If I'd watched that scene by myself, I would have still found it hot, but Harper next to me magnified everything, and I wished so much that we could have been those two characters. After I came back, I made sure to sit closer to her so my leg fell back into hers. She tossed the blanket back over me as if helping me settle back in.

And then five minutes later, the characters started taking off their clothes for their first sex scene. Harper squeezed my leg, letting out a muted squeal. She was quick to take her hand back, but she left me with a buzz pulsating where she'd touched me.

Harper looked over, and when our eyes locked, she did a double take, smiling wider the longer our stares held. "What? You're missing the hot sex scene."

When her eyes fell to my lips, that was when I knew I had to act. If I was waiting for the perfect moment, this was it, hidden in the darkness, our legs meshed together, my knee still vibrating from her touch, and right after an attempt to steal a glimpse of my lips. I slowly leaned in, waiting for her to pull back if she wanted to, but she didn't. Her smile faded as her eyes zeroed in and darkened on me. I might not have had a lot of experience in the kissing department, but I was smart enough to know that the look Harper gave me was one that begged for me to act.

So I acted. My stomach floated up to my chest when she kissed me back. She slid a hand along my cheek and slipped her tongue in my mouth, and feeling it graze the tip of mine sent a potent warmth traveling through my veins and down my arms and legs. As her tongue searched for more, I thought I would collapse. Her rhythms were unhurried and gentle. I could feel the kiss in the pit of my stomach as if it had been shaken awake from a deep sleep. She held my cheek, causing me to melt into her completely. The feelings landing in my gut danced around like ballroom dancers.

Something about that pushed me on top of her, and Harper welcomed it by spreading her legs as I sandwiched in between. All I could think about were her hands skimming underneath the hem of my shirt. My breath hitched when her fingertips met my waistline, all while her tongue continued to dance with mine. When she started to softly rock her hips, I melted into her and allowed myself to search for something to relieve the throbbing in between my legs. She continued to slide her hands up my shirt, leaving a trail of goose bumps from her soft fingertips. I wanted to feel more of her too, so I followed her lead. With one hand holding her face, I used my free hand to skim underneath her shirt. Her skin was so soft, and the more I felt, the more goose bumps rose from my touch. Her body tensed for a second until she rocked faster against me, and the pressure building inside me was starting to become overwhelming.

I knew what was happening. I knew that all the tongue swipes, hands underneath shirts inching toward the bras, and the grinding was about to send me flying like a shooting star.

I didn't know how long we kissed. The only indicators of time passing were my lips becoming increasingly chapped and pleasure throbbing between my legs. I didn't know that I could feel so overwhelmed from kissing and touching, things I'd never felt before. A few more rocks and I was going to burst from the euphoria. I had to pull away to stop it from happening, and when I did, Harper opened her eyes, examined me for a moment, and then laughed.

"Wow," she said with a ragged breath.

I fell to my side, propped up my head, and filled my lungs with much needed oxygen. "I know."

"That was an amazing way to spend an hour."

"Wait, was it?"

"We didn't even finish the movie." She pointed to her TV that was back on the menu on Netflix.

Holy shit, it really was an hour.

"I'm sorry," I said and tried my puppy dog eyes. "Watching them make out inspired me."

"I'm glad it inspired you. I really benefited from it." She ran her thumb down my chapped lips, and it was sexy as hell. It reignited everything all over again.

"Sorry, I needed to breathe, but I'm done now," I said.

"Good, because I want to keep going." She pushed herself on top of me. Her hair dangled in front of my face, and it smelled so fucking wonderful.

I'd soaked my lips in ChapStick right before I left, and while I enjoyed the bike ride back to Serena's, the cool midnight breeze smacked against my lips, reminding me of all the wonderful and welcome damage Harper caused. It was like her mouth left lipstick stains on every inch of skin she'd kissed, and any spot she'd touched radiated a glow like a blacklight. I wondered if passing cars noticed that I'd been kissed for over an hour. I felt like a different person than when I first walked into her house. If I felt different, did that mean I looked different?

I didn't find the answer until I checked myself out in my bathroom mirror and smiled at my lips still red and swollen and the ChapStick still shimmering in the light. Then, at the nape of my neck—and the spot I could still feel Harper sucking on—I found the smallest purple bruise. My eyes widened while I leaned into the mirror to examine my first hickey more closely. It was a small one that would remind me of Harper on top, her hips rocking on mine, and the soft murmurs that escaped her when our tongues clashed.

I bit back my smile and savored the little souvenir.

I liked eating my scrambled eggs and hash browns, fully doused in equal parts Tabasco and ketchup.

"Hope you're in the mood for some breakfast," Dad said and gestured to the empty seat.

"Theo was nice enough to surprise us with it," Serena said, and it almost seemed like a forced smile, as if to try to convince me how redeeming her son was.

Theo stood next to me with the pot of coffee, flashing a grin I wanted to punch. "Coffee?"

"No, I'm good," I said flatly, not buying his act or trusting what was exactly in the pot.

"You sure? I made more just for you."

"Positive."

Right as I scooped a small spoonful of eggs, Dad said, "Remi, the four of us are going to have a family day."

I shot him a look. After our conversation about how I didn't feel safe around Theo or that I simply didn't want to be around him, and Dad had said he understood, we were going to have a "family" day? Serena and Theo were not my family. Theo was *not* my family. The fact that Dad even referred to all four of us as a family sent a shiver of disgust down my spine.

"We're going to take Serena's boat out for a few hours."

"I figured it would be fun," Serena said. "It's supposed to be such a nice day, and why not spend it out on the water?"

I wasn't sure what would make me more nauseous, the seasickness or bonding with my new "family."

"I get seasick," I said.

"I know," Dad said. "Which is why I went ahead and bought you a patch."

"But I already have plans today."

"You'll cancel them. You've been here for a month, and we haven't done anything together."

"It'll be only a few hours," Serena said, her voice dropping lower as if she could hear my disappointment. Seeing her smile fade the smallest degree really packed a punch. I didn't mean to hurt her feelings. All of that was wrapped up for Theo. "I'm not asking for a whole day. Just an afternoon."

"Also, I have something to say," Theo said and sat across from me. "Remi, I apologize for my behavior the other night. I was a little intoxicated, and it was completely unacceptable."

Dad and Serena then looked at me with hopeful eyes, as if that fictitious apology was enough for the four of us to get on her boat and sail into the sunset together.

I had been bullied during elementary school and all of middle school, and I didn't do one thing to stand up to Chris Murray or the other kids. I saw the way Harper stood up for herself on the boardwalk and spoke to Theo like the child he was. I was envious. I wanted that superpower of looking a bully in the eye and telling them to fuck off. She made it seem so easy. Why couldn't I do it? Why hadn't I done it? I was so tired of rolling over and playing nice with someone who, yet again, felt the need to make my life miserable. I'd spent eighteen years doing that. Now was my time to finally stand up for myself and make up for all those years of acquiesced deference.

"You were bullying an eighteen-year-old girl," I said and stared him straight in the eye. I wasn't afraid of him now with Dad and Serena around me. I knew that with them by my side, my words would actually hold some kind of power.

He nervously chuckled as light pink tinted his cheeks. "What? What are you—"

"You told her that you liked watching people pass by the Acadian like it was a beggar."

Serena gasped and shot him a scowl. "Theo."

"I...I don't remember saying that," he said like a dog with its tail in between its legs.

It was empowering to see how fast he whimpered. It was like watching him keel over after I'd smacked his gut. I wanted more of it.

"Well, I do because I heard it," I said, louder and more confidently. "And apparently, you do this all the time to this girl, like the time you asked her where all her customers were? You remember saying that?"

He blinked a couple times. I could tell he stifled his anger by how his jaw clenched. "No, I don't."

"You're not a reputable source, so I don't believe you, and I don't believe that you're sorry."

"Are you kidding me?"

"No, I'm not."

I caught a glimpse of Dad, who glanced at his plate in silence. Serena's stare intensified on her son, and she slowly shook her head in what looked to be disbelief and embarrassment.

Theo turned to his mom. "What? You don't actually believe her, do you? I don't even know the girl she's talking about."

"Lovely," I said right as Serena opened her mouth to respond. "You bully random girls on the boardwalk for no reason then? How pleasant."

"Remi—" Dad said as if he was tired of my antics.

"What? He bullied a girl and then grabbed me when I defended her. Making breakfast and saying sorry isn't going to undo any of it. Hate to burst the bubble."

Serena and Dad shared a defeated look while Theo's defined jawline tightened, and his eyes bore into me as if trying to telepathically tell me to accept his apology or else. As bad as I felt ruining something Dad and Serena seemed excited about, Theo was a dick, and he wasn't going to get a pitiful slap on the wrist. I wasn't going to be guilted into silence like I was with Chris Murray or when Dad practically forced me to come down to Gaslight Shores.

I was so tired of being expected to shut up and go with the flow for the sake of minimizing drama. My feelings were valid, and it was about time I voiced them.

Honestly, I was surprised that I had the confidence to say something. It wasn't really until all my words hung over the kitchen table and drenched the room in a palpable awkwardness that I realized how proud I was for finally defending myself. It'd never happened before, not in school, not with Dad when he was being an ass during the divorce, not ever. I sometimes wondered if I even had it in me to stand up for what was right and wrong.

I guess I did.

"Maybe this isn't a good idea after all," Serena whispered to Dad, but her stare remained on her lap.

Dad reached for her hand and squeezed it. "I'm sorry, hon."

Serena shook her head and left the table. The air became thicker while her heavy footsteps up the stairs echoed in the foyer. Dad shot me a glare and then one at Theo.

"She really wanted to do this," he said sternly to us before following her. Like when I was kid, a burning sensation washed through me knowing how disappointed I'd made him, even though the decision I made was right for me...and for Harper.

"Cool, Remi, look what you did," Theo said. The absence of his mom seemed to wash away the fake remorse he'd painted on moments before.

"Look what *I* did? You're the asshole who created this mess. See, I knew you weren't sorry at all."

"What more do you want from me? I said I was sorry, and because of you, this whole stupid day was ruined. All she wanted was a few hours on a fucking boat."

"I'm sure all she wanted was a nice son who contributed positively to the world, so let's focus on that more than a few hours on the boat." He laughed like I'd gone mad, and God, something about that made my anger boil. "You can tell me whatever you want. It's not going to make me feel bad for calling you out." I screeched my chair against the wood. There was no point in sitting there longer with him. "By the way, your breakfast sucks."

"By the way, cute hickey on your neck."

An inferno traveled like wildfire on my face, and I knew it colored my neck in ugly red blotches. Theo coughed up a cackle. I stormed out of the house and into my apartment, making sure that both doors leading to it were locked.

At least I got hickeys. The only marks girls left on Theo were to reprimand him for being an asshole.

The mood for the rest of the day was off. The drama from the Fourth colliding with the drama from the morning stacked onto my sternum. I had no idea what to do. My world with Harper and my world with Serena and Theo were now threaded together. I didn't emerge from my apartment because I was too busy weighing all the pros and cons of telling Harper the truth. Maybe she would actually see me as a separate entity from Serena, Theo, and Envie. Or maybe, given the freshness of what happened with Theo, it would be salt in the wounds.

I decided I had to do something. I texted her that I needed an escape from everyone, so she suggested we mini golf after her shift. I met her outside of the Acadian at seven sharp. We hopped in her car and drove the two miles to the mini golf course, and I lectured myself the whole way there that I had to come clean about something.

"I'm not trying to brag," Harper said while placing her light blue golf ball on the tee off pad. She straightened her back, and a mischievous smile formed. "Okay, I'm totally trying to brag. I'm pretty amazing at mini golf. Just to warn you."

"I'll be the judge."

"It's not a matter of judgment, Remi. It's a fact. No one has beaten me in four years."

"Mini golf is basically math and physics, and guess who aced AP physics and AP calc? This chick," I hooked a thumb at my chest. "Not to brag, but I was valedictorian, and I'm going to MIT. Oh, and some girl called me a genius one time. She kinda looked like you, actually."

Harper rolled her eyes, but I noticed her suppressing a grin. "You think you can beat a mini golf maestro based on calculus and physics?"

"It's a possibility, yes."

I knew I was going to lose. I was terrible at mini golf and hadn't played in years. Actually, the last time I remembered playing was with Dad when he and mom were still together. But if I was going to lose to Harper, and she was going to enjoy every moment of it, I was determined to squeeze in my own victorious moments by teasing her.

"If you're so confident, want to raise the stakes?" Harper said. "Loser of the game has to buy us something from South Pole after?"

I stuck out my hand, and she shook it. "Deal."

Apparently, when a person tried really hard to win at mini golf, they were even worse at it. Harper was rightfully bragging. She either made par or putted one or two under. By the ninth hole, halfway into the game, I was losing by a pathetic eleven points, and Harper's victorious grin grew with each hole.

"Tell me more about physics and calc," she said, bumping her hip into mine before setting her ball on the pad.

"Someone is a poor winner."

"Nah, just with you."

She putted, and I cringed when the ball perfectly turned the corner and then bounced into the correct tunnel. We both left our spots to watch her ball come out the other side, stopping a few inches from the hole. She sighed, probably bummed that she came so close to a hole-in-one, and even though she hadn't, she was almost guaranteed to make it in two putts, with the par being four.

I shook my head, walked back to the tee pad, and begrudgingly placed my lime green ball on the mat. Harper giggled from the side. Right as I gripped my club and was about to wind up, I heard a familiar cackle infiltrating the thick, smoggy air. Only one person's laugh could make me cringe like that. I lowered my club and checked over my shoulder to find Theo four courses behind, and with the winding paths of the sidewalks and the other courses, we were doomed to run into each other. He was with a blond girl who was way too beautiful for him. While the blonde observed the invisible path to the hole, he cocked his head and raked his stare down to her ass. When she turned, he snapped his eyes to hers.

"Fuck," I muttered under my breath.

"What?"

I glanced back at Harper. "The..." I caught myself. I wasn't supposed to know his name. He was just a random guy to me. *Crap.* "That guy...the one from the boardwalk, he's right over there."

Harper craned her neck to look. I knew when she found him because her stare rounded. "Shit." Her shoulders slumped in defeat. I hated so much that one look at Theo ruined her smile and vibrant energy. "I think we should bail."

"Wait, what?"

As much as I wanted to avoid Theo, I didn't want him to have all this control. He'd already ruined one night, I didn't want him to ruin yet another, the first night Harper and I had spent together alone after we'd kissed. I couldn't let Theo ruin a maybe-date.

"I don't want him ruining a night that was supposed to be fun," I said.

"It doesn't mean we have to call it a night. It means we won't have to worry about him making a scene. That's what Theo Bradly does. He makes a scene when he doesn't get attention from anyone else. I'm over being his punchline. If we stay, we risk having me be a joke yet again."

I checked over my shoulder again and felt the guilt pressing into my sternum. "Yeah, let's leave," I said and snatched my ball off the ground.

We didn't say much when we dropped our stuff off at the hut. The silence stayed with us until we reached her car. It shouldn't have been like this. Harper and I shouldn't have had our date compromised because Theo was a loose cannon.

"We don't have to call it a night," she said. "You still owe me dessert, and look at the sky." She pointed up. "Another good night for stargazing."

How she was able to power through Theo's bullying and find a silver lining to our ruined plans made my chest swell. It was sexy as hell, actually. Harper knew her worth and didn't accept anything less, whereas at moments of insecurity, I let others determine mine. I learned so much from her in those moments. I was who I was, I liked what I liked, and she made me feel like being unique was a great quality.

We drove back to the boardwalk, and Harper parked behind the Acadian. When we both got out, she slipped her fingers in mine and walked me to the sidewalk. My heart thrummed at the unexpected contact. I floated next to her and focused on how soft her fingers were and how gently she held my hand. She guided us through the crowds, and since Theo was still at mini golf, I let the salty wind blow away the fear of being caught. It gave me the confidence to determine that I had to tell her that I knew Theo before the night ended.

Even when we stood in the five-person deep line at South Pole Treats, her hand never wavered. My heart rate twitched like it had when I drank my first cup of coffee. The only difference between that time when I was sixteen and now was that I didn't want to go back to a normal heart rate. I wanted my body to adjust to it. Life was more exciting at that pace.

With my peanut butter supreme sundae and her Oreo hurricane, we walked across the boardwalk and found a spot in the sand. By the time we polished off our desserts, the sky was dark enough for Jupiter and Saturn to pop through. We didn't come prepared with a blanket or a telescope, but the cool sand felt good against my legs. Harper sat close and extended her hands back like me. Like on the Fourth of July, her hand searched through the sand until it found mine. I basked in the thrilling anticipation of when she would kiss me or when I would kiss her. I'd never kissed on the beach in complete darkness with a beautiful sky above me, but I could only imagine how wonderful it was.

"You know that you can see a shooting star every ten minutes?" I said.

"I was today years old when I learned that tidbit," Harper said. "So many shooting stars I haven't seen."

"That's what I'm here for. All your sky and space knowledge needs. We'll make sure you see one tonight."

"While we wait, you should tell me another space fact."

I had to tell her something else, but I'd take advantage of the space fact she desperately wanted to hear to buy myself more time.

"Okay, so over here," I said, pointing straight at the eastern sky in front of us but keeping my other hand secured under hers. "There is this thing called the Summer Triangle, made up of these three stars: Vega, Deneb, and Altair. Once you find those three stars, you can use it as a roadmap to find the Milky Way."

"Well, damn, I want to see the Milky Way. How do we do that?"

"We have to find a place with no light pollution. I've been stargazing since I was a kid and have never seen it. The sky needs to be the darkest it can get."

"Let's make this happen then." She hooked her arm around mine and rested her chin on my shoulder. That sweet and innocent gesture turned me to putty. "We can both see something together for the first time."

Honestly, if she'd asked me to rob a bank like that, I probably would have said yes.

I tightened my arm around hers, securing her in her spot so she didn't shift away. "If we're serious about this, I'll have to look up a light pollution map and the next new moon. The moon can't be out either."

"I'm dead serious."

I laughed at how eager she was. I didn't even have to say anything else to sell her. "Okay, one second."

With her still wrapped around my arm, I used my free hand to do a quick search on my phone. The nearest green spot on the light pollution map was Hunting Island, and the next new moon was the last weekend of July, almost three weeks away.

"It's a date, okay?" Harper asked as if she wanted to make a promise.

I loved how she looked resting against my shoulder and giving me pleading eyes, as if I seriously needed to be convinced. My heart tugged so much, I closed my eyes and softly kissed her forehead. As my lips lingered a little longer, she let out a deep sigh.

I could feel her turn into putty too.

The thunderstorm that had passed through the night before brought a little chill in the soft breeze. Harper pressing into my side provided some welcome warmth. The waves were quieter than usual, delicately crawling up the shore. There was something about the moonlight and bold stars that made the simplest thing twenty times more special.

We sat like that for a couple of silent moments. I knew that the moment provided the transition to tell her about Theo. I had to do it, or the pain would never leave my chest.

I unhooked my arm, and Harper looked over as if she felt the loss. "Hey...um...I need to tell you something."

Her eyebrows furrowed, and I already hated so much that the softness detailing her facial features seconds before became sharper. "Okay…"

A lump sprouted in my throat. I forced a cough to try to loosen it, but I knew it wouldn't go away until I gave her something. "It's about Theo."

"What about him?"

I turned to the ocean for a moment and watched the low tide lick the shore. "I worked at Envie…until a few days ago, that is."

The silence became sharp and painful. I faced Harper and saw her scooting away while a detailed frowned directed at me only fueled the pressure behind my ribs. "What?"

Her voice was soft yet so harsh, demanding answers.

"I've been working at Envie. It's why I was so intrigued with trying the Acadian. I wanted to see why this restaurant rivalry was a thing. Theo was my manager and—"

"He was your manager?" Her voice rose.

I froze. The anger that laced through her words made my brain glitch. *See. You already ruined everything.*

"Yes, but after the Fourth, I quit. I'm not going to work there anymore because I don't feel safe around him."

"I can't…why…why didn't you tell me this?"

"Because you said that Envie is ruining everything. I'm not from here. I knew from working at Envie that there was some rivalry, and I thought it was like all the other restaurant rivalries, like the pizza one back home—"

"It's not just some restaurant rivalry, Remi. This is my life. This is my parents' life, and the Acadian is practically dead. Give it until Labor Day, and it will be dead. The only job my parents ever knew is going to be gone, which leaves them to do what?"

She left the question hanging, and I couldn't tell if it was rhetorical or not, but I felt the need to try to answer. "I…I don't know," I said.

"Exactly."

"See, this is why I didn't say anything. I was set up with this job, and I took it. This was all before I met you and found out about how it's affecting your life, and by then, I was worried that you would see me as the bad guy when I'm anything but. I have no allegiance to Envie. I'm on your side, Harper. Through all of it, and I'm so sorry."

Despite my apology, Harper turned to face the ocean, tucked her knees into her chest, and hugged them. The kind of silence that took over killed the sound of the waves. All I could do was fixate on each quiet minute that ticked by without her saying anything or looking at me. As painful as it was, I knew I needed to give her the time to process…at least this piece of info. By the way she reacted to just working at Envie, I knew that telling her about Serena would propel her off the beach. I needed to do it one step at a time. If she decided to talk to me again, maybe she would eventually see me as me—and nothing else—and would learn that Envie meant nothing to me and that she and the Acadian meant everything. When that finally happened, then I would tell her about Serena. I had to before the summer ended, but I wanted it to be at the right time.

"Do you ever talk about the Acadian?" she asked, barely above a whisper.

"To Theo? Absolutely not. I came in, made very mediocre sandwiches, and left. The only time I talked about the Acadian was with Aaron, the guy who came in to have the po'boys with me, but that's only because he said he used to go to the Acadian all the time and kept telling me how much he loved it."

She grunted. "And now he works at Envie instead? Some loyalty."

"Apparently, they pay more, but that doesn't matter. He loves the Acadian. The only time it was mentioned in Envie, at least when I was working, was when Aaron would talk about how he liked it better than Envie. Harper, I started the job before I met you, before you told me about everything. I'm one-hundred-percent done with that place. There's no way I'm going back, especially after what Theo did on the Fourth. I promise."

She ran her fingers along her forehead, down to her temples as if kneading out the tension building in them. "You punched him in the stomach and then quit?"

"Yeah. Well, I didn't show up to my shift the next day. I stood him up and quit that way."

She turned and looked at me like I'd gone mad. We shared a confused stare for a second before the faintest smile finally broke. "You just didn't show up to work?"

I shrugged. "No."

She let out another laugh. "That's pretty bold."

"He's an asshole and deserves nothing more. But I'm done working there, Harper. I'm free for the rest of the summer, and the only way I want to spend it is eating at the Acadian and all the other food on the boardwalk with you."

Her grin grew. "That's how I want to spend it too."

"Do you forgive me?"

"I think I need to process it a little more, but yeah. Thank you for telling me. I mean, you were only working for the devil for... what...a few weeks? And your exit was pretty grand."

"I don't even care. I'd do it that way again if I had the chance."

She scooted closer and closed the gap between us. "You're too good for Envie anyway. I'm glad you broke free."

She faltered, observed my face, and as if something settled in her, she leaned in to kiss me. I was stunned, not expecting it after telling her about Envie. But I'd take it. I closed my eyes and followed her cautious lead. Her kiss was soft and hesitant, like she was still processing the truth at the same time she was trying to push it out of sight. I hoped that meant she forgave me.

Like a switch, my mind turned off and tuned out everything, the argument, any onlookers on the beach, the shooting stars. As her tongue brushed mine, it felt like the goose bumps on my arms inverted inside me. I held her face to keep her in place, and like before, an unknown amount of time passed before she pulled away.

"Look!" Harper said and jolted straight up, finger pointed. Right as I looked, I saw a speck flit across the sky. "Oh my God, did you see that?"

I'd seen a million shooting stars, but they never got old.

I smiled at her enthusiasm and wondered if she was always this interested in stars or if I had some influence. I wanted to believe it was a little bit of both.

"You have to make a wish," I said.

"Okay." She sealed her lips and eyes for a moment before looking over. "Done."

She looked at my mouth instead of the sky, and I was amazed that whatever force emanated from her was powerful enough to draw my gaze away from my favorite sight of all time. It was like the sky didn't even exist. Only Harper.

When I leaned back in, Harper laughed and stopped my chest. "I can't believe Remi Brenner doesn't care about the sky anymore. Am I really that alluring?"

"Shh. Don't be like Betelgeuse and lose your brightness because you used too much energy talking—"

She yanked on my shirt until my lips collided with hers. Right as I sunk into her mouth again, she pulled back just a whisper. "Remi."

I smiled while basking in the feeling of her words brushing my lips. "What?"

She felt one of my curls, looped it around her finger, and gently reeled me back in. "Nothing."

I had no idea how long we made out, but when I pulled away for some air, my lips were chapped, and my whole body was tingly. I looked around the beach and was shocked that hardly anyone was taking advantage of the beautiful night and sky. But then again, we weren't taking advantage of the sky either.

Harper checked the time on her phone, and the screen cast a dim light on her puffy lips. "It's ten thirteen."

I looked at my phone and noticed a text from my dad sent forty minutes ago. Before I left, I'd texted him I was going out with friends, so my silence didn't make things worse.

Hey where are you? It doesn't look like you're back? Just want to know if you're still out and safe.

I quickly texted back. *I went out with some friends. At the boardwalk right now. Will be back by 11.*

"Yeah, unfortunately, I should head back," I said regretfully.

"If we leave now, we can sneak in some time making out in my car. The Acadian is closed, and everyone is usually gone by now, which means, empty parking lot." She waggled her eyebrows.

I stood up and held out my hand. "I don't need any more convincing."

The best part about making out with a local? She knew the best spots to get away with it. Her car was the only one in the back parking lot behind the Acadian, Sully's, and the arcade. We both got in the back seat, and my heart stuttered at the anticipation of all the room Harper suspected we would need.

The kiss resumed with much more fervidity than on the beach. I placed my hands on her waist for a moment before too much need overcame me, and I had to slip them under the hem of her shirt to touch her skin. Harper pushed me on my back and crawled on top. Her hair enveloped us in a small world of only her face and her fruity shampoo. I traced the swell of her breasts, and she sent a soft murmur into my mouth. I kept replaying that sound over and over again as the heat on my lips wandered downward.

The temperature in the car rose while Harper sucked the nape of my neck, the same spot where my little hickey had taken up residence. Then it was my turn for a sound to fly out of me. At first, I was embarrassed because I didn't want to seem so easy, but God, she was just so good at making my whole body light up. She repositioned and slipped a leg in between mine. All those feelings migrated downward when I felt her pelvis resting against mine, and like our make outs before, she slowly moved along with the rhythms of our kiss. I held her back and let my hands wander. Her bra strap helped guide me around her sides and to her chest, and when her breasts were in my palms, her breathing hitched at the same time as mine, and another groan rose from her throat.

I knew if we didn't stop, we would get too carried away. I retrieved my hands and cupped her face, giving her one last kiss.

My body hated so much that my brain took over because God, did I want to keep going. I had no idea that kissing and being pressed against someone like that could feel so good. But my brain reminded me that we were in a car behind the Acadian. I'd also told my dad I'd be home in less than an hour, and I knew that time had already flown by; that was what happened whenever I was around Harper Hebert.

"I think we need to get going before this intensifies," I said through ragged breaths.

"Wanna put your bike in my trunk, and I can drop you off?"

"Sure, give me a second."

I kissed her before getting out of the car to go around the corner to the bike rack.

She held my hand the entire ride back to the Palms. The roads were desolate, and some kind of country station played through the speakers. Even though I hated country music, it was already starting to remind me of Harper and the summer that was quickly morphing into ours.

CHAPTER TEN

Not working at Envie anymore did have a downside. I was free all the time and didn't have any excuses to not do something. When Serena suggested that we have a "girls' day," I acquiesced because there was nothing else to do except to finish reading or hang out with Harper, who was working.

I guess it would free me from the guilt about the failed boat trip.

We drove into downtown Charleston, and I was amazed by how adorable the city was. The architecture was beautiful, some were even painted in bold pastel colors, and like Gaslight Shores, palm trees lined the streets. Serena veered off the route to the spa to show off the cobblestone roads still intact. Charleston was like Gaslight Shores's older cousin but with more people, history, and opulence.

The spa was located on a part of King Street known as the Fashion District, Serena said. The street was one of the main downtown roads that housed all the restaurants, hotels, art galleries, and shops. Serena handed her Range Rover keys to the valet, and we walked around the corner with the sun beating down on us. She lowered her Prada sunglasses, and my ten-dollar glasses from Target made me feel completely inadequate walking beside her. When she opened the door to the spa, the employees greeted her by name with big hugs, and I wondered how often she came here.

"This is my stepdaughter, Remi," Serena said, perching her sunglasses on the top of her head. I was surprised how her calling me her stepdaughter didn't feel like chugging sour milk anymore. "Remi, this is Caroline, the owner. She's wonderful."

"This is the famous stepdaughter of yours. Serena, she's just pretty as a peach."

"I wish I could take some credit, but I can't. She got Dennis's good genes. She's a smart one too. Just graduated high school as valedictorian, starting her freshman year at MIT next month."

"Well, that's lovely, my dear. Congratulations. I know just the thing to celebrate. Y'all follow me."

Caroline ushered us to one of the manicure tables. Serena's eyes widened at me as if trying to get me pumped up for the treat, and I wanted to die inside. I'd never had a manicure before and barely had nails, but I forced a smile to appease her. She was at least trying to get to know me, and none of that went unnoticed. Dad could have married someone who didn't give two shits about me, so part of me was grateful that she cared.

As we got situated in our seats, Caroline brought over a flute of champagne for Serena and sparkling grape juice for me. The two nail technicians took their seats and instructed us to give them one of our hands. Once the technician started massaging my hand, my skeptical attitude started to dissolve like the tension I apparently had in my hands and fingers.

Okay, maybe Serena was on to something with these manicures.

"I'm so glad you agreed to do this," Serena said and took a sip of champagne. "It means a lot, you know. Getting to know each other."

Her eyes held so much sincerity that I had to turn away and watch the technician massage my hand. I felt bad for not trying until now, halfway into my stay, disliking her son so much that it had wedged us apart.

"I'm glad too," I said and truly meant it. "Thanks for bringing me out, and I'm sorry about Sunday."

"Oh, honey, it's fine. I thought that it was a good idea in the moment, but I don't blame you for not wanting to be around Theo. It's just…well…" She let out a deep exhale. "I'm so sorry about what he did. I know I shouldn't have to apologize for him, but…

well...he's struggling right now and taking it out on others. It isn't acceptable at all, and I'm trying to work on it."

"It's not your fault."

She offered a thin smile that didn't reach her eyes. "I'm his mother. It's a reflection on me as well."

"I don't think it is. He's a grown adult."

"His father really resents me...for a lot of things, really. They have that father-son bond, and it seems like the more he grows up, the more he acts out. I think to get back at me for not being there all the time while he was growing up. You know, because of all the traveling with my job. Who really knows?" She exhaled again and then forced a smile. "Anyway, I'm sorry for putting you in any position that made you uncomfortable."

"It's okay."

It took great humility to apologize not only for her behavior, but for someone else's. I didn't think Serena needed to apologize on behalf of her twenty-two-year-old son. But she did anyway.

"It's not, but I appreciate it," she said with a wink. "What really needs to happen is that I need to go talk to the Hebert girl. Harper. You said she told you this wasn't the first time?"

At the mention of her name, I felt the warmth crawl over my face, and I hoped that it didn't match the dark red nail polish bottles on the wall behind the technicians. Whatever shade it was, Serena seemed to notice, by the sudden furrow of her eyebrows. If Dad knew Harper's name and what she looked like, it shouldn't have shocked me so much that Serena did too.

"That's what she told me. Anytime they run into each other."

Serena scoffed and shook her head. "Unbelievable. How embarrassing."

"Can I ask you something?"

"Yeah, sure. You can ask me anything."

I paused for a moment, one last attempt to gauge if I should really ask the question or not. We were already on the subject of the Heberts, so why not hear it from Serena DeLuca herself? Today's spa day was about getting to know each other, and if I didn't jump on the moment, I didn't know if I'd ever have another chance. "Why did you open up Envie? Why open up a fast-food joint when you have all these fancy restaurants?"

"I always wanted to open up a quick bites place, one with full meal customization. They're becoming so popular now. It was an opportunity to expand."

"But you had to have known that there was already a po'boy place on the boardwalk."

Her smile faded. "Are you talking about the Acadian?"

"Yeah. Wasn't it a Gaslight Shores staple before Envie came along?"

"It was. It's a great restaurant—"

"Then why build Envie? Why build a competitor to something that's been around for seventy years? You know how much it's suffering because of Envie?"

She studied me a little more intently as her eyebrows pulled together. "Remi, why are you asking about this? You seem upset."

Yeah, I guess I was upset. I was upset that this insane rivalry was greatly affecting the Heberts. I was upset that telling Harper I worked at Envie for a month almost scared her away. I was upset that there was so much damage done by Serena, Theo, and Envie that it terrified me to tell Harper that they were my stepfamily because I had this unsettling feeling in my gut that it would scare her away from me.

"When I was talking to Harper, she told me how Envie is taking away their customers, and now they might have to close down."

She exhaled and took another encouraging sip of her drink. "I had my eyes on opening something up on the boardwalk ever since I bought the house years ago. I almost went through with an upscale restaurant but decided against it. I wanted something fresh to add to my resume and already have Axis in New York and LA. I knew it was the perfect spot for my fast-food place. Of course, I knew about the Acadian and its history. That's why I sought it out. I offered to invest in it."

My eyes widened at the brand-new information. "Wait, what?"

"I pitched the Heberts my entire business proposal. Told them how my help would benefit their restaurant, what improvements they needed to make to stay up with current industry trends, and if they agreed to a partnership, they would have access to my contacts that could bottle their famous Debris Sauce so we could get it on the shelves. It's won countless awards over the years. That's a huge missed opportunity to get more people exposed to it. I was confident that we could make the Acadian a spot that would have people from out of town coming in droves, people who've never even been to Gaslight Shores before. We'd been chatting for at least three months about the possibility, and I thought it was going to happen, but they declined it."

"They declined it? What? Why?" I didn't understand. How could you decline that offer? It sounded amazing to me.

"Oh yes, they declined it," she said with a small chuckle. "'The Acadian has been around for over seventy years,' Tim Hebert said. He wanted to keep the place how his grandfather created it. A simple menu, which is outdated. The food industry right now is all about customization, and they didn't want to conform. Bottling their sauce would help them make money during the off-season, but they didn't want to do it. An interior design facelift, they didn't want to do that. I upped my offer, and they still declined. They weren't interested in anything I had to bring to the table. Honestly, I kind of felt led on."

I didn't realize my mouth hung open until that moment. I wanted to ask Harper about her family's side of the story. Now that she knew I worked with Theo, I could say that I heard him mention the rejected deal.

I had a million more questions than I started with.

"I didn't know that," I said softly, feeling a little deceived that Harper didn't share that part with me. I got a taste of my own medicine, and it made me really think hard about how the hell to tell her about Serena, but anytime I tried, I was at a loss. Was there even a perfect time to tell her? No matter how I did it, she was going to be pissed, and honestly, I didn't blame her at all.

"Yeah, it was pretty unfortunate for all of us. But they weren't interested, and I wasn't going to miss the potential I saw. So I opened Envie. It has a wider range of selections and isn't a niche to po'boys. I'm sad to hear that the Acadian isn't doing well, but if it wasn't Envie, it would have been another sandwich place, and if the Heberts aren't willing to keep up with the times, then they're setting themselves up for failure. I wish they would have at least taken my advice. Trends change all the time, and the businesses that refuse to adjust never make it."

I glanced over at the nail technician, who'd started filing and shaping my right hand. This whole summer, I'd believed that Serena was this heartless woman, ruining staples of beloved summer towns, but that wasn't the case at all. I felt like my brain was betraying Harper and the Heberts for understanding where Serena was coming from. She'd acknowledged the importance of the Acadian and offered to help it. She was right. If the Heberts weren't willing to keep up with the times, there was only so much Serena could do to help save it.

I felt like a traitor for saying that in my head, scratching off Envie as one of the reasons why I had a problem with Serena. She'd defended and listened to me when Theo was being an asshole. She'd apologized for him. She'd offered to help take the Acadian to the next level that would have had the Heberts financially set for life. The only other thing on my list of reasons to not like my new stepmom was because she was the first woman after Mom, and that wasn't anything personal.

"Would you consider making another offer to them?" I asked, deciding to go out on a limb.

She gave a forced smile that told me everything I needed to know before she even spoke. "It's too late for that, Remi. Envie exists. I came to them, left them my card if they changed their mind. Ball is in their court. I do wish them the best, though. Very nice family. Stubborn but nice." The technicians instructed us to dip our massaged hand in a cup of warm water that was scented with lavender oil while they moved on to our left hand. "Okay, enough about that. I want the tea," Serena said, smirking over at me. "Who is this mystery person you keep hanging out with? I have a feeling that it's someone special because this person is nameless. Your dad thinks it's just a friend, but men are kind of clueless, am I right?"

She wiggled her dark blond eyebrows as if she'd crossed her legs in a girls' sleepover gossip circle.

I felt my whole face flush even worse than when she dropped Harper's name. "You've talked about this with my dad?" I was mortified. I didn't even think Dad and Serena noticed, honestly. Apparently, I was wrong about so many things.

"Of course," she said like it should have been obvious. "You've been so mysterious about your whereabouts. Now spill or you're covering this manicure."

I really wished I had access to both of my hands so I could hide my warm face behind them. "I'm not—"

"Remi, honey, you can fool your dad but not me. I've seen the smiles when you're on your phone and how irritable you get when your dad asks who you're hanging out with. I was your age once. So who's the boy?"

I couldn't believe what I considered telling her. She'd done such a good job being real and honest ever since the beginning of the summer, and I was too stubborn to notice until now. It didn't feel as painful to be honest with her anymore. She was making such an effort; I could at least do the same. Building a relationship was a two-way street, and since Theo had done a really good job making things awkward inside the house, it would be too much effort to maintain the distance with Serena.

Also, I wasn't sure if I wanted the distance with her anymore.

"Who says it's a boy?"

She blinked several times in a row, and her eyebrows folded as one side of her smile curved. "Wait. Are you…"

"Gay? No. I like who I like. Boy. Girl. Someone in between."

And then she laughed. It wasn't quite the reaction I expected, but the smile on her face told me the laugh wasn't in mockery. It was like she was laughing at herself for thinking otherwise. The smallest bit of doubt unclenched in my chest from knowing that she wasn't going to tell me how I needed to bathe in holy water. "I'm so sorry, Remi," she said through her chuckle. "I had no idea. I shouldn't have assumed you were talking to a boy."

"It's all good."

"Your father never told me, so I'm surprised, that's all. But I guess that's not his place to tell, is it? Well, okay then, do I get any details about the lucky lady?"

I actually loved how easygoing and nonjudgmental Serena was, how easy she was to connect with, how she really listened when I spoke, and how optimistic she was about everything. After we selected our nail polish—she went with "complimentary wine" and I chose "boyfriend jeans"—she faced me again as if to remind me to spill.

By that moment, I really did want to tell her about the girl I'd been talking to all summer because I had no one else to talk to about her, at least, not in-person. The closer I got to both Harper and Serena, the guiltier I felt for trying to wedge more space in between them. Telling Serena was a step closer to closing that gap. The smaller the space between Serena and Harper, the easier it would maybe be to tell Harper the rest of the truth.

I exhaled a long sigh that came from the pit of my gut. "If I tell you, can you promise not to tell anyone? Especially Theo?"

"After Theo's behavior, I know better than to tell him anything about you. This is our girl time. All this kind of stuff stays between us. I promise."

I sucked in more air and held it in. "It's Harper Hebert."

Serena's eyes widened, but the curve of her lips didn't waver. "Wow. Well...I wasn't expecting that. She's a pretty girl. You both did good."

I let out the air I'd held in. She didn't seem upset at all. Hell, she looked even more invested in our "girl time" than moments before. It felt good to finally allow the truth out. Keeping all of that in from three different parties was hard, and it was starting to take its toll. I felt lighter when I told her, and when she smiled back at me, talking about Harper was more exciting.

"How did you two meet?" Serena asked.

"I...um...well...I wanted to try a po'boy. Aaron and Theo kept hyping up the rivalry, and I wanted to form my own opinion."

"Very scientific of you." She added a wink.

"Yeah, I guess. We hit it off immediately and have been hanging out ever since."

"So is this a summer romance?" she said in a teasing tone.

I rolled my eyes. "Serena, don't make this weird."

She laughed. "When can we meet her? Bring her over for dinner, or hell, how about we take her out to dinner? You, me, and your dad."

"Oh yeah. About that," I said and focused my attention on my nails drying under the light. I barely recognized my fingers with nail polish, but I really did love the dark-blue-almost-black color. "She doesn't know."

"Remi..." Her chipper tone deflated into a soft, lecturing one.

"I know it's bad, okay? I told her the other day I worked at Envie, and she seemed visibly upset. Rightfully so because her family's really hurting. She had dreams to go to culinary school, to get out of this town and finally make a name for herself, and now she can't because the Acadian is probably not going to survive past this summer. She's so upset about it. She seems okay now knowing that I quit Envie but...if I still worked there? I really don't think she would have handled it that well. I have no idea how to tell her the rest of the truth."

"The truth meaning me?"

I looked up and noticed a glimmer of hurt in her brown eyes. It was enough emotion to remind me of why I kept things to myself. I didn't want to hurt anyone. Harper. Serena. My dad. Anyone...with the exception of Theo. "Yeah. That."

She thinned her smile. "Where did she want to go? To culinary school, I mean."

"I don't know. Somewhere not here. She's never been out of this town. She wants to go to culinary school and learn French cooking, maybe study abroad for a year in France. She's been making French pastries every time I come over, and she's really good at it. She has all this passion and was on the path to achieve all of that until Envie opened up, and instead, the family's money went into keeping the Acadian alive."

"There's only so much I can do, Remi. I offered my help, and they didn't want it. I don't know what else to do."

"Yeah, but you're going to be fine whether Envie exists or not. You have Axis, your name, your clout. The Heberts won't. Their family legacy won't. Harper's dreams won't. This is all the family has ever known, and it's about to be gone. They have no idea what they're going to do after this. Their options are extremely limited. Yours aren't."

Serena looked at her hands glimmering in a purplish-red color. The mood shifted from the "girl talk" that strung us together to the truth now snipping all the progress in half. For the first time, I felt the loss of our connection. Once I knew what it felt like to open up to her and to try to establish some kind of bond, I wanted to reel it back in.

"I could always give you some flyers for the Fournier School of Culinary Arts," she said, still looking at her drying nails. "I'm on the board. Doesn't hurt to look into it, you know?"

"Isn't that in New York City?"

"It is, but it's no more than in-state tuition. And Fournier's program focuses half on cooking techniques and half on business management. It's one of a kind." She finally faced me again. "How about I gather some info, and you can give it to her, show her that she has affordable options. There are plenty of scholarships and financial aid. Plus, Fournier is ranked one of the top culinary schools in the country. She doesn't have to know that I gave it to you. I doubt she knows I'm on the board. Most people don't."

I shrugged. Did Harper know that Serena was on the board for the Fournier School of Culinary Arts? Would she be offended if I gave her those resources? I really wanted Harper to be happy. I wanted her to feel fulfilled. She always worried about her family, the Acadian, her family's legacy, but she needed to worry about her own life too. If her dream was to go to culinary school and learn more about French cooking, she should be able to do that. She said she wanted to see the world, and I wanted that for her.

"Yeah, I guess it doesn't hurt. Thank you, Serena."

"You're welcome. And two more things. One, please be safe. Think long and hard about what you do and don't do—"

"Oh my God," I muttered, wanting so badly to retrieve my hands to hide my mortified face. But since my nails were still drying, I had no other choice but to turn away.

Serena laughed. "You're eighteen and have been hanging around a beautiful girl all summer. I know what's on your mind, and I know eighteen-year-olds have sex. It's no secret. Remember, I was eighteen once."

"Serena, can we stop talking about this? Oh my God."

She snickered as if finding entertainment in my chagrin. "Not yet. Be careful, okay? Just promise me you'll think before you do. You're an adult. You can make your own decisions, and don't worry, I won't be discussing this with your dad."

I exhaled a heavy breath. "Oh, thank God."

"And two, you need to tell her the truth."

"What?"

"It needs to happen soon. It sounds like Envie and no business deal with her parents is really affecting her, and honestly, I would hold a slight grudge against me too. I don't blame her. You can't control who your dad marries, but you can control how honest and dishonest you are. The longer you hide it, the more you're going to hurt her, and I don't think you want that, do you?"

"Not at all. That's why I haven't told her. I don't want to hurt her. I just didn't want it to prevent us from being friends. I wanted her to see me as my own person."

"And you can still prove that to her. That's my only suggestion to you. A very strong suggestion. What you do with it is your decision, but you need to prepare yourself for the consequence of whatever decision you make. Think about it." She exhaled. "Now, I'm done. I promise. Do we have a deal?"

I glanced over at my sparkling grape juice and how my throat desperately needed something to make it feel less swollen, dry, and scratchy. "Yes, we have a deal. Now can we talk about...I don't know...puppies or something?"

She tossed her head back and laughed. "Puppies. Yes, Remi, we can talk about puppies."

We didn't talk about puppies. We shared a laugh before the technician came back and turned off the lights. Serena paid, we went to her favorite bistro a few blocks away for lunch, and we talked about nothing too deep for the rest of our day. I did, however, ask if she knew where Reagan Moore lived. My own curiosity was getting to me, and Serena was the holder of the knowledge.

"Are you a Reagan fan?" she asked as she stabbed a large forkful of salad.

Of course I was a Reagan Moore fan. Ninety percent of people my age were fans. Her songs were all over the radio, they were catchy, they were relatable. More importantly, she was queer and told the world that while there were still people and parts of the world who shamed us for who we loved, we could still be successful and influential.

"Of course I am."

Serena smiled. "Reagan lives in the next cul-de-sac over."

"What? Seriously?"

The Palms was a big development. Reagan Moore could have lived anywhere, but I had no idea she was only one street over this whole time.

"Seriously. Would you like to say hi?"

"I…um…I mean…"

Yes and no. Of course I wanted to say hi, but I also had no idea what to say. I didn't know how to speak properly when I was nervous, and the last thing I wanted was for Reagan Moore to think I was painfully awkward. Also, I wanted Harper next to me, but I had no idea how to do that without Serena's intervention.

"I think she's in LA right now, but I know she's coming back before the summer ends."

"Are you on…talking terms with her?"

Serena laughed. "Of course. She's my summer neighbor. Plus, she's come to Axis LA a couple of times with her girlfriend. Very sweet girl. I'll keep this in mind next time she's back in town."

My heart raced. Even if I couldn't have Harper beside me, maybe I could sneak in a moment of seeing if Reagan Moore had ever been to the Acadian. Maybe I could even send her there while Harper was working. It was a long shot, I told myself, but I wasn't going to be deterred. I had plenty of time to think of a plan, even if the chances of the plan working were slim to none. I imagined Reagan Moore walking into the Acadian, people taking pictures, and having it spread on the internet. People would flock to the Acadian because Reagan Moore went there. Maybe it would give them a much-needed boost to survive the summer.

Maybe. Just maybe.

CHAPTER ELEVEN

*H*oly crap, I'm sleeping over tonight.
   Once Harper and I made the plans, my heart hadn't stopped racing. If "Netflix and chill" was code for "let's make out," then I knew exactly what "let's have a sleepover" meant.

I packed my pj's, a toothbrush, and a pack of gum in my bookbag because Brie told me to. I wanted to buy a travel bottle of mouthwash, but Brie told me that would be too obvious, so I opted for gum that I'd already started chewing to get ahead of the game. Any sort of bad breath bacteria was going to stay out of my mouth for the next twelve hours. I was adamant about it.

As I got out of the shower and slipped into a cute tank top and short jean shorts, two cars pulled into the driveway with pounding bass. I glanced out the window to find Theo getting out of his Jeep, with a Ford pickup with tires too big for it parking behind. Two guys came out of the truck, the same douchey faces from the boardwalk on the Fourth. Theo pulled out a case of Bud Light from the trunk and passed out cans to his friends. One of them started blasting rap music from a Bluetooth speaker that wasn't in view, but I definitely heard it as the deep bass jiggled my windows to the smallest degree. They leaned against the cars and continued laughing and chatting away.

I grunted when I knew I had to make a mad dash down the driveway as fast as I could so they wouldn't harass me.

Once I stepped outside, they fixed their stares on me. I darted into the garage to grab my bike and bought myself time by sending Harper the world's slowest text until I mustered enough courage to deal with them.

I kept my eyes on the front bike wheel and kicked the stand up. As I took a seat, I noticed Theo pushing himself off the back of his Jeep.

"Oh, don't you look pretty as a peach," he said in a mocking accent.

I hated how three pairs of sleazy eyes raked down my body, and in doing so, I already had the need to take another shower. I regretted wearing a tank top that showed off my shoulders and the smallest bit of cleavage, but with Theo and his friends eyeing me, it felt like it revealed everything. I should have espoused Billie Eilish's style, one she purposely wore so she wouldn't be oversexualized in Hollywood.

"Is someone dressed for a special occasion? Or a special someone?" A painful heat washed over me. It must have shown because the three of them cackled and drank more beer as if it was their entertainment refreshment. "Are you hanging out with the boy who gave you the hickey? Guys, get this, she had a baby hickey on her neck, just, like, hanging right there."

His two friends rolled with laughter.

"Would you shut up?" I said.

"Can I meet the guy who's been hooking up with my favorite stepsister? Oh, is the mysterious boyfriend Aaron? Did Aaron give you the hickey?"

"Why the hell would I tell you?"

"Because this is a small town. I'll find out eventually."

"I doubt that you're smart enough." I pushed off the sidewalk and rode down the driveway.

"Challenge accepted," he shouted.

I flipped him off and pedaled fast. I checked over my shoulders a couple of times to make sure no one was following me and then decided to take the long way to Harper's if they decided to follow me on Route 7.

By the time I got to the Heberts, my heart had turned into a brick thumping against my rib cage. I sucked in hot, stale air as a clamoring wave of cicada buzzing filtered through the trees.

"Oh, hey," Harper said when she answered the door, and the blast of the air-conditioning brought a bit of relief from my perspiring face and body.

Riding a bike while trying to look good for my first sleepover with the girl I was talking to was the worst idea I ever had. If MIT knew that, they might have recanted my acceptance.

"Hurry up and get in here so you don't melt. It's humid as fuck. I think there's a storm coming. My mom won't shut up about it."

I caught a glimpse of the gray clouds forming in the pockets of the canopy right before Harper grabbed my clammy hand and tugged me inside.

In the kitchen, Mr. Hebert jiggled popcorn kernels in a pot over the stove, and Mrs. Hebert was in front of him at the kitchen island, scattering pizza rolls on a tin-foil-covered tray. Once they greeted me, she placed the tray in the oven.

"There's a big storm brewing out there," Mrs. Hebert said.

"I know. Tell me about it," I said, fanning myself. "I'm ready for the storm to get rid of this humidity."

"Oh, honey, nothing gets rid of it, unfortunately. Now, if it gets severe, I want you girls to come downstairs, all right? I'll call up if you two need to come down."

Harper opened the bag of tortilla chips, popped one in her mouth, and then offered me the bag. "Okay, Mom. I'm sure it will be fine." Harper opened the fridge and pulled out a glass container of what looked to be mousse. "Oh, I made some chocolate mousse." She opened the lid and scooped some on her finger, and the way she sucked it into her mouth made my cheeks warm. I don't even think she meant to make me react because why would she in front of her parents?

"Harper, use a spoon," her mom said through her laugh and slid her one across the island.

Harper handed me the spoon, and as a chocolate lover, I didn't need to take a modest spoonful. I scooped as much as I could, tasted it, and almost turned into chocolate mousse. "Oh wow."

"I'm pretty proud of how this turned out."

"You should be."

We both ate a small plate of mousse while the popcorn and pizza rolls finished, and once they were, we stacked all the snacks in our arms as if we were experienced servers and scurried upstairs.

"Before we start anything," Harper said and cautiously placed the food on the edge of her bed. Her eyes followed the modest dip the tank top created in front of my chest, and a whirl of heat found its way back to me again. "Only pj's are allowed."

I put my hands up to surrender. "You don't have to ask me twice, but before I get too comfortable, can we talk about something?"

Serena's voice never left my head. Before the night started, I wanted to try to talk about everything. If she was still processing me working at Envie, if she knew about the business deal Serena tried to make with her parents. I couldn't ignore everything.

"Sure, what's up?"

"Can we talk about Envie?"

Harper grunted. "Do we have to? Envie is the last thing I want to talk about. It's very draining. Look, I forgive you, Remi, and looking back at all of it, I get why you were afraid to tell me. But right now, I don't want to dwell on it. I've been trying not to dwell on things out of my control. You're my escape from all of it, and it would be awesome to not think about it for the rest of the night, you know?"

She closed the space between us and looped her fingers through my belt loops, pulling me in closer.

"I understand but—"

Her kiss hushed me right up. She pulled away, and her mouth hovered right under my lips. "No Envie. No Theo. No Serena. This is our time. I very much like our time."

I gave up. If not talking about it was what she wanted and needed for her mental health, forcing her into talking about it would be wrong. Apparently, this wasn't the time to do it, and I needed to accept that.

After another quick peck on the lips, Harper said, "Real clothes. Off. Now."

And with that, I followed Harper's lead and flushed everything about Envie out of my brain.

Even though I'd originally attempted to look cute, the bike ride through a brewing storm made me sweat off any sort of cuteness. But if Harper wanted me in comfortable clothes, I'd cooperate. Plus, the navy blue T-shirt with GSHS in white lettering across her breasts made her extra adorable and soft.

If I was into Harper in a worn shirt and mesh white shorts that lingered high on her toned legs, then I'm sure she probably would think the same thing about me in my pj's.

I sat close beside her on her bed, relaxing my leg into hers so some part of me was touching her. Her leg was silky smooth, hinting to me that she'd recently shaved, probably that morning, like I had. Feeling her warm skin made my gut twirl and dance.

"Okay, what did you say to your parents?" I asked. "How did you get them to agree to a sleepover?"

She laughed and popped a pizza roll in her mouth. "I'm allowed to have a sleepover. My mom just gave me one condition."

Of course there had to be a condition. I knew the situation was too good to be true. "And what's that?"

"We have to leave the door open." She motioned to the door, which was wide open and propped against the wall. "But don't worry," she said, dropping to a whisper. "Their bedroom is downstairs, and they usually go to bed around midnight. Maybe we can actually watch a movie and then have fun of our own a little later." She bounced her eyebrows.

She clicked the remote and told me she was in the mood to watch something gay. She recommended watching *Carol* since I'd never seen it, and she said by the end of the movie, I'd have a crush on Cate Blanchett.

Like the movies we'd tried watching before, I only half paid attention to it. The shared blanket caused a great distraction because no matter how alluring Cate Blanchett was, I kept focusing on the leg equally relaxed into mine. The storm had arrived. Rain splattered against the windows, and thunder rumbled in the distance. It made her bed even cozier, under the blankets with her body heat warming up my leg.

Something felt different about this movie night. Maybe it was because I was spending the night, and that opened up so many possibilities about all the things that could happen. I had a feeling that once I grabbed her hand, we wouldn't be paying attention to Cate Blanchett and all her lesbian glory. But the thing was, I didn't care about Cate Blanchett or the movie. I wanted to skirt the edge of what was right and what wasn't for the first time in my life. I wanted to rebel against the open door and feel my heart stammer and twitch while kissing her while knowing that her parents were only a floor below.

I snuck a glance at her. She slowly tossed popcorn into her mouth while keeping her eyes fixed on the screen. I swallowed back the lump and took control of the situation because I wanted to feel more than just her leg. I grabbed her hand, and without even looking at me, she squeezed back. I smiled, and that was good enough for the time being. We watched the rest of the movie like that. Even when we needed to adjust, our bodies moved, but our hands stayed intertwined.

It was the first movie we'd actually finished. It made me wonder if we were both really into it or too nervous to do anything but watch. For me, at least, I was too nervous to do anything else. My heart thrummed the whole time we'd held hands, wondering what the hell we would do after the credits played. When that moment came, she stopped the TV and retrieved her hand, turning to me and crossing her legs.

"Truth or dare."

"Wait, what?" I nervously chuckled and scratched the back of my head. "Are we fourteen?"

She playfully smacked my knee. "We're passing the time until they go to sleep. You have a better idea?"

A crack of lightning sparked outside and jolted us in our spots. I glanced outside her window and noticed the trees bending and billowing with the whistling winds, causing the nightstand light to flicker.

"No. Is your mom going to be asking us to come down?"

She rolled her eyes. "Not unless there's a tornado warning. We'll hear the alarm blaring on the TV before she tells us to come downstairs. Now answer the question. Truth or dare?"

I let out a playful grunt. "Fine. Truth." Her jaw set, as if she was hoping for me to pick a dare. "What? Why the hell would I pick dare on the literal first question?"

"To be fun."

"No, I'm not making it easy for you. It's your game, so you're going to have to deal with my decisions. Truth."

"Ugh. Fine," she said and let out a grunt. As she thought about it, she looked up at her ceiling. Once the question came to her, she perked up, met my gaze, and smiled at her quick accomplishment. "Have you kissed any girls before me?"

Crap. One question in, and I already had to reveal my cards... or lack thereof. I hoped by answering the question that my barely existing dating life didn't scare her away from whatever she wanted to gain from playing truth or dare. I knew it was an irrational thought, but I still couldn't prevent the worry from scrolling through my mind.

"No," I said softly, and I hated how much my insecurity rang through the confession. I took a sip of Cheerwine to erase the nervous rattling.

Harper's eyes widened. "No?"

"I mean...I realized I was bi a few months ago, after I dated this guy for two months. Well, I guess, in a way, I always knew it, but it didn't click until a few months ago. Truth or dare?"

I was desperate to jump to the next one so we didn't have to focus on all my inexperience.

"Truth."

I looked up at the ceiling fan spinning cool air. Thank God for it because my temperature kept rising. "Have you kissed any other slocals besides me?"

"I try to kiss one from each state. I'm glad I've finally checked off Connecticut. Only four more states to go." I could feel my face fall, and Harper laughed. "I'm joking. You're my only one. I promise."

I put my hand over my heart. "I'm honored."

"As you should. Now, truth or dare?"

"Dare."

Harper's eyes rounded. I didn't blame her. I was a little surprised by my willingness for a dare so early in the game. She tapped her fingers against her chin, and a fleet of butterflies fluttered in my chest at the excitement and anticipation of what it would be. I was ready for any dare she wanted to give me.

"I dare you to unhook my bra."

How confidently she said it made a swirl of nerves quiver in my throat and taste like bile. We were about to jump right into this with the door wide open. I could hear the TV downstairs faintly playing, which had to mean that her parents could hear us if we could hear them. Her lips curved upward against the soft glow of the Netflix main menu. I thought we would have a few more dares to warm us up to anything steamy, but no, Harper jumped right in.

"What about your parents?" I asked in a whisper, my heart hammering hard and steady. Now that I was on the line of law-abiding and rebellious, I started questioning myself all over again.

She waved me off. "They have no reason to come up here. I swear this open door is just a scare tactic."

How confident she seemed in her dare was gravity that sucked me right in. I gulped nonexistent saliva that clawed down my throat as I stared at the hem of her shirt. She had to have known I'd never unhooked someone's bra before. Hell, I hadn't unhooked my bra. I just pulled it over and tossed it to the ground like a heathen. Well, I'd been doing that all wrong because maybe if I unhooked it and took care of my bras, I would have actually acquired some skills that would come in handy when trying to impress bold and beautiful girls like Harper. But no, I had nothing but a knot of nerves coiling tightly in my stomach.

I sucked in a heavy breath as I wandered under her shirt, and my breath juddered when I touched her skin and gently grazed up her body. Already, my body was lighting up the same way the heat lightning staggered through the sky. Our eyes held the whole journey up, and when I finally reached the bra hook, her breath hitched and landed on my lips. I attempted to unhook it with one hand like I knew I was supposed to do, like how all the movies and gifs on Tumblr made me truly believe I could do, but I failed miserably.

"I think I have to do it with two hands."

And without flinching her gaze, Harper said, "I don't care."

The way she said it sounded like a demand, like she truly didn't care how I removed it. She just wanted me to do it. I wrapped both hands around her back, and it drew me in until I was only a breath away from her mouth. I stared at her lips as I undid each hook, feeling each of her ragged breaths landing and causing a charge in between our mouths. It was my first indication of how nervous she was. Turned out, I wasn't the only one who was off-balance. The clasps broke apart and fell to the sides. I finally let out that heavy exhale, skimming my fingers from her back to her front, and accidentally felt the bottom swell of her breasts. She zeroed in on me and gently guided my wrists until my palms covered her breasts. I forgot how to breathe. How could I when every inch of her breasts was in my palms, and my thumbs traced over her nipples. She hadn't done anything to me yet, and I was already unwound.

Then, the downstairs lights flickered off. The dark shadows around Harper's face faded, camouflaged with the darkness that enveloped the room, plucking us away and into our own world that I was so ready to explore. I froze with her breasts in hand, listening carefully to her parents shuffling around. Then the footsteps stopped abruptly but only for a moment before they continued into the bedroom.

"Truth or dare," I whispered.

"Dare."

Now that her parents had gone to bed and the rest of the night was ours, her confidence had softened. Her voice was low and trembled. It was like we were finally on equal playing fields: eager yet scared to continue.

"I dare you to shut the door," I barely said through my croak.

Without any hesitation, she got up, closed the door, and once the handle clicked, she said, "I dare you to lie down."

My heart had never raced as fast and hard as it did until I laid my head on a pillow. She sat on my pelvis and slowly peeled my shirt over my head, as if carefully taking in each inch of my body as she did so. The air-conditioning sent goose bumps all over my arms and back. A cold shiver snaked through me as her delicate stare skimmed my face and raked down my body, tearing me open and making me breathless.

She took me in for a moment before tracing my collarbone, almost as if she knew that insecurities needed to be put out like a hazardous flame. "Are you doing okay?" she asked, her voice hoarse.

My throat was too dry to speak. All I could do was nod. With that, she lowered herself onto me, and she felt like a blanket warming me up. I closed my eyes and reveled in the kisses she dotted on my face and neck, each one removing a morsel of insecurity.

"Are you nervous?" she asked when she pulled away.

"I…I just…I haven't done this before."

"Not at all?"

"No."

The admission made me feel like I'd stripped myself raw. Even though only my shirt was off, I felt naked, transparent, and worried that Harper would find me repulsive.

"Do you want to keep going?" she asked, and her words seemed as delicate as I felt.

Of course I want to keep going. The real question is, do you?

"Yes," I said. "But I don't know what I'm doing."

She laughed. "Neither do I."

"But you've done this before."

"You don't do it one time and then become a master. I think it's all about finding out what the other person likes and dislikes."

"How do you know?"

Harper shrugged. "I don't know. We just tell each other. Do you trust me?"

I nodded. "I do. Do you trust me?"

"I do. Now take my shirt off."

She raised her hands up, allowing me better access, and my whole chest exploded and filled with another fleet of butterflies that were a mixture of nervousness and complete amazement of how beautiful she was. All I could do was stare at her beautiful collarbone, her breasts, her magenta belly button ring moving with her uneven breaths. When she lowered herself on me, she captured my mouth, and her naked top molded with mine. There were so many new feelings piling inside me all at once that I had to pull away for a second to fill my lungs with enough oxygen.

"You good?" she asked, and even though this was the fourth time she'd checked in, every question ensured me that she was treating me like a ball of glass instead of something easily disposed of. It made me surer that going further was what I wanted.

I nodded and tugged her face back into mine. She draped over me, and every one of my senses was heightened. The wind blistered through the trees and some twigs tapped on the side of the house. I heard every crack of lightning, grumble of thunder, and every splatter of large raindrops against the window. I felt every inch of my body pressed up against hers, and one flick of her tongue on mine sent something through me I never felt before, like the only legal ecstasy on Earth.

She kissed my neck, then my collarbone, and then wandered lower. I had to collect all my strength to swallow every moan of pleasure that threatened to escape. She stopped when she kissed past my belly button and her mouth hovered over the top of my shorts. She unbuttoned them and then looked up. I swear I didn't think Harper could look any more beautiful, but she did. The way her disheveled hair draped over most of her face and the vulnerability scintillated her dark eyes.

"Is this still okay?"

"Mm-hmm," was all I could say.

"Can I continue?"

"Please."

She looped her fingers under the top of my shorts. "You promise to tell me if you want to stop?"

"I promise."

"And tell me if you don't like something?"

"I promise."

"Okay." She kissed my skin right above them before taking off my shorts and underwear.

When Harper put her mouth on me, she made me forget about everything else happening in our world. The only thing I could hear were the murmurs colliding against my tightly sealed mouth. I could only taste her kiss lingering on my lips, only smell the remnants of her body wash on my face, only see dots of different colored circles on the inside of my eyelids. But I felt everything. Her warm mouth, her fingers moving inside me, every nerve ending lighting up my insides like a crack of lightning bolting across the sky, the tears filling up my eyes like the sidewalks outside.

Every one of my muscles tensed and then released in a bliss I'd never felt before. I opened my eyes to find her looking up with a smile of pure awe, and the way she stared made me feel strangely sexy. I'd never felt sexy in my life until that exact moment. The way she looked at me as I collected my breath made me feel like the most miraculous thing she'd ever seen.

"Wow," I said, breathing raggedly with an arm slung over my eyes.

She kissed up my stomach until she hovered above me. "Was that okay?"

"That..." I paused because it felt like my heart was about to spring out of my chest, and I needed to tame it back in. "Was amazing." I cupped her face and brought her in for a kiss to thank her for everything she did, for making me feel like that, for being gentle, for treating me like I mattered. Now it was my turn to make her feel the same, the way that her first time should have been, and she never got. I'd make sure I'd erase that memory and patch it up with a better one. "I want to try now."

She pulled away with rounded eyes. "You do?"

"I do. Is that okay?"

"More than okay."

We switched spots. I waited until she relaxed in my indent before removing the rest of her clothes. I still had no idea what to do or if I was doing it right, but I got the sense that Harper liked it by how she moved her hips a little, how her mouth parted silently, and how a soft murmur crept out a few moments later. Her hand found mine and curled around my fingertips, and even though I was the one giving her the pleasure, she still took complete control of me. I listened to her sounds, I asked if she was okay, and continued when she encouraged me to do so. Everything about her was so damn sexy and beautiful, and I couldn't believe the power I had to make someone feel as amazing as Harper had made me feel. She helped direct me where with hip movements, releasing sounds of pleasure and grabbing a little fistful of my hair. Once we fell into the same rhythms, it wasn't as scary. It was actually pretty fucking wonderful.

Afterward, we threw our clothes back on and buried ourselves in her bed. I cuddled into her side, my head on her chest, listening to her heart softly beating as the rain continued to clatter onto the house. She kissed me softly on the forehead, sending another hum of pure contentment through me. It was a soft kiss, but the sentiment was heavy enough to root me in the now, the truest thing anyone would ever know. I needed to focus on that. Our now in a myriad of nows. Nothing else. No past, no future, those didn't exist.

Only this did. Harper, the thunderstorm, and the cocktail of bliss she made me feel.

CHAPTER TWELVE

"Good morning," Harper's groggy voice whispered into my ear.

I slowly opened my eyes. Harper's head rested on my shoulder, her arm slung over my body, and her silky-smooth leg sprawled across mine. Even though she sounded a little bit like a robotic monster, it still made me smile. She was even prettier in the morning with her sleepy eyes and the small blemishes more noticeable on her face.

"Oh, hi," I said, and I flipped over onto my side. "How did you sleep?"

"Wonderful. I kind of forgot there was a thunderstorm last night. What about you?"

"About the same."

Honestly, that morning hit differently than all the other mornings. Something in the air was lighter yet more static. My body still hummed with pleasure and seeing Harper's smile first thing warmed me up like the first sip of fresh warm coffee.

She squeezed my hand before turning over to check her phone. "Looks like my parents are at the shop surveying the damage on the boardwalk. I guess the storm was a little stronger than I thought it was. I was a little preoccupied, you know?" She winked, and it hit me instantly on the cheeks. "They're cleaning up some debris before they open, which means..." She lifted herself up and leaned in for a soft kiss. "We get the kitchen to ourselves, and that means pancakes."

After brushing our teeth, we scampered downstairs, and I watched Harper take over the kitchen like the pro she was. I offered to help, but she insisted that I was her guest, and I was to stand there, sip orange juice, and look pretty while she fixed breakfast. Her confidence had replenished, and she worked the kitchen like she was destined to. With nothing to do except watch her be a sexy chef, I stole chocolate chips. She swatted at my wrists like I was a pesky housefly. I tossed one down her shirt, and then pulled her in for a kiss, pinning her back against the kitchen counter, and we got lost in the kiss like we seemed to always do. It wasn't until we smelled something burning that we pulled away and had to throw out the burned pancake.

"No kissing," she said, directing the spatula at me. "I'm trying to be sweet and cook you breakfast and…stop." She smacked my hand with the spatula as I tried sneaking in another chocolate chip, "Stop eating the chocolate chips."

"If I can't have your lips, I need the chocolate chips."

The banana chocolate chip pancakes were the best I'd ever had, and it had nothing to do with the eternal bliss still radiating through my whole insides from the night before. They were so fluffy and rich. Harper said the secret was all about the eggs. When she was making them, I did wonder why she separated the egg yolks into the dry ingredients and then whipped the egg whites separately. Apparently, it was the secret.

"You're a culinary genius," I said after swallowing a bite.

"I'll take it. But I also read it online. Lots of trials and errors. I'm getting into a pastry kick, and trust me, I've had to suppress a lot of temper tantrums after spending all that time making it just for it to be a disaster."

"What kind of pastries?"

"Well, I made a perfect batch of chocolate éclairs earlier this week. I'm pretty proud of myself."

"Are you going to become a pastry chef in Paris?"

"Maybe. That's kind of the dream. To spend a year in Paris and learn everything I can."

"You're going to have a little flat in Paris overlooking the Eiffel Tower?"

"Obviously."

"Can I come visit?"

She nodded. "Of course. Just land your space shuttle on Champ de Mars, and I'll have some fresh pastries waiting for you."

"Perfect because I'm going to be so over freeze-dried ice cream by then."

"And I'll treat you to homemade macarons, creme brulee, or chocolate truffles."

"Or all of the above?"

She laughed. "Or all of the above."

As the scene of the distant future played out in my mind, the realization of the near future popped my daze. The morning continued to hit differently because the summer daze started fading when I realized I only had two weeks left until I went back home to prepare for my move to Cambridge.

What the hell would happen to us? Were we even an us? Whatever we were, I didn't want it to end.

I buried the thought, knowing that Harper wouldn't want me to worry about the future or Envie at this present moment. This was still the escape we both needed.

After breakfast, we scurried upstairs and dove into her bed, getting tangled up in each other's limbs yet again. Right after she sent me to the same place as the night before, my body vibrated and tingled. But then the thought of our ticking clock exploded in my head again, and the worry stung my eyes.

"Hey, you okay?" she asked, holding my face.

I hesitated for a moment and weighed the pros and cons of ruining our perfect sleepover with questions and anxiety. But the thing was, the last eighteen hours were my favorite hours of the summer. Harper and I dove into something so much deeper than a fun summer fling. After what had happened the night before, I didn't want this to end. I wanted more nights like that, more mornings filled with kisses and banana chocolate chip pancakes. I really wanted to watch her whip up all her favorite French desserts in her Paris flat.

"I don't know. I'm worried about what happens after the summer ends. I kind of forgot how this will all end soon. Like in two weeks."

Harper thinned her lips and pulled away, resting her back against the headboard and staring off at something on the other side of the room. "Yeah, me too. It's crazy how fast the summer went by."

"What do you want to happen?"

She thought about it for a moment before turning to me. "I don't want anything to happen. I want everything to stay the same, like how it is right now." She squeezed my hand. "How come the girl I really like has to leave to study aerospace engineering at MIT? As badass as that sounds, I want to be selfish."

"I like the selfishness. Can I bring you with me?"

"I wish."

The conversation with Serena popped up in my mind, and then she invaded it. The guilt choked and burned my chest, and a panic started bubbling behind my sternum. No, I couldn't tell her now.

"You know...um..." I said, and a cough rose up my throat, almost as if my body voluntarily wanted to purge the truth. "There's amazing culinary schools in New York City. Hell, there's a good one even in Boston."

"Yeah, I bet, but my family can't afford it."

"Just because it's in New York doesn't mean it costs an arm and a leg. I did some research and found a school that's a little bit more than the community college you're going to. If you applied for some scholarships, you'd probably pay the same amount as you would staying here."

"Really?" Interest fluctuated her voice.

"Really. I can show you if you really want."

"I don't know...I mean, I guess I knew my parents were struggling, so I didn't try too hard to look at every single school and its tuition. I didn't want to look at all the schools I could have gone to if Envie didn't freakin' exist." *Yup, now was definitely not the time to tell her.* "Let's say, by some miracle, I got scholarships, and the price would be the same as community college here, what about my parents? I can't leave them high and dry when this is probably the Acadian's last summer."

I wanted to tell her that whether she stayed in Gaslight Shores wasn't going to make or break the Acadian. It needed much more than Harper, unfortunately. It needed money, and that was something an eighteen-year-old couldn't make happen.

"You have your own life too, Harper," I said instead and grabbed both her hands. "You can't give up your whole life for others. You deserve to do what you want to do. Following your dreams isn't leaving your parents high and dry. I think your parents would agree too."

"I just..." She looked at our hands. "I don't know what they're going to do without the Acadian. Some people are meant to see the world, and some aren't. You're meant to literally see the world, and maybe I'm meant to stay here in Gaslight Shores."

"But it doesn't have to be like that. What if you at least tried? I can help you. I'm pretty good at scholarship applications. I got a bunch, and don't tell anyone, but I helped my best friend Brie too. One of the pluses of not having a social life in high school: I'm the CEO of scholarship applications. I still have my spreadsheet I can share with you, and you can at least try. That way, you can see how far you can actually go, and maybe if you get an acceptance letter, it might change how you think."

She hesitated for a moment and loosened her grip. "Remi, why do you care so much about where I go to school?"

She said it so softly, like she was scared to ask but was still genuinely curious. The question hit me hard and forced me to think. Maybe part of me wanted her in New York because that meant we actually stood a chance to stay together. But the truth was, I was falling pretty hard for her, and I wanted her to be truly happy because I genuinely believed she deserved it. She wouldn't be happy in Gaslight Shores or at the Acadian for the rest of her life. She didn't deserve to have all her dreams demoted to sacrifices.

"I care about you," I said and reached to hold her hand. It was the only thing I could offer her for a moment of relief. She stared at her fingers curled over mine, and for a split second, she seemed calmer.

"And I want you to be happy and to feel like you're good enough. You're good enough, Harper, and you deserve all those things you want out of your life. What you want is valid too. Remember when we were on top of the Ferris wheel? You said that Gaslight Shores was too small for you. Applying and trying is looking at college from the Ferris wheel. It will let you see everything that's in your reach."

She squeezed my hand and glanced up, and finally, I got a glimpse of that beautiful smile. "I want to try."

"Then let's try."

I met Harper at a coffee shop a few blocks away from the boardwalk the next day. It smelled like roasted coffee and chai tea. Something about the smell really encouraged me to sit and get to work. That was, until Harper came in looking extra pretty with her brown hair falling past her shoulders and jean shorts that rode up her toned legs. How were we supposed to dive into my sexy college scholarship spreadsheet if I was going to be this distracted?

"You're not supposed to look so pretty when we have lots of work to do," I said when she slid into the booth.

I loved how her cheeks turned pink. I wanted to kiss them all over but stopped myself since we were in public. "I'm sorry. I didn't mean to."

"I know. That's the problem."

It was a good thing we'd decided to meet in a neutral setting rather than attempt to work at her house. I could only imagine the urges of sneaking in a quick make out that I knew wouldn't be quick at all.

While we nursed our iced chai lattes, I proudly showed off my Excel sheets, a sacred document I hadn't shown anyone else in fear I would have a bigger nerd label taped to my forehead. Organized by scholarship name, the URL, due date, if an essay was required, and all the eligibly requirements. After we took a shot of espresso to get our brains going, we checked off all the scholarships Harper was able to apply for and gathered up the schools she was interested in. Four in New York City, three in Boston, one in Philadelphia, and one in Chicago.

Over the week, when Harper wasn't working, we met up at the coffee shop and polished the essays and applications, and I went in and tweaked her essays in a shared Google Doc like we were coauthoring our first novel together. And by the end of the week, many chai lattes, shots of espresso, and hours later, Harper had applied to four schools and seven scholarships, and if she got a scholarship, it would make her tuition as much as the community college on the other side of the bridge.

Amped up on all the caffeine, we decided to walk our extra energy off on the boardwalk. Harper suggested we go on the Ferris wheel. I'd gotten to know her as a pretty confident person, but when it came time to chase her dreams and apply to colleges, she'd seemed anything but. By the time we were trapped in our cabin and jolted up, there was a different glow to her smile. There was hope, like she'd cleaned the dust off her culinary dreams and saw them for what they actually were. Shiny, valuable, and realistic.

The wheel stopped, and another gorgeous view of Gaslight Shores sparkled below us, with lamps and neon lights from the arcade mixing with the lights from the other stores. Harper's back wasn't glued to the seat, her hands didn't clench the railing, and her eyes were open wide, taking in as much below her as I was. I swore I was looking at a brand-new Harper Hebert, and I loved it.

"You've mastered the college application process, and now you've mastered the Ferris wheel?"

She glanced over, and a soft breeze blew back the tresses that hadn't made it to her messy bun. She reached for my hand and held it tightly. "I guess I didn't think it was possible."

"Of course it is. Those colleges aren't going to be rejecting someone with a three-point eight GPA, and your essays about working at the Acadian are so good. I have a good feeling about this."

"I really want this to work out," she said and looked back out at the town below. "College, I mean. I wasn't excited about it because

I wanted it so badly but never thought it was possible. But you've made it seem possible, and now I want it even more. Because it can actually be."

"You'll tell me when you get your letters, right?"

She looked back, and a hint of sadness rounded her eyes. The countdown timer squeezed in between us and made itself known again. "What? Of course I will. You spent five days applying to colleges with me. Who the hell volunteers to help someone apply to colleges and write essays?"

"I don't know. Some weirdo, probably."

She palmed my face. "You're not weird, Remi Brenner. I promise you that."

Now it was my turn to kiss her. We made out until the wheel jerked up a couple minutes later, spun us around, and stopped us halfway up.

"When are you going to tell your parents?" I asked.

She shrugged. "I don't know. I'm not afraid that they'll be upset. I'm afraid that they'll worry while scrounging pennies to save the Acadian. I might not tell them until I get a letter, you know? I want to tell them when it's the right time."

I knew about that all too well...as much as I wished I didn't. I had seven more days left, and the ticking was now as loud as a siren in my head about the right time to tell Harper. Not when we were on the Ferris wheel, witnessing the issues on the ground shrink, not when the confidence of applying to college still ran through her veins, and not tomorrow, when we would venture to see the Milky Way. I wanted to squeeze out the last bit of whatever wonderful thing was happening between us.

And then I'd tell her.

I just hoped it wasn't too late.

CHAPTER THIRTEEN

The amount of thought that went into our last weekend made my heart inflate with so much happiness, I thought I would burst at the same time I was deflating from so much sadness.

How was this our last weekend?

We drove up to Hunting Island, and what I thought would be a long night searching for the Milky Way and coming back to Gaslight Shores at three in the morning turned into a spontaneous camping trip.

"The surprise," Harper said as we drove past the state park sign that told us the campground was to the right. "How about we camp under the Milky Way instead?"

And my heart exploded.

The only time I went camping was in my backyard with my dad, and he was always the one to set up the tent and start a fire. I had no idea how to put a tent together, and it took Harper and me at least forty-five minutes to figure out the poles, but we laughed the whole time. She'd brought two sleeping bags, two pillows, and a large queen comforter to share while we stargazed. Inside the cooler were bottles of Cheerwine, hot dogs, ketchup and mustard, a bag of kettle-cooked chips, and Harper had even made a whole Tupperware of *pain au chocolat.*

"A little something to impress you," she said.

I grabbed one of the rolls, ripped it in half, and watched the chocolate center ooze. One taste and I melted into my seat. "Oh my God, this is amazing."

"Right? A preview for when you visit me in Paris." She winked, and it made my heart soar.

I never expected my heart to tug when watching her make a fire, but it did. Talk about a primal instinct. I never thought someone making a fire, patiently waiting and observing the flame licking and catching, would be sexy. Her eyes and my attraction to her grew with the fire, and she looked at the flames as if amazed she could create that with her hands...and a starter log. But still, we had to start somewhere.

Once the flames absorbed the logs, she stood and victoriously tossed her hands up. "I made fire. Look! My first fire."

I clapped. "What a survivalist."

"I think this means I can go on *Naked and Afraid* now," she said and placed a log delicately over the fire.

"I'll definitely watch that episode."

She winked and flitted her gaze back to her creation.

We searched for sticks to help us grill hot dogs, and while we waited for them to cook, we debated which was the proper way to heat marshmallows over the fire. Harper liked them burned; I liked both them and the hotdogs a beautiful shade of toasted brown. Bugs chirped and hissed from the nearby palm trees. I made sure to sit and take in everything around me. I never thought Gaslight Shores would grow on me. When I'd first stepped off the plane, I was disgusted by the humidity and the palmetto bugs zipping past my ears. I hated the restaurant rivalry and the categorization of golfies, slocals, and chummers. I wanted my summer to be with Brie, carrying out all the plans we'd made with each other and our friends one last time before we veered down different paths.

But then something unexpected had happened. I'd met Harper, and without really trying, she'd made me appreciate the town and its small-town vibe, how laid-back things could be around here if you found the right people. It also helped that I'd tried with my dad and Serena. Giving Dad a second chance and Serena the benefit of the doubt had saved my sanity. I was going to miss most of it. How loud the cicadas were in the day and how loud the crickets and frogs were at night, the forest of speckles from the lightning bugs, all the delicious fried and sugary foods of the boardwalk, how the sky looked from the beach with the waves as the soundtrack to our nights.

Using our phones as flashlights, we walked over to the beach; the bag on my back held two Cheerwines, the Tupperware, the telescope, and a present I was going to surprise Harper with. A little something I'd bought online that would, hopefully, forever root us in this summer.

Right as the trees opened up to the beach, I looked up, and my stomach plummeted in the best way.

"Oh my God," I said under my breath.

I'd never seen the sky look so beautiful before. Right above us was the Milky Way band of gossamer beauty, a cluster of millions of stars slicing through the night sky. It was the purest glance of the universe I'd ever seen. The expansiveness of it opened up something in me too, cutting me as deep as the stars traveled. All the moments I'd spent before this one looking up at the twinkling specks were only a thin observation of the surface of the universe. Seeing the Milky Way deepened the view, reminding me how expansive it really was.

I could feel myself falling in love with the sky all over again.

"Is that it?" Harper asked, sounding as starstruck as I was.

"That's it. That's…that's really the Milky Way."

We tossed the blanket haphazardly onto the sand. I was too distracted to spread it out and make sure there were minimal creases. But I didn't care. Not when the most beautiful thing I'd ever seen was right there, right above me, and it felt like it was as close to me as a nine-foot ceiling. I fumbled as I set up the telescope, as if the Milky Way would fly across the sky in a second like a shooting star.

I looked in the eyepiece, and it looked like someone had tossed glitter at the black sky. Pulling away, I observed the difference, and honestly, there was no bad view. No matter how I looked at the Milky Way, it stole my breath and pleasantly squeezed my chest. I motioned for Harper to look, and she let out another gasp.

South Carolina gave me the best view of our galaxy from Earth. The only other place that could compete with this view was on the International Space Station.

I was surprised by how much I was going to miss this place.

I lay on my back, and Harper did the same, cuddling next to me with her head in between my shoulder and armpit. We stared up and lay in silence for a while. The silence wasn't uncomfortable at all. If anything, it was fully necessary to take in the cloudy trail of stars. For a second, I almost forgot that I was on Earth and not in space.

"I can't believe one day you'll be up there," Harper finally said. "You're going to have a front row view to the whole universe."

I smiled at the thought. It seemed like such a pipe dream that it was hard to even imagine, but it was the thing I wanted most in my life. I wouldn't stop until I reached the stars.

The sky wasn't the limit. For me, it was only the beginning.

"I really hope so," I said. "I have to compete with so many people to get in an astronaut class, but I'm going to keep at it until they tell me I have to stop, or they'll call security."

"It's going to happen. You'll step foot on the moon…or maybe Mars."

I sat up and reached in my bookbag for the Cheerwine, opened one for each of us, and took a long, cold, bubbling sip of what was quickly turning into my new favorite soda. The cherry cola would always remind me of Harper and Gaslight Shores.

I stole another peek at the telescope and got lost in what looked to be stardust. "If I go to the moon, Brie wants me to write her full name in the dust because it will stay there for a million years because there's no wind. The footprints from Neil Armstrong and his crew are still there right now."

When I turned to her, I saw Harper's rounded eyes. "Really? Can we see it through the telescope?"

"No, they're too small and far away, but you have to trust me."

"I trust you." She slipped her fingers in between mine and rested her head against my shoulder. My chest swelled at the contact and the soft breeze of her shampoo filling up my nose. "Then, could you write my name too?"

"I'll write 'Remi hearts Harper' with an infinity sign."

"You promise?"

"Of course. I promised Brie. I'll definitely promise you that."

She pulled away, and the moment became softer. "Even if it's, like, twenty years in the future? Hell, we probably won't even be talking then."

The softness attacked me when she said that, a reminder of the sirens blaring in my ears from the clock that I didn't know how to stop—the clock that wasn't supposed to exist. Not according to astrophysics, anyway. As the end of summer neared, I felt the weight of the end slowly pushing down on my chest.

If time was supposedly an illusion, why could I feel it passing?

"Don't say that."

Harper chuckled, not one of amusement but one that sounded like disappointment. "I'm being realistic."

It wasn't like she was the only one who'd thought about this. Ever since our sleepover, I'd thought about our now breaking off and becoming our past. Seven days from now, I'd be back home with Mom, spending the last two weeks of the summer with her until I moved to Cambridge. As much as I couldn't wait to start college, that meant I had to give up my current now for a new one. I didn't understand. If life was a myriad of infinite nows, how the hell did you keep living in one? I wanted to keep living in this one: ocean in front of me, Harper around my arm, and the Milky Way glowing above.

I was dedicated to salvaging everything that had happened in our summer. Luckily, I came prepared.

"I got something for you," I said before I reached back into my bookbag and pulled out the present wrapped in dark blue wrapping paper with gold constellations on it.

When I handed her the gift, she studied it by shining her phone light on it, and then looked back up with a creased brow. "You got me a present?"

"Yes. You're not the only one with surprises up your sleeves. Now open it."

I lifted the blanket over the present and held her phone so she could unwrap it as I kept the phone flashlight hidden, making sure the light stayed underneath the blanket to not annoy others on the beach. Harper opened the box and found two clear quartz crystals wrapped around gold wire, attached to gold chain necklaces. "Wow, this is a really pretty necklace," she said, taking one of them out to study it. "What is it?"

"It's a quartz. Quartz crystals are used in watches to keep precise time because in all other watches and clocks, gravity and the temperature affect how they track time. It's like every kind of clock is on a slightly different pace. But not quartz watches. Electricity makes the quartz vibrate at a consistent rate, so it's the most accurate clock we have. I don't have enough money to buy a quartz watch, but now we both have a quartz necklace, so when I leave, it doesn't matter where we are, we'll always be in sync, on the same time and on the same trajectory, and nothing can get in the way. Not weather, not distance, and not the strongest force in the whole universe. These quartz necklaces will make our summer infinite."

My explanation hung in the air for a moment as she rolled the necklace between her fingers. The breeze curled into the shore with the tide and billowed back our hair, and the soft phone light cast toward her face allowed me to have a better view of her and the softness in her eyes while she took in the necklace and my words.

"Remi," she said hoarsely. She slid her hand along my cheek and pulled me in, kissing me so softly yet so intimately that I felt like she turned me inside out, my emotions laid out like a poker hand while I waited to see if I'd win the pot. I had no idea if we would win, but it was worth the gamble for me. And the way she looked at me, the way she kissed me, I could tell she felt the same.

When she pulled away, she pressed her forehead against mine, and her soft breaths landed on my tingling lips. "You're making this really hard. I really don't want this summer to end."

"I don't either. I promise, I'll do everything to keep it going."

Harper picked up one of the necklaces and wrapped it around my neck. When it was secured, she tucked her hair back into a ponytail and gestured to me to do the same. Right then, I felt time passing so quickly, I felt like a piece of debris caught up in the strong wind. Harper tightened her grip around my arm and rested her head on my shoulder, locking me back in the now. I could feel her inhaling and exhaling slowly, as if she was as content as I was.

The quartz necklace was a promise to keep the summer going even when the leaves turned colors, the blazing heat cooled into a breeze, and the days became increasingly shorter. None of that mattered to quartzes. Though I could feel the last six days squeezing all the air out of my lungs, the quartz dangling over my chest absorbed that promise.

Was falling for someone supposed to be this scary? My pulse and heart raced for control, and I couldn't figure out how to feel. The movies made it seem like this fairytale: easy, carefree, and fun. Was it supposed to? Was I falling for Harper in all the wrong ways? It didn't feel wrong until the future kept poking me, reminding me that it existed just as much as the now, and I needed to worry.

"Harper?"

She looked up, and the movement brought the comforting smell of her shampoo. How could it be so scary when she smelled like that. "Hm?"

"Truth or dare?"

She pulled away. "Truth." It was too dark to make out a smile, but I could hear it in her voice.

"Have you ever felt this way about someone?"

Surely, this wasn't unrequited love. I could feel it in the way she looked at me, spoke to me, snuggled into me, that she must have been right with me or at least a few steps behind.

"No," she said in such a Harper way, so confidently that I felt it in my bones. "Have you?"

"No." I paused and looked at the starry strip streaking across the sky, trying to pluck myself from the ground and put myself at a higher altitude so everything seemed less scary and fake. "Are you scared?"

"Terrified but, like, the same feeling as when I went on the Ferris wheel: ready to conquer it."

When I saw the necklace dangling on her, my stomach whirled up to my lungs. I came to Gaslight Shores not wanting to, and by the end of the summer, I had more feelings about leaving the town than I did about being forced to spend a summer in it. Harper was the first girl I'd kissed, the first person I'd slept with, the first person

I had feelings for that traveled deeper than a simple crush brushing along the surface of my chest. Anytime I saw her, anytime I was with her, I could feel it hugging my insides. That had to mean that part of our summer would always be infinite. First loves left their name on a heart the same way astronauts left their footprints on the moon. A piece of my heart would forever be rooted to Harper and Gaslight Shores.

I grabbed her quartz necklace and reeled her in to kiss me under the bands of the galaxy.

I didn't know if I was in love with her, but I knew that the now launched me toward it.

CHAPTER FOURTEEN

Stephen Hawking pointed out to me how fucked I was. I knew that I was fucked with Serena DeLuca as my stepmom and the fact that I'd fallen for Harper. But when Hawking put it in fascinating, scientific terms that translated very well in my really weird brain, I realized how much withholding the truth about my stepfamily would threaten my whole summer.

The moment happened when I lay out on the lawn chair after taking a dip in the pool, collecting some sun while waiting for Harper to get off work. We were going to have dinner at the Purple Cactus, one of the last restaurants I needed to try on the boardwalk. After all the other chapters of *A Brief History of Time*, I decided to save Chapter Six: Black Holes, as the reward for finishing my summer read. The topic that was so unbelievably fascinating to me. There wasn't a single thing that made black holes boring. They were a blob of mystery. Scientists didn't even know what was inside one.

Well, Chapter Six was anything but a reward because it blatantly told me that I'd severely fucked up, more than I had even thought.

Hawking discussed event horizons, boundaries around a black hole. The speed of light was the only universal constant in space, and nothing could travel faster than light. Once light hit a black hole's event horizon, it would never be seen again. Light couldn't even travel through a black hole; light had no effect on it. The observer of a black hole could no longer see light once it hit the event horizon, and light wouldn't come out the other end. It was lost inside.

Then Hawking went on to tell me that event horizons of black holes could only get bigger; they never shrank. They grew every time something fell into one. This was because of something called the Second Law of Thermodynamics, which sounded absolutely boring at first glance, but when I continued reading, Hawking had me sitting straight in the lawn chair. Basically, the law said that a spontaneous process generated disorder. In an isolated system—like the universe—disorder could never be decreased. It would only increase over time.

I lowered the book and thought about everything I'd just read. My universe right now was Gaslight Shores. That was my isolated system. I pulled my gaze from Hawking's words to the ripples in the pool moving along with the light breeze. Every day that ticked away created more disorder in my relationship with Harper, whether it was apparent or not. Every time I told her to drop me off at the gate or mentioned my stepmom and stepbrother but never named them. Every day that I could have told her the truth or when she begged me not to talk about Envie, it all generated disorder.

I knew that I owed Harper the truth, but I was so terrified to lose her. She'd become my whole summer, the reason why I tolerated Gaslight Shores, the sole reason I was dreading leaving it. How much disorder would it take to disrupt my relationship with her…or our whole summer, for that matter?

The real question was, did my lies create an event horizon? Because if they did, that would mean my apology wouldn't affect Harper. Nothing could affect the observer on the other end of the lies. If the damage had been done, if I'd really created an event horizon, the other side to telling the truth would be heartbreak.

I had to fix it. And I had to do it tonight.

All day, I practiced what I would say to her, but no matter how many times I combed over the apology in my head, my gut told me I was already screwed and heading directly into an event horizon, never to be seen again.

My hands shook as I locked my bike around the rack in front of Grandpop's and Mia's. I was so focused on the lump rapidly growing in my throat that I didn't even remember walking to the Purple

Cactus until I noticed the purple awning on my left. Underneath it, I found Harper waving from an elevated table that faced the boardwalk. Next to her were two pina colada-looking drinks and a basket of chips and salsa.

As I turned the corner, out of Harper's sight for the briefest moment, I inhaled a deep breath of fried oil, charcoal, and salt air before exhaling, hoping that the breath would relieve some nerves.

"Did you suddenly turn twenty-one?" I asked while taking my seat, swallowing the nerves threatening to change my voice.

"They're virgin pina coladas. I figured we should treat ourselves. You know, something to cheer us up."

I needed a lot more than one virgin pina colada to cheer me up.

I bought some time avoiding the subject when I looked at the Purple Cactus's extensive taco menu. They had everything from chicken, steak, and shrimp to fried catfish, bourbon-glazed mushrooms and pineapples, to beef tongue and actual crispy cactus tacos. As intrigued as I was by the cactus option, I already had a pool of nerves churning in my stomach. There wasn't enough space for new food. I settled for something I knew was easy on my stomach: chicken. Harper went with the fried catfish, and after the server put in our order, I stalled even more by trying my drink.

Harper took a sip too and twirled the purple umbrella. "Are you okay? You seem…off."

I pulled a large gulp, and then it attacked back with brain freeze. I winced and held my throbbing head in my hands, and Harper rubbed my back. Karma was already coming after me.

"I'm stressed," I said with my hands still wrapped around my aching temples.

"Why?"

The pain in my head subsided and traveled south to my stomach.

Her hand dropped off my back, and I couldn't tell if its absence made my stomachache worse or relieved it. "Try not to think about it. We still have tonight and a few more days. Let's just focus on now."

The now. Focus on the now. It was easier to think time was an illusion when there was nothing to lose.

I couldn't focus on the now. I could only see the past and all the times I should have told her, and the future that would be distorted because of all the times I hadn't.

"Do you...could we go to the beach after this? And...I don't know...talk?" I pulled a long sip from my drink. "I think we need to talk."

Harper's eyebrows pulled together. "Yeah...sure."

Something uncomfortable settled between us. It was so foreign that the awkwardness felt like warm wax dripping down my back. The server helped relieve it a bit when he brought out our tacos. Harper dove right into eating them, but all I could do was feel the nerves and guilt stack on top of each other like bricks building a sturdy wall.

"Remi...are you sure you're okay? You're not even eating," Harper said.

My eyes started stinging from the question and how she'd asked so delicately. Our looming talk was going to be anything but delicate. I wanted to close my eyes and repeat the way she'd asked me, as if I deserved to feel anything but okay.

"My stomach just hurts."

"I can get you a to-go box if you want. You don't have to eat it if you're not feeling it."

"Oh shit, Johnny. You were right."

I snapped in the direction of the snickering voice. Theo pushed up from the railing next door. Seeing him drill his beady eyes into mine with what seemed to be his only two friends next to him made the bricks of nerves and guilt tumble in a disintegrated heap in my gut. It was like my intuition knew he was near, and whatever was happening inside me clambered up in my throat and tasted like bile.

"See, I told you I would find out eventually," Theo said, wagging his finger at me. Now he stood on the other side of our table, a foot separating us, close enough for me to smell his awful cologne. He turned to his friend with the blond shaggy hair. "Was this the chick you saw her with the other night at the Ferris wheel?"

"I did. And they were holding hands."

My chest compressed, and there was no air for me to suck in and refill my lungs. Theo looked back at me, and his sneer became darker and more sinister. He bellowed his blood-curdling cackle. "Oh shit. Seriously? I can't believe it. What a find, man." He patted his friend's back, and the friend smiled like it was the ultimate reward. "And you said I wasn't smart enough to find out. Well guess what, Remi? I found out. Who's the dumbass now?"

"Oh, fuck off," Harper said.

"You could have done better with your selection," Theo said, ignoring Harper. "Don't you want a chick who'll be able to financially support you? Because she sure as hell can't."

"Find a different insult. That one is severely overused and quite boring now."

Theo pulled his face back and then turned to me, but I couldn't look him in the eye. I stared intently at my uneaten chicken tacos as his stare drilled into the side of my face. "I'm surprised that you got her to talk to you, Remi. After where you came from."

"She worked at Envie. I know. That's old news. You can go away now."

Theo cackled. "That's it? That's all you know?"

The question hanging between us was more palpable than Spanish moss dripping over live oak trees. From the corner of my eye, I saw Harper waiting for my explanation, but I couldn't believe it either. I couldn't believe that this was how all my secrets would come out. In the worst possible way: from Theo.

"Shut the fuck up," I muttered through my clenched jaw, but that only entertained Theo more. His smirk reached his earlobes, and I wished that I had long enough nails so I could scratch it off his face.

"That's all I know? What does that even mean?" Harper whispered to me.

But it wasn't soft enough for Theo not to hear it. "She only knows that you worked at Envie. Nothing else? Oh my God. This is amazing."

This was the start of my event horizon, and nothing I could say would affect Harper. I could tell by the way her eyes were soaked in a thick, glossy layer of hurt. We were heading straight into a black hole, like the ticking clock had been warning me the whole summer, and I'd chosen to keep it on snooze.

Theo crossed his arms. "Go on, tell her how we *really* know each other."

My throat started constricting, and the hot tears stung my eyelids. I had no control over it. The things I could control were long gone, and all I could do was watch myself get sucked into the black hole.

"Remi?" Harper said, no longer whispering. Now she was demanding answers as I tried keeping all my roiling emotions inside, ready to burst at the seams. One crack and it would only encourage Theo.

"He's...um..." I swiped away the tears falling down my cheeks, but it wasn't any use. My eyes kept leaking. "That's what I wanted to talk to you about. He's...um...my stepbrother."

"What?"

I saw something flash across her eyes I'd never seen before. Betrayal. The crack in her voice sucker punched me in the gut.

"I can explain—"

"I never thought Miss MIT, I-wanna-be-an-astronaut-when-I-grow-up, was too dumb to tell her girlfriend that the reason her family's restaurant sucks is because of her stepmom."

I finally pierced a glare at Theo despite my blurry vision. "Fuck you," I said as the anger took hold of me like I was its marionette.

Harper shook her head, grabbed her basket of tacos, and tossed them upside down in the trash. She bolted down the boardwalk, leaving me alone to watch Theo and his friend roaring with laughter.

"Damn, this is even better than I thought," Theo said. "You spent the whole summer making me out to be the bad guy, and never once did you look at yourself in the mirror?"

"You're a piece of shit, and even your own mother knows that," I yelled, and finally, his smile loosened. "That's why she doesn't trust you with Envie, why you're a twenty-two-year-old who's completely dependent on your mommy's connections. You're too incompetent to do anything by yourself. It's actually really sad."

I tossed my tacos in the trash, barely even touching them or having any sort of opinion on the Purple Cactus like I wanted to. There wasn't enough time, not when I had to race down the boardwalk and swim against the current of all the pedestrians.

By the time I reached the parking lot behind the Acadian, Harper had started her car. One last sprint and I made it to the driver's side and pounded on the window. She flinched and jerked away. Her tears streamed as freely as the sweat dripping down my back.

"Harper, wait! Please...please let me explain." I said between gasps.

She rolled the window down a fourth of the way, keeping a literal guard between us. Dusk had already started falling, which meant the parking lot lights had turned on and shone a spotlight on her watery eyes.

I hated so much how thick her tears brimmed. One blink had them rolling down her cheeks, and it tore me in two. "This whole time...this whole summer...you...you were lying to me?"

"I wasn't lying—"

"Oh, so you just forgot to mention that Serena DeLuca and Theo Bradly are your stepmother and brother?"

"Please, let me explain. Harper...please—"

"You had the whole summer to explain, Remi. Clearly, explaining wasn't a priority for you."

She rolled up her window before zipping out the other end of the parking lot. I wasted no time running to my bike, unlocking it, and speeding as fast as I could to her house.

I followed the path Harper and I had walked a handful of times. The first time we ever walked together played in my mind. Fourth of July, the night I realized in hindsight I should have told her. But even as the thought sprouted, if I'd told her then, would our summer have happened? Would she still have kissed me? Would that have turned into distracted movie nights, getting lost in the stars, and falling for each other? Would it still have turned into the summer I was willing to slow down?

Theo was right. I'd spent the whole summer thinking he was the bad guy, and here I was owning the title myself.

"And how many times did you think about it and how wrong it was?"

"A lot." It was my turn to wipe the steady flow of tears. "Every day. Believe me when I say that I felt so bad for doing it."

"Every day?" She laughed, and her eyes darkened as she stepped forward to close the gap. "You felt bad every day of the summer, but that was still better than just being honest with me?"

I opened my mouth but then realized I had nothing to say. She'd painted an even worse picture of me than what I saw myself. "How was I supposed to know you would still talk to me? You made it very clear that you hated Serena, and I was trying to protect you."

"Don't say that lying to me is protecting me. You didn't protect me at all. You fucking hurt me, and now I feel like such a fucking idiot."

I'd never seen her that angry before, and it terrified me knowing how badly I'd hurt her and how badly I'd ruined us. Her tears rolled sideways down her face, and she didn't even try to hide or stop them anymore.

"Harper, I'm…I'm so sorry."

"We really had something, and you—" She jabbed her finger in my chest, and the snarl on her face and the strength of her jab squeezed more tears out of me. "You stomped all over it. I opened up to you. I told you things I hadn't told my best friends. I trusted you with everything! I thought you were different."

"I am different."

"How? How are you different from Autumn?"

My mouth dropped. I could name a million reasons why I was different from Autumn. I cared about Harper. I wasn't ashamed of her. I saw her worth and all the things she could achieve. I wanted to be around her every second. But all those differences knotted around each other so tightly that I didn't know which one to pick and say, the right reasoning to mend everything that was breaking in front of us.

"I'm so sorry, Harper," I said through my cries. "Please, believe me. I didn't know how to tell you. I was scared. I was—" I took a step toward her to comfort her, but like all the other times within the past forty-five minutes, she put her hand up and took a few steps back to avoid my touch, as if I was repulsive.

"Don't touch me. I...I need to go." She headed back inside, and I didn't try to stop her.

Somehow, I made it back to my bed in one piece, but the moment I collapsed on the mattress, my whole body broke. My veins were on fire, my limbs wobbled as I cried, my chest caved in, and my stomach spiraled out of control.

I thought my summer would be boring, something not even the palm trees and the ocean could fix. I expected it to be forced and forgettable. But then I'd met Harper, and we'd spent the long days stitching a beautiful tapestry to cloak over my dulled expectations, and my summer became so much more colorful, something worth hanging up and admiring. Until the day I'd ripped it apart.

CHAPTER FIFTEEN

I didn't wake up until one in the afternoon when there was a knock on my door, and my dad called my name on the other side. I hadn't gone to the bathroom yet, but I already knew what my face must look like by the burning in my eyes. I didn't want my dad to see what I looked like because then I'd have to tell him everything, and I wasn't sure if I was strong enough. Not when everything was still so fresh.

"Remi? Is everything okay? You're not picking up your phone." When I couldn't answer, he continued. "It's one in the afternoon. Can I come in to make sure you're alive?"

Once I opened the door, Dad's reaction served as a mirror because his eyes widened, and his eyebrows furrowed tightly. I bet my face looked like a hot mess. It felt like one.

"What's wrong, kiddo?"

As if I didn't cry everything out of my system the night before, just hearing the sympathetic tone in his voice made me break again, and my dad was quick to scoop me up in his arms. I couldn't believe I was crying on his shirt. It had never happened before, at least since I became a teenager. The last time I remembered crying in front of him was when Chris Murray did his desk bit, and Dad had squeezed onto my twin bed and held me until I had settled down.

And that was exactly what happened this time. I told him everything in a chaotic, nonlinear order, and I had no idea how he kept up with all of it. He didn't ask any questions until his shirt held all my tears, and what was left in me were crying convulsions rattling through my body.

When I looked at him, the first thing I noticed was his tight jaw. He stared at the ground and shook his head. His look was the same as when he'd processed what Chris Murray had done to my desk. The Chris Murray incident might have happened eight years ago, but Dad hardly ever got mad enough to visually express it. That was why that look had been burned into my memory, and why it had the same effect on me when I saw it consume his face yet again.

Dad was about to lose his shit.

"I'm done with that kid," he said, his anger quiet and tamed... at least for the time being. I knew that it was all temporary, though. "I'm so done with that kid."

He gave my shoulder a tight squeeze before stomping toward the door.

"What...what are you doing?"

"I'm not letting him get away with this."

Right as Dad left, another door shut. I glanced outside the window and saw Theo getting out of his Jeep in a cutoff T-shirt that showed off his muscles, basketball shorts, tennis shoes, and a protein shake bottle in his hand. He was fresh from the gym, and despite having several inches on Dad—and definitely several more pounds of muscle—Dad marched over to him like he was a zero threat.

Oh shit.

I cracked open my window to hear Dad's wrath.

"Hey Dennis," Theo said, acting like nothing happened the night before.

"You have a lot of nerve talking to me right now," Dad said and directed a firm point Theo's way.

I crouched behind the windowsill so neither could see me watching.

"What are you talking about?"

"You've humiliated my daughter twice now?"

"What?"

"Don't play dumb. This is the second time you've humiliated Remi this summer. You didn't learn your lesson after harassing

Harper Hebert?" Like a coward, Theo backed into his Jeep with his hands up in surrender. "You really get enjoyment out of this kind of stuff, huh?"

"Hey, man, it's not my fault your daughter didn't tell her girlfriend the truth."

"So you thought that gave you the right to ruin their night yet again? You'd already done that once this summer. That wasn't enough? I'm sick and tired of your crap and so is your mom. Remember what she told you after the Fourth? Next antic you pull, you're out of the house? Cut off until you get your act together? I'd start packing my bags if I were you."

"You want me to go up there and apologize or something?"

Of course, at the mention of being cut off, he whimpered like a puppy.

"No. Don't you dare talk to my daughter."

Dad headed into the house, and Theo chased him. Even though my eyes were still swollen and hot from all the crying, and my chest and stomach were still so tight, watching Theo try to redeem any last bit of undeserved privilege made me feel the slightest bit better. My dad telling him all the things I wish I could say and actually witnessing it affect Theo made my heart swell.

I tried calling Harper again, and when she didn't pick up, I sent her a text pleading to talk. An hour passed with nothing. I stood in the shower and allowed the hot water to detangle the pain still throbbing deep inside me. When I got out, I wiped the steam off the mirror and assessed the damage to my face: puffy eyes and burst blood vessels speckling under them. That was what my shame looked like, and it wasn't pretty.

The long shower wasn't long enough to get a text from Harper. The only one I got was Serena asking if she could stop by to talk. The only person I wanted to talk to was Harper. I didn't want to retell the story and feel shittier than I already did. I didn't want to hold my breath in fear of judgment from Serena or my dad because what I'd done was wrong, truly wrong, and Serena had warned me. I knew I'd fucked up, but hearing from others about how much wouldn't help. If anything, it would weigh me down and prevent me from trying to make it better, to piece back together the perfect summer I'd destroyed because I was too much of a coward to tell Harper from the beginning.

Serena came into the apartment with a plate of fresh chocolate chip cookies. She practically tiptoed to the foot of my bed. The nice gesture of baked sugar should have brought me a minute of ease, but it only reminded me of Harper and all the desserts she'd made me over the summer.

Serena gave me a sympathetic look and extended the plate, gesturing for me to grab a cookie. I did it to appease her, but I wasn't hungry. I picked at it instead and watched the crumbs fall onto the plate.

"How are you feeling, sweetie?"

I didn't answer. I shrugged and curled up in a tighter ball, cookie still in hand, and the leftover tears warmed my eyes.

"Your dad told me everything, and I'm so sorry for what Theo did…again. I'm not going to let this slide, all right? I already spoke to his dad, and he's flying out to New York in the morning. It's time for him to start acting like an adult, get his own job, make his own money. He doesn't appreciate my help, so why continue?"

I stopped picking at the cookie and looked up, shocked by how fast she'd moved. She must have really been done with his behavior, and I felt another round of tears brewing knowing how seriously she was taking this, how seriously she was taking me.

I couldn't believe I'd ever had some gratuitous grudge against her when she turned out to be a really incredible woman, someone I was glad was in my life.

"Don't be sorry," I said and wiped my face with the back of my wrist. "None of it was your fault. I should have told her. This is karma for me not saying anything."

She patted my knee. "Why didn't you tell her, Remi? I thought you were going to."

Her tone was gentle but sounded confused and disappointed, and I knew how much I appreciated her by how that disappointed tone unfurled in my stomach. I hated disappointing people and couldn't handle it when I did it to Mom and Dad. Turns out, I couldn't handle it with Serena, either, and I knew that meant something.

My eyes started to leak again. "I was scared." I cried, and Serena scooted over to pull me in for an embrace. Her expensive perfume that was probably something ridiculous like Dior or Chanel swaddled me along with her arms. "Every time I thought about it, I didn't want it to ruin the moment, and I kept running out of moments. I...I was going to tell her yesterday but...Theo beat me," I said in between my hiccupping sobs.

Her rubbing hand never wavered on my back, even as I admitted my fault, my huge fault: the fact that I was the antagonist in my own summer romance.

"Give her some time, hon," Serena said soothingly.

"I don't have any more time. I leave in two days, and she won't text me. She hasn't given me the chance to explain myself."

"Remi, she needs time to process, okay? I imagine it's a lot to take in, especially given how it was revealed. Give her the rest of today and try again tomorrow."

"But—"

She broke the hug and squeezed my knee, giving me a firm stare. I needed to listen to what she said. I hushed instantly. "Trust me, okay? You don't want to overwhelm her with too many texts. Take it easy for the day and try again tomorrow. Now, I have a surprise for you tomorrow," she said as she got off the bed. "Whenever you're ready to cash it in, you let me know, okay?"

"A surprise?"

The last thing I deserved was a surprise. Unless it was Harper outside my door willing to forgive me, I didn't care what it was. I didn't want it.

Her smile grew. "Yes, a surprise." She took a glance at her silver and rose gold watch. "I'm thinking we should walk over in the early afternoon. Does that sound okay?"

"Walk over?"

She winked. "Let me know. I think it might help cheer you up a bit. Remember, give her time, and maybe things will be better tomorrow. You let me know if you need anything, all right?"

I loved Serena's optimism. I wished so much that what she'd told me was true, that all Harper needed was time to realize that she was able to see past my fuckup because she loved me so much.

And then I grunted and tossed on my bed. *Loved.* What a punch to the gut. I knew I was only eighteen, and saying that I was in love with Harper was a stretch, but I knew whatever I felt about her was one-hundred-percent real. It was the realest thing I'd ever felt, and whatever the name for the emotion, it was a strong force.

I tossed and turned while trying to fall asleep that night. After a few hours of being unsuccessful, I ended up laying my head on the foot of the bed and stared at the framed Europa poster on the wall. The only thing that interrupted my tumbling thoughts about Harper was my complete fascination with black holes. Like the argument, the chapter I'd read was still so fresh, still reconstructing everything I thought the universe was.

Black holes formed after stars collapsed under their own weight, and they left behind a small but dense core. Black holes were the scars of the universe, and it felt like a scar was forming in my chest with how much it literally hurt, like my lungs had shrunk to a fraction of their size, and all the deep breaths I'd been trying to take were painfully stretching them out. All I could think about were all the things I could have done differently and how I'd be spending my night if I'd been honest with her from the beginning.

It was so much more emotion than when I'd broken up with Owen. I didn't even cry, then. The only other heartbreak I'd known was when I'd watched my family fade and then crumble. I thought about the day that Dad had moved out when I was fourteen and wondered if a breakup was like a black hole for a human heart. Months had passed where Mom was a shell of herself, and the things she'd once loved couldn't pull her out of bed. Although Mom was better now, she'd told me that once you loved someone, they were a part of your life forever, whether you liked it or not. Heartbreaks changed a person, and she'd said that unfortunately, I would eventually learn that too. It made me afraid of falling in love. Were people supposed to be afraid to fall in love even if they had no idea what being in love was like? Did you know that you were falling in love when you started becoming scared?

I already had one heartbreak down, and I wondered how many my heart would collect in my lifetime.

❖

Dad and I drove to the boardwalk on my last morning to enjoy the sunrise.

It was something that he suggested at the beginning of the summer, but like hell I was going to wake up at six to watch the sun climb up the sky. Not when there weren't any stars, and I could have been sleeping in bed.

The last morning hit differently than all the others. The day didn't feel real, and despite not starting classes for another three weeks, it still felt like the last day of summer vacation. I never thought in a million years that I would be sad to leave Gaslight Shores. The second I had landed in Charleston and felt the thick air, I'd wanted to leave. I didn't want to have a relationship with Serena. I had only come for a visit to appease my dad enough to help pay for college, and I certainly didn't expect to meet a girl who'd made every single day in a town I didn't want to be in worthwhile.

But everything I didn't want or didn't expect had happened, and I was so grateful for all of it that leaving tightened my chest. I wanted another month, needed it, actually, and I was already combing through the calendar in my mind of when I could come back again and maybe try with Harper. But my gut told me that it was a lost cause. She lived too far away.

Dad and I planted ourselves in sand still cold from absorbing the night. The ocean was quiet from a low tide, and after all the noise in my head from the last two days, it helped calm everything around me...for a moment. I sucked in a deep breath of that salty morning air I'd grown to love, held it in so it could absorb my stress, and blew it out.

"I can't believe how fast the summer went, kiddo," Dad said.

I couldn't believe how fast it went either. It wasn't supposed to. It was supposed to drag on until it drove me mad, but instead, it had done the opposite.

I grabbed a handful of sand and enjoyed how it felt falling through my fingers. "Yeah, I know."

He put his arm around me. "I'm really glad you came to visit. It meant so much to me." He paused and let out an exhale. I studied him and could see a lot of thoughts tumbling behind his blank stare at the sunrise.

"What are you thinking?" I asked.

He laughed. "A lot of things." He shook his head and stared at his lap. "I know the divorce was hard on you, kiddo. It wasn't enjoyable for anyone, and I know I did some pretty dumb things to you and your mom that I'm ashamed of, and for that, I'm sorry."

I turned and saw the hurt in his eyes. It was the first time he'd showed any sort of remorse. Before, it had seemed like a game to him, how much he could win and take from Mom. But everything I thought was stripped away, and my dad looked at me not like the winner of the divorce but like a guy who'd lost his family and was desperate to get a semblance of it back.

"And I'm so sorry I got rid of the telescope. I really wasn't thinking."

"It'll be okay."

He squeezed my shoulder and gave me the smallest smile. "I've been thinking a lot...this whole summer, actually. I'm so glad that we had this chance to be together again, you know? I've really missed you."

"I missed you too."

"And I'm so sorry that I made you feel obligated to come down. Hon, I was desperate to see you again, and I thought that... well...I knew the only way to get you to consider your old man again was to bring up college, and that was so incredibly wrong." He ran a hand through his hair. The soft morning light highlighted the gray starting to show against his brown hair, a reminder of how Dad was aging like I was, how he was still growing and learning too. "Listen, I'm not perfect. Far from perfect. I might be old, but I still make mistakes, and those mistakes shouldn't have to fall on you. I regret a lot of things that happened over the years. Ever since I told you about the telescope, I couldn't stop feeling bad about it, and I feel even worse for how I convinced you to come down here. It's not okay. You don't need to worry about college, Remi. I'm so sorry that I ever planted that seed in your head. It was very wrong."

I picked up another handful of sand. "I don't even know what happened." I looked up at him, clenching the sand in my fist. "What even happened? With you and Mom?"

He thinned his lips. "We just drifted apart, kiddo."

"But how? You were married for twenty years."

"That's the thing. We'd been together for twenty-four years. We met when we were twenty-six. We were two totally different people back then."

"Yeah but..." I stopped myself and thought about my next words. I couldn't shake how different Dad acted around Serena from how he ever had with Mom. As scared as I was to find out the truth, I also wanted to know it so I could stop wondering, so maybe I could fully move on. "Did you even love Mom?"

His eyebrows pulled together. "What? Of course I loved her."

"But you...you and Serena act so differently. You and Mom never acted the way you and Serena do."

He faced the ocean and let out a deep sigh. He was quiet for a moment, as if carefully formatting his next sentence. I didn't blame him for taking the time to construct it. It wasn't an easy question, but it was one I had to ask. I wanted to understand how people could fall in love and then years later fall out of love, how they could go from a twenty-four-year bond to fighting over the living room couch to tossing darts at each other and hoping to nail the bullseye. I wanted to know and understand so I could make sure that it never happened to me.

"Remi, some people have different connections," Dad finally said, exhaling. "Your mom and I...we...I did love her...and we were good partners, raising you, doing life together. But I don't know, we felt like that was all we had. A good partnership. Marriage is so much more than that, or at least, it should be. I love your mom as a person, I always will, but we both agreed that we weren't soulmates."

The truth hurt. I appreciated his honesty and talking about Mom in a civil way, without that nasty tone he'd always used. I appreciated that he spoke to me like an adult and trusted me with the truth, but it didn't mean it didn't hurt any less.

I dumped the handful of sand and wiped the remainder against my legs. "If you both agreed on that, why was it so ugly? It didn't seem like you agreed on anything."

He shook his head. "I don't know, hon. I think we were both just scared and ashamed. No one ever wants to experience a divorce. No one ever expects that it could happen to them. I can't speak for your mother, but I felt like a complete failure. I felt like twenty-four years of my life were wasted. I felt like a failure, that the relationship I'd had with your mom worked, but it wasn't the relationship it could be, a partnership with passion and affection. I felt like a failure for upsetting her, for losing all my time with you, wondering if taking the job in Brooklyn was the right move because I would see you less. It got ugly because we were scared. It doesn't make some of the things I said and did right, but I was terrified of losing everything, Remi. There was a point in time when I felt like I'd really lost everything."

The sun peered over the horizon, lighting the sky up in light pinks and yellows, pulling both of our gazes back to it. As hurt as I was about the telescope and the bribery, I could see the regret in his eyes, hear it in his tone, and most importantly, I could feel it. None of that was ever going to be okay. But it wasn't until that moment on the beach when the emotion finally surfaced in his eyes that I could see all the things he'd been hiding under. I guessed that was what people did when they were scared. They built a bunch of walls made up of their biggest flaws, some flaws they didn't even know they had, and hid under them.

As I picked up another handful of sand, watched it fall through my fingers, and repeated, I thought about it. I was sure losing a twenty-year marriage and a once tight-knit bond with his only daughter had been terrifying. I was sure that growing up like Theo, with his mother constantly working and never being around, had been scary. And although I didn't have to condone Dad's choices or forgive Theo, it made more sense as to why they'd done the horrible things they'd done. No one ever thought they were the bad guy. We all had what we thought were "justifiable" reasons for whatever actions. I thought being afraid of losing Harper was a justifiable reason for not telling her Serena and Theo were my stepfamily. Zero part of my decision to keep quiet would ever be right, and that was the guilt I had to deal with. That was the consequence. I was sure Dad felt the same way about his decisions, and that was what made me finally forgive him. For everything.

"I'm sorry that I stopped talking to you," I said. "I forgive you, though." When I said those words, the tightness in my lungs released.

His thin smile grew a bit. "We both made some mistakes. We both hurt each other, but I think what this summer brought us was something to clean our slates. At least, I hope?"

"Well, you can clean your slate. But I've dirtied mine up."

"She still hasn't texted you back?"

I shook my head. "I don't blame her. I probably would ignore me too."

"Give her time."

I grunted and ran a hand through my hair flying back from the ocean wind. "That's what Serena said."

We sat with that for a few silent moments. I checked my phone again, a nervous habit I'd developed over the span of thirty-five hours, hoping that a text from Harper would take over my screen. But like all the other moments, my phone was blank.

"How about this: maybe for Christmas, I'll make it up to you and buy you the latest and coolest Celestron telescope. We can look at the thing together like old times."

I smiled. "That would be awesome."

"Just act surprised when you unwrap it, keep the Christmas spirit alive."

"I will. I promise."

He put his arm around me and pulled me in. I'd forgotten how much I loved his strong embraces. When I put my head on his shoulder, he kissed the top of my hair. "I love you to the moon and back, kiddo. Always have. Always will."

Why say that you loved someone to the moon and back? I'd never understood the saying. The moon was a little under five hundred thousand miles, a six-day round trip on a space shuttle.

Saying you loved someone to the moon and back was like telling them you tolerated them for six days. I felt like my parents' "I love yous" to each other over the course of their twenty-four-year relationship were "to the moon and back." I wanted my "I love yous" to mean so much more than a six-day trip around the moon. I wanted to love someone to Betelgeuse and back, and I wanted someone to love *me* to Betelgeuse and back. It would take sixteen million years for a round trip, over twelve hundred light years. That was infinite love.

I hoped that Dad found that person in Serena, I hoped that Mom would eventually find her person to say it to, and I definitely couldn't wait to find my person and add their name to the list of names to write on the moon. Brie, my best friend. Harper, my first everything, and the love of my life.

"I love you to Europa and back," I said with a small smile and bumped into his side.

Of course, I loved my dad with everything, but I would reserve Betelgeuse for the love of my life. To Europa and back was still a ridiculous amount of distance. It would take twelve years round-trip, but Europa had my dad's heart, and I knew using it would mean more than the literal distance between it and the Earth.

He laughed. "That's much better than saying to the moon and back, right?"

"It's, like, a difference of over seven hundred million miles, so I'd say yes."

Dad ruffled my hair. "Then I love you to Europa and back, kiddo."

As we headed back to the car, I couldn't stop searching for the Acadian standing in the silence over the boardwalk. It was seven a.m., and the store wouldn't open until eleven. Harper and the rest of the employees wouldn't be there until ten, and my heart sunk knowing that three hours separated us from a good-bye I so desperately wanted to have. I grabbed my quartz necklace as we walked closer and hoped that touching it would help veer us back on the same trajectory, like we were supposed to be.

❖

"Dad's not coming?" I asked when I met Serena on the driveway at noon for whatever she was up to.

She smiled and wrapped her arm around me. "No. He said this was our thing."

I was even more confused as to what this surprise was.

I followed her down the street, and when the cul-de-sac poured into another road, we took a left. I still had no idea where we were going, but apparently, we were going on a walk through the neighborhood. I observed the huge homes and wondered what the owners did for a living. How did people own these homes if they weren't celebrities like Serena and Reagan Moore?

And then it hit me.

Right as the epiphany settled, we walked up a circular driveway to another enormous mansion, probably the size of Serena's, definitely larger than the other homes we'd passed on our walk. Serena approached the double wooden door and rang the doorbell.

"What's going on?" I asked through my clenched jaw.

"A little pick-me-up," Serena said and then smiled when the front door opened.

And there stood pop sensation Reagan Moore. My mouth fell. Somehow, even though she'd dressed like a normal person in jean shorts, a black tank top, and black flip-flops I could've sworn were from Old Navy, her fame and clout still radiated from her like a halo. The blurred, ant-sized celebrity that I had seen from the back of Madison Square Garden was now two feet away from me, and all those facial features I had memorized like any huge Reagan Moore fan were now all real.

"You must be Remi," Reagan Moore said and extended her arms out to hug me. And then she did, and I couldn't believe I hugged her back. She was the same height as me and so freakin beautiful that I didn't feel like I belonged next to her or Serena. "Serena has told me so much about you." All I could do was look at Serena with—what I was sure was—a dumbfounded look. "Come on in. Blair just made a blueberry cobbler."

Blair Bennett was in the house too? As in, Reagan Moore's rockstar girlfriend? Surely this was a dream, and I hadn't woken up from my nap yet.

The what-had-to-have-been-a-lucid-dream seemed even more real when I stood in Reagan Moore's kitchen and smelled the sweet, delicious cobbler wafting from its casserole dish on top of the stove. Blair Bennett trotted around the kitchen counter wearing a black apron and held her arms out for a hug. I saw the sleeve tattoo that added to her look, proving that she was the real Blair Bennett. She slid me a plate of fresh cobbler, and as starstruck as I was, all I could think about was Harper and how much she would have loved this moment, probably more than me, and I was a *big* fan.

The stomachache started churning again.

Serena bragged about how I was about to head back home to start college at MIT, and while I witnessed Reagan Moore and Blair Bennett congratulate me on my achievement and tell me how impressive it was, I willed the tears to go away.

God, I wish I could text her about this. Harper should be here right now.

"I think we just met one of the first women to ever go on Mars," Reagan said to Blair.

"That's so freakin' cool," Blair said, and I thought she was the epitome of cool. She could play like nine different instruments, she had cool tattoos, and was dating the biggest pop star in the world. She was cool, and I was a nerd. A horrible, lying nerd who'd blown it.

Serena's phone went off, and she excused herself to take it, navigating Reagan Moore's house like she'd been inside before.

"I...um...I went to your show once," I said, mumbling like an idiot, trying to fill in the silence even though there had only been a nanosecond of it. I took a bite of cobbler and melted in my seat. I couldn't believe I was eating something Blair Bennett made and with Reagan Moore's fork. "At Madison Square Garden...when Midnight Konfusion opened." The two exchanged a look as if speaking in their own code. "Your tickets are incredibly hard to get."

I couldn't believe how incredibly dumb I sounded. I was thankful that Serena bragging about MIT hopefully made up for it.

The two of them laughed. "How about this, next time you want to come to a show, just let your stepmom know, and we'll see what we can do?" Reagan said with a wink. "We have connections."

I knew I had to act. I had no idea how long I would have by myself with Reagan Moore and Blair Bennett, but all I could think about was how much Harper loved them and how much she wanted them to stop by the Acadian, and they both had the clout to put it on the map again.

"I have a random question," I said and stabbed at the dessert.

"We love random questions," Blair Bennett said and leaned into the kitchen island. "Go for it."

"Have you...um...have you heard of the Acadian?"

"Of course," Reagan Moore said.

That instantly pulled my gaze. "Wait, really?"

She laughed. "It's the po'boy place on the boardwalk." She turned to Blair. "It's, like, super famous in town."

She knew about the Acadian this whole time?

"So...um...well...my friend—" I cringed when I candy-coated the word. Harper was so much more than a friend. So much more and so much less, thanks to me. "Her family owns it, and she's... well...she's a really big fan. Has always wanted to go to a concert but has never gotten lucky enough to get a ticket. And the Acadian is really struggling right now, and she's feeling really down." I blew out a breath. This entire proposal was ridiculous, but I knew I needed to finish what I started. A giant fuckup needed as big of a make up, and asking Reagan Moore this question was as big as I could get. It was the only thing I could do that could maybe help the Heberts. "I know this is going to be a ridiculous ask, but I don't know, if you maybe had the time to stop by or something, I know it would make her whole day. I know you're busy and all and probably can't, but I had to ask."

Blair turned to Reagan. "Why didn't you ever take me to get a po'boy? Why is this the first I've heard of this?" Her tone was teasing and light.

"I think this is something we could do," Reagan said with a smile. "I have heard wonderful things about it."

"Really?"

"Really. What's your friend's name?"

"Harper. Harper Hebert. She's always working. Has straight brown hair a little past her shoulders, a few freckles on her nose, brown eyes that are kind of like a chestnut color."

A wide mischievous smile spread across Blair's face, and it sent a heatwave through me. She propped her head up with her fist. "Sounds like she means a lot to you." I swore that grin she flashed was a signal that she saw right through me.

"She does," I said, and guilt twisted my insides when I admitted that to myself. "She means everything."

Then why didn't you tell her earlier? She could have been next to you if you'd told her.

Blair flashed a knowing grin to Reagan, and heat sprawled across my face when she wiggled her dark brown eyebrows at Reagan, who matched her girlfriend's smile and faced me.

"Consider it done," Reagan said and then faced Blair. "I mean, we don't explore the boardwalk as often as we should. Disguising ourselves is a lot of work."

"But I want to go on the Ferris wheel," Blair said. "Take me on it, damn it."

Serena came back shortly after, and once I finished my cobbler, Reagan and Blair led me to the recording studio that apparently was in her house. Of course Reagan Moore had a recording studio, with a baby grand piano, five acoustic guitars, seven electric guitars, a drum set, and two bass guitars. They even let me play a couple, and when Serena and I finally left, I walked away feeling an incredible high at the same time my chest and stomach still ached from what had happened two nights before.

I felt guilty for feeling happy, like I didn't deserve the treat that Serena gifted me, despite agreeing to it back when we had our manicures.

"Thank you for that, Serena," I said on our walk back. "It really meant a lot. They seem really cool in person."

She tossed her arm over my shoulders for a quick hug. "Not a problem, sweetie. I thought you could have used a little pick-me-up. Something to get you out of bed and put a smile on your face. And I know they were happy to do it."

We didn't say much until we walked up the driveway, and right as I veered to the right to go back in the apartment, Serena said, "Remi, I hope all of this Theo nonsense doesn't scare you from coming to visit more often. I really enjoyed our summer together, and I know your dad really did too."

"It's not going to scare me away. I promise."

And I really meant it. I'd met an amazing girl who made each day exciting, I felt closer to my dad than I felt in years, and I'd made an unexpected friend in Serena, and she'd shown me that I could trust her with things I couldn't necessarily tell my dad or mom or anyone else. She was like a friend and a second mother, and I really cherished the relationship we'd formed.

The second I made it back to my apartment, I decided to send Harper one last text, a Hail Mary to salvage something of our summer.

I'm heading to the airport at 7 a.m. tomorrow. Can I please say good-bye? I'm really sorry, Harper.

My heart plummeted when the gray texting bubble appeared. I shot straight up in my bed, feeling the staccato heartbeats twitching in my neck. She was typing. She was actually typing. I silently begged for her to write faster so our text thread finally evened out with something from her, but just as I thought she would finally send the text, the bubble disappeared.

"What? No!"

I grabbed the quartz necklace and ran it along the chain, willing its magical powers to put us back on the same trajectory like it was supposed to do, like we were supposed to be. Then, the bubble appeared once more, and my heart hammered so fast that I thought it was going to fly out of my chest. It appeared and disappeared multiple times, and each time, the tears threatened as I waited and got nothing. She had our thread open. She was thinking of me. She was writing a response…and then she never sent it. The bubble disappeared. I cried as I stared at my screen for ten minutes, waiting for it to appear again and give me the gift of a text. Even if the text told me to fuck off, at least I would get a text back, something that was better than silence, something that offered a modicum of closure.

Minutes formed and turned into an hour, and then a whole night of sporadic sleeping passed. The ticking clock was so powerful, it woke me up almost every hour to check my phone to see if that response came. I wanted to wake up and see it. I wanted to know she had trouble sleeping too, thinking of me and all the good things that had happened this summer. There was more good than bad, I thought. We'd had so many amazing nows.

But before I knew it, I woke up again, the alarm literally going off. And that was that. The summer was over.

I carried my two suitcases down the steps and into the back of the Range Rover. As I opened the door, I checked my phone one last time. The only thing that existed on my screen was the time: 6:57.

All our nows had officially turned into memories.

"You ready, kiddo?" Dad asked from the driver's seat. Both he and Serena, who was in the passenger seat, glanced in the rearview mirror.

I wasn't ready, but I had no other choice. I nodded, and Dad backed out of the driveway. As we pulled out of the Palms gate one last time, I thought of all the times I'd met Harper on the other side of it. I choked back as many tears as I could, but some still slipped through. I quickly swatted at my face every time a new one rolled down my cheek, knowing that Dad kept stealing glimpses from the mirror, probably to make sure I was okay.

But I wasn't because I'd just learned that Einstein was full of shit. Time *did* exist because I'd run out of it.

CHAPTER SIXTEEN

Coming back to Gaslight Shores for Thanksgiving had the same kind of energy as visiting one of my old schools after I'd moved on from it. It felt different yet strangely familiar. All the tiny details sprouted in my mind, long forgotten but still memorized, and the place didn't feel like mine. A summer resort town in the middle of November was a completely different place. All the cars parked up and down Main and Front Street were gone, the bike racks were empty, and it felt odd to be wearing jeans and an MIT hoodie and not the usual tank top, shorts, and flip-flops.

When Dad drove us back to the house, I said hello to Serena, who was freshly tan from traveling around South America the last two months, filming the third season of *Chef Queens*. Luckily, Theo was still in Brooklyn, living with his dad and figuring out his life, Dad quickly said in passing on the way back from the airport. Not having to worry about Theo around the house—or anywhere in town, for that matter—made the air seem lighter than it ever had before. I felt like I could actually take in a full breath in the house.

The three of us ate an early dinner, and I filled them in on all the college updates they asked for. Yes, I was acing all my classes, loved my roommate, Hailey, and the group of friends we'd made on our floor. And no, I didn't have a boyfriend or girlfriend.

I didn't tell them this, but there were a lot of attractive people on my floor, and I'd flirted with a few of them during the first couple of weeks. I mean, there were attractive nerdy people in my classes who loved all the things I loved. We could flirt with each other using chemistry or calc class as our common denominator. I could make stupid space jokes as a way to make them laugh, and they wouldn't think I was weird, like most people in high school had made me feel. But as fun as flirting was, my mind was focused on school. I tried moving on from the summer, and with each day that passed without hearing from Harper, I lost more hope that I would ever get the chance to truly apologize. Especially when I found out that Reagan Moore really had visited the Acadian and had posted it on her Instagram account. I thought that would be the catalyst to our make up because of all the times we'd talked about Reagan Moore coming to visit. But I hadn't heard anything from her, and that was the clearest indication that we were absolutely done and that I needed to move on.

Talking to other people and trying to put myself out there was too damn difficult when my mind and heart were still set on Harper. The flirting would be light and meaningless until my heart was ready to let someone new in.

It was easier to distract my brain with school than dwell on something that wasn't in my control anymore.

"Have you heard from Harper?" Serena asked after I told her I wasn't seeing anyone.

I hadn't heard her name in three months, and hearing it again sent a pang through my chest.

"Nope. Nothing," I said.

Serena made a face. "I'm shocked by that."

"Why? I did a really good job screwing it up. I don't blame her." She and my dad shared a look. "What?"

"You know that the Acadian didn't close, right?" Dad asked.

I felt my eyes involuntarily round. "Wait, what?"

"I went to talk to the Heberts after you left," Serena said. "I wanted to personally apologize to Harper for everything Theo did."

"What? Why didn't you tell me?" My voice rose.

"I didn't think that was something you wanted to hear. You were so upset...I was afraid mentioning anything would make things worse."

I imagined how I would have felt if Serena had called and told me. The fact that she got to see and talk to Harper when she wouldn't talk to me would have sent so much jealousy coursing through me at a time when I was trying so hard to accept what had happened and move on from it.

I deflated in my seat when I realized Serena was probably right.

"How…how didn't they close?" I asked, still processing all the heavy knowledge.

Serena shrugged. "They asked for help. Asked if I was still interested in being their partner. I told them I was, but I would have to relocate Envie. It would be a huge conflict of interest having both restaurants on the boardwalk."

My mouth dropped. "So…did you relocate?"

"I'm in the process. I've been gone since the beginning of October, so there was only so much I could do before I left, but I found an adorable space in Charleston in Harleston Village. I love it, and I get the best of both worlds. A place in Charleston and a spot on the boardwalk. It's a little pain to relocate, but I actually think this works out for the best."

"I can't believe…I had no idea."

"It's pretty exciting, really. I shared all these ideas with the Heberts, and Tim and Alice seemed on board with everything. I made it clear that keeping the Acadian true to its roots was important, and we would make sure it stays like that because its rich history is what makes it an amazing place. We haven't been able to make too much of a dent since I was away, but after New Year's, all guns blazing."

I had no idea what to be more shocked about: the fact that the Heberts teamed up with Serena or the fact that Harper had never told me. I guess she didn't have to. She didn't owe me anything.

Knowing all of those details, my heart was set even more than it was before. Now that I was in Gaslight Shores for the long weekend, I desperately wanted to find some kind of closure at the very least. I wanted to see Harper. I wanted her to know that even though I ruined the summer and kept Serena a secret, I didn't hide my heart. It was out there on display the whole time, and I meant every word I'd said and meant every kiss.

She had to know that.

I brushed off the thin layer of dust that accumulated on my bike tucked away in the garage and pedaled the same route I'd taken every day to the boardwalk.

Without the bikes, convertibles, and runners throughout the town, Gaslight Shores was a skeleton of a summer resort town, the vibrancy of the summer long gone, but the charm still visible from the rows of gas lamps, palmettos, and pastel paints coloring the shops. It was a town that had constantly smelled like salt, sunscreen, and fried oil, and now, only the salt remained, leaving the rest of the air dull.

It was weird to lock my bike on an empty rack. Mia's and Sully's Fries had the metal rolling shutters closed, and to the left sat an empty boardwalk free from lines, and on the right, the Ferris wheel sat still and dark. There were a few people running on the boardwalk and the beach, but I counted a total of five as opposed to the hundreds I was used to.

First, I checked out Envie to see if what Serena told me was true, and sure enough, there was a commercial For Sale sign hanging in the window along with a smaller sign taped on the inside of the purple front door. "Don't worry! Envie hasn't closed. We've relocated to Charleston. The same sandwiches you love will be waiting for you. Please follow us on Facebook and Instagram for updates on the new opening."

So much had already changed since August. The trees in Cambridge had turned into yellows, reds, and oranges, and crunchy leaves littered the streets and sidewalks. The brisk fall wind nipped at me through my sweatshirt, and I crossed my arms to retain more body heat. Gaslight Shores had gone from a popular resort to a small coastal town of twenty thousand year-round residents. So much had changed in three months, but my feelings for Harper hadn't wavered. If anything, they'd grown. I missed her so much, and the knot of that pain never untangled in my chest.

The Acadian still stood bold and proud, cementing its legacy on the boardwalk, one of the few places that wasn't closed. I stared at its dark red door, and already, my heart leapt at the anticipation of hearing the bell and finally seeing Harper again. I ran through everything I wanted to say that I'd practiced in case she texted or called me out of the blue. But all the words I had memorized and once thought were good enough fell flat when I stood in front of the building. My heart stuttered just imagining seeing Harper and her cute, freckled nose and smile that was no longer reserved for me.

I filled my lungs with cool briny air and opened the door. The bell jingled like it did every time, and unlike the desolate dining room I was used to, all the booths and tables were occupied, with the exception of two. I smiled and allowed the happiness to pleasantly tug at my chest as I soaked up the unfamiliar but welcome sight.

"Welcome to the Acadian," a teenage girl in a red apron said, smiling at me with her braces. "How may I help you?"

"Hi…um…could I uh…could I get The Original?"

"Sure thing."

She reached for the French bread below the counter, sliced it in half, and proceeded to prepare it. I wasn't hungry at all. Not when Serena had fixed up a "simple" chicken parmesan for dinner, but it didn't feel right to stop in and not get a po'boy.

"Anything else?" the chipper teen asked.

"A side of hush puppies and some Debris Sauce please."

"Would you like a cup or a bottle?"

My eyebrows furrowed. "You have bottles?"

"Yes." She stepped aside and gestured to the fridge that used to hold the bottled beverages, only now, the top row was packed with Debris Sauce bottles branded with the Acadian logo. When the Heberts had decided to partner with Serena, they must have finally agreed to selling their sauce.

"I'll take a bottle," I said and reached for my credit card. "Also, is…um…is Harper working today? Harper Hebert?"

"Yeah, she's in the back," she said, swiped my card, and then handed it back. "Want me to go get her?"

My stomach dropped. "Yeah, sure."

The girl went to the kitchen while heat crawled up my spine and wrapped around my back. I clutched my to-go bag tightly, and not even the smell of fresh hush puppies seeping through could put me at ease.

As I waited for them to come out, I noticed a new addition on the wall to the left. Another frame hung next to the soda machine. I walked over to check it out and found Harper, her parents, and a few other young people I assumed were employees next to Reagan Moore and Blair Bennett. Reagan had her arm around Harper, and Harper had the widest smile on her face. I could feel it in my stomach. Reagan and Blair had signed the picture in the upper right and left corners, and I couldn't help but smile at how happy Harper looked.

"Remi?"

Harper appeared from the kitchen, and my heart free-fell to my gut. She wiped her hands on her red apron and seemed as shocked as I was, despite me being the one to ask for her.

The memories of us went off like fireworks in my head, and all I could do was raise my hand to give her an awkward wave. "Hi," I said, my throat closing in around my words.

She opened and then closed her mouth, as if there were a million things she wanted to say but wanted to stop them pouring out. It was like watching that text bubble appear and disappear in person. "What...what are you doing here?"

"I'm here for Thanksgiving, and I wanted to..." I stopped myself for a moment. "Could we...um...do you have a minute?"

She looked over at the girl at the assembly line and then observed the crowded dining room. "I only have a minute."

"Can we go outside?"

"Give me a second."

She went to the kitchen and came out moments later without her apron. She followed me to an empty bench right outside the restaurant. When we took a seat, the lost three months wedged a giant silence in between us. It felt like the bench was made of nails, and after trying to adjust myself to get comfortable, I gave up, knowing that this was going to be anything but.

"How have you been doing?" I asked, scratching at the back of my head and having no idea how to smoothly start the conversation.

The wind coming in with the tide whipped back the baby hairs that didn't make it in her ponytail. She attempted to tuck one of the tresses behind her ear but failed. All I wanted to do was reach out and help, but I didn't. "Good."

"Yeah?"

She hesitated for a moment, staring out at the ocean as if trying to collect her words like seashells along the shore. "I think you know how it's been going."

I let out a chuckle but not because I thought anything was funny. Because my brain was still processing what had been happening. I was lucky that I was updated before I found Harper. "I didn't know until literally an hour ago."

She frowned. "Really?"

"Well, you didn't tell me so how would I have found out?" I said matter-of-factly.

"Your dad? Serena?"

"My dad never mentioned it. Plus, Serena has been out of the country for the last two months."

As much as I wanted to know about Harper and the Acadian, I knew asking Dad about updates would hurt me. It would tear open the wounds that had started to close up, and despite thinking about Harper every day since I'd left, I'd finally accepted what had transpired. I'd severely fucked up, and I had to live with the guilt and my actions. Harper had every right to be mad, and I had to give her space, no matter how badly I wanted to text her. I'd sent at least five balls into her court with my unanswered texts and missed calls. I wasn't going to keep tossing.

"You sent Reagan Moore and Blair Bennett to the Acadian?"

I noticed the freckles on her nose again, and being reacquainted with them made waves of nerves curl around in my stomach. My gaze accidently slipped down to her mouth, and once I realized I scanned each inch of her lips, I forced them back up.

"I lightly suggested they go visit."

"Blair Bennett pulled me aside and said a girl with curly hair told her there was a girl who worked at the Acadian with freckles and chestnut-colored eyes who was a fan, and then she proceeded to wiggle her eyebrows and said that the curly-headed girl said that I meant everything to her."

That explained why Blair Bennett had given me that wide, impish grin after I'd said that. She'd totally known that I'd liked Harper, and the memory spread a warmth across my cheeks. "I might have said something like that," I said, trying to play it as coy as possible.

"You know, we had so many people coming in after that day. Long after the season ended on Labor Day."

"That's really good."

She pulled her gaze away from me and stared at the ocean. "I thought about texting you but…I don't know. I thought it was too late."

"Why didn't you send that text? I saw the bubble."

She swatted at her eyes so quickly, I didn't even see a tear falling. A pang of regret lodged in my chest knowing that the emotions had surfaced in her. She shrugged and looked at me in defeat. "You were leaving. I was staying. I thought it was pointless."

"What? How the hell was that pointless? I knew I messed up, but I felt like you could have at least said something back. Just one simple text."

"One text back wasn't simple, just like telling me the truth wasn't simple."

There was a squeezing in my chest from her jab. "You have every right to be mad at me," I said softly and looked at my hands. "I don't blame you, but I tried so hard to fix things. All I wanted was a chance to explain so you didn't think I did this purposely to hurt you."

"I was still so mad. I had no idea what parts of my summer were true."

"All my feelings for you were the realest things I've ever experienced. Why would I lie about that?"

She faltered for a moment. "I don't know." She ran her hand through her hair, and the sight made my breath hitch. She was still so beautiful. "Listen, I really need to get back to work—"

"When do you get off?"

She faltered as her eyebrows drew together. "Nine. I'm closing."

"Can we finish this talk after? I was going to come here to stargaze. Betelgeuse is out, you know."

Her knitted eyebrows loosened. "Is it?"

It was like one mention of Betelgeuse lowered the smallest part of her guard, letting me get a glimpse of how she truly felt. There seemed to be hope, maybe a bit of regret. It was only a brief moment, but her curiosity in that question and the way she softened at the mention of Betelgeuse made me believe that there was still something left of our summer.

"It's going to be my first time seeing it through my telescope," I said. "I'll probably bring this and look around." I pulled up my po'boy bag.

"Okay."

My heart stuttered. Her agreeing to meet me after work felt as rewarding as that text message would have made me feel if she'd ever sent it. "Wait, really?"

"Really. I want to see the dying star. See if it's worth the wait. And...well...you, of course."

And you, of course.

She said it like it was supposed to be obvious, but I had no idea what was obvious or where she stood. But I'd take her willingness to meet me as a victory. That had to mean something.

I came back to the beach at nine with my po'boy, telescope, and lots of blankets. It was weird being at the beach wearing long sleeves underneath my sweatshirt, all bundled up to protect me from the chilly air. I laid out a blanket to sit on and another to cover my legs as I set up the telescope and pointed to Orion's left shoulder. Betelgeuse's orange color was visible from Earth, the only colored dot in the constellation. When I looked in the eyepiece, I was amazed all over again. A ball of orange against all the black. Somehow, that little ball was as wide as the distance between Mercury and the asteroid belt. Something about staring at it with the telescope helped recenter me, like flying in an airplane or riding the Ferris wheel. It settled the riptide of nerves in my stomach ever since I'd left Harper so she could go back to work, wondering what the hell would happen when we finished our talk.

"I found you."

I turned to find Harper behind me, bundled up in a coat with an Acadian to-go bag in her grip. She took a seat next to me, and I tried hard not to unravel so easily when I smelled her shampoo scenting the salty breeze. It made my mind glitch for a nanosecond, as if this was a moment from the summer.

I swallowed hard and eyed my telescope. All the uncertainty hanging like question marks made it almost impossible to look her in the eye. "Want to see Betelgeuse? It's looking beautiful tonight."

I leaned on my favorite star to help break the ice. We'd only cracked the surface a couple of hours ago, but if looking at the star made us a little more comfortable with each other, then I was going to use it as a crutch.

"Wow, that's the dying star?" she asked, looking into the telescope.

"Yup. Would have never known, right?"

"I don't think I would have cared about this star if it weren't for you."

She pulled away, stole a glance, and when our eyes locked, she flitted them away and back into the eyepiece. "It's so beautiful."

"Remember, if relocated, it would take up all the space between Mercury and the asteroid belt. It's nine hundred and fifty times larger than the sun."

"Damn." She stared at it for a few more moments before backing away and opening her wrapped-up po'boy.

I followed her, and the heavy silence from a few hours ago squeezed back in like we were a dynamic trio.

I thought the fact that she'd agreed to meet me meant something, but how we both struggled to say our next words terrified me. I wanted to know what was going on in her head, hell, what had been going on in her head for the last three months. I learned then that Harper Hebert had a very sturdy guard when it was up, and I hated so much being on the other side of it.

"Can we finish our talk?"

She swallowed a bite and nodded.

I gave up waiting on her to toss all those balls I'd swatted into her court back to me. She was hiding behind her guard, and honestly, I didn't blame her. "Okay. I'll start. I know I brought all of this on myself, but I was really scared that you wouldn't want to talk to me anymore. I was instantly drawn to you from the very beginning, and I didn't want someone like Serena, who I'd literally just met, to ruin that. It's not an excuse for lying. I know that was wrong, but my intentions weren't to hurt you or manipulate you. I really had no malice behind it."

She lowered her po'boy, and her gaze drifted off me to her lap. "Serena came to our house a few days after you left to apologize about Theo and everything. She told me that you were really upset leaving with things unresolved."

"I was more than upset. I was heartbroken."

"I was too, Remi. Because I thought I knew you, I thought I could fully trust you, and you lied to me for two months."

"I'm so sorry, Harper. If I could do it again, I would have told you."

She didn't say anything. Instead, she wrapped her po'boy back up in the sandwich paper and slid it back in the plastic bag.

"I've really missed you," I said.

It was enough for her to look at me. My stomach flipped upside down at the sudden eye contact and the way she stared at me with lingering hope. "I missed you too," she said so softly as a wave crashed onto the shore. It was so quiet, I had to replay the words to make sure she said what I'd thought she said, what I'd hoped she said.

"You do?"

She looked at me like I should have known. "Of course I do."

"Then why didn't you text me back? We could have had closure. We both deserve that. Don't you think that what we had deserves some kind of closure?"

"I didn't want closure. Closure means it's over, and I didn't want it to be."

She pulled out the quartz necklace I'd given her from underneath her shirt, and my heart swelled so much, I thought it would rocket out of my chest. I couldn't believe she still wore the necklace after how we'd ended things. I'd kept mine on my desk, dangling from my closed *A Brief History of Time* book as a bookmark to Chapter 6: Black Holes, and the dolphin keychain she'd got me rested on top of the book. I wanted to remember my summer and the time that I'd fallen hard for a girl, and even though I didn't think she was mine anymore, I still wanted to remember. But if she still wore hers, then that must have meant she still clung to us.

"You kept the necklace?" I asked.

"Of course I did. You didn't?"

"I keep mine on my desk, stuck it in the book I read this summer. I thought we were over, so I didn't wear it. I guess I kept it out because we didn't feel completely finished either."

"Because we were meant to stay on the same trajectory," Harper said. "You told me that Einstein said that the past, present, and future exist simultaneously."

"Yeah, but Einstein also said time was an illusion, but clearly it's not because we ran out of it."

"Did we, though? I never stopped feeling it. It never felt over to me. It was like it was still happening at the same time it was over."

That was exactly how I felt too. I just didn't know how to put it in words. I thought it was because I couldn't move on because we'd never had closure, but Harper said it perfectly. Our past was still alive.

She glanced at the necklace and twirled the quartz in between her fingers. "I got into culinary school. All of them except one of the New York ones. I also got two scholarships."

"Wait, seriously?"

She looked up and gave me the start of a smile. "Seriously. I'm going to the Fournier School in January."

My mouth hung open. She was really doing it. She was going to culinary school in New York City. I'd never been so proud of someone else's accomplishment; it felt so much like my own. She must have noticed my shocked reaction because her smile grew, and she tried hiding it by pressing her lips together.

"Oh my God, Harper, that's…amazing. I'm so proud of you."

She shrugged. "It helps when someone believes in you and really encourages you to do it. You made me really believe that I deserve it. I don't know. It's like I didn't think I could ever go to culinary school. My parents supported my dreams, but it was like the financial burden really weighed down their excitement for me. And then you came along," she said, and finally, those eyes looked at me the way they had all summer. The way she stared gave me hope that there was still something left. "And you made me actually believe I could do it."

"And guess what? You're doing it."

"I know. I can't believe it. I wonder if it was the power of the quartz," Harper said with a little laugh and looked at the necklace still between her fingers. "I tried so hard to forget about you, Remi. I thought by telling myself that it was too late that it would make it easier, but no matter how hard I tried, my mind kept going back to you." She paused for a moment and then glanced back up. She still had the power to put my stomach on spin cycle with just a simple look. "Is it too late?"

Was it too late? Was three months of silence too much time? I'd already accepted that she was out of my life, but just because I'd accepted it didn't mean that I was okay with it. I'd never once let the quartz necklace out of my sight because I wanted to get back on the same time trajectory as Harper in case I still stood a chance. Turns out, the whole time I'd stared at it and wished, she'd had it around her neck.

Maybe that was what kept us strung together.

Harper's stare held mine so tightly, it caused my stomach to flutter. "I really fell hard for you, Remi. I—" She glanced at her fidgeting hands and chewed the inside of her lip.

I decided to help calm her anxiety by grabbing her hand, and it caused a whirl of all the emotions I'd tried suppressing since August to bubble in my chest. I sucked in my bottom lip to attempt to stabilize myself. When I noticed her looking back, we shifted back into place. I could feel it rising up my gut like a roller coaster.

"I thought of texting you back so many times, but I was scared."

"About what?"

She shrugged. "I don't know. That you'd moved on? You started college. There are so many people that you probably met, so some two-month fling with me wasn't anything noteworthy."

"I never had something with anybody like what I had with you. I meant what I said when I talked to Blair Bennett. It meant everything to me. *You* mean everything to me. I really fell hard for you too. Actually, I'm still falling."

The smile she had been biting back finally claimed her face. She tightened her grip around my hand and held it up to her chest. "I think we should do something about this. Cambridge is only three and a half hours away from New York, you know?"

I laughed. "I know. Did you look it up?"

"I did. When I got accepted and then debated on texting you. I wanted to see if there was a possibility of getting back together, if we still stood a chance."

"My dad and Serena live in the city. My mom lives an hour and a half away from both of us. We have so many places we could meet up and spend the weekend at. We could resume this if you want it."

I didn't realize how close we were until I saw her smile that was so expressive, I felt it in my chest. "I really want it. More than anything."

I finally had the courage to tuck in the baby hairs blowing back in the breeze. Harper closed her eyes and leaned into my touch. "If we do this, I think I need to make a trip on your first weekend in the city."

She shot her eyes open. "Wait? Really?"

"Someone has to teach the South Carolinian the New York subway system. I can't have you standing on the left."

Her eyebrows furrowed, but the intrigue never dimmed from her eyes. "What does that even mean?"

"My point exactly. And do you know how to get a taxi?"

"Isn't that what Uber and Lyft are for?"

"You can't live in the city without at least hailing a taxi. You aren't allowed the ride sharing services until you graduate from taxi hailing first. It's a rule. Also, in New York, it's soda, not Coke. Time to adapt to our rules."

"But what if your rules are wrong?"

"They're not, trust me, and you don't want to test a New Yorker. They're scary. Oh, and pizza. We need to introduce you to New Haven pizza. If we need a trip away from the city, my mom's house is halfway between us, and I can talk to you about the New

Haven pizza rivalry. Don't worry, it's a friendly one, but I'll need your thoughts on both of the pizzas at stake."

"What about the sky? There aren't any stars in New York City."

"No, but there are skyscrapers. It half makes up for the lack of stars. We can just go on the observation deck of the Empire State Building and look at the stars on the ground. All the buildings and the city flickering around us. It won't be the Milky Way on Hunting Island, but it will be a different kind of beautiful."

"I really like the sound of all of this. You'll really come that weekend?"

I grazed her soft cheek with my thumb and was so relieved to touch her again. The feelings piling in me became overwhelming, and I had to kiss her. Our lips met in a gentle and simple reacquaintance, and at first, we moved over each other's lips with hesitancy. I could feel her heartbreak, her relief, and the last three silent months on her lips at the same time I could feel our summer stitching up and healing, a burst of light to make up for the darkness.

When I pulled away, I rested my forehead against hers. "I promise. I have to give my girlfriend a proper welcome."

She looked at me the way she used to all summer. "I'm your girlfriend?"

"I really hope so."

She leaned in slowly, enough time to watch her eyes close and her smile curl in anticipation. Her lips landed on me so softly, like we were having our first kiss all over again, and maybe we were. The first time everything was out in the open, no secrets buried in the sand, the first time we had the world at our fingertips, the first time as girlfriends.

I couldn't believe it. I had a girlfriend.

Our kiss was simple and gentle but still told so much. I didn't know how starved I was for her until our patterns became synced, the same rhythms I'd danced to during the humid summer nights. It only lasted a few moments but long enough that it formed an unspoken promise. The excitement swirled inside me. While everyone else would mope about going back to school after the two-week Christmas break and starting yet another semester, I got to look forward to my girlfriend moving to the big city, her first taste of life beyond Gaslight Shores. She'd upgrade from slocals, golfies, and chummers to stereotypical people of each borough, upgrade from driving her old Corolla to learning all about the subway and never standing on the left, and upgrade from making po'boys to learning everything she'd ever wanted to learn about cuisine.

She would be a simple bus ride away. We had so much ahead of us.

"I'm here until Sunday, you know," I said. "Maybe we can have another stargazing date? Like in Serena's backyard? The stars are great over there, and we can have a firepit too, cuddle under some blankets?"

She scooted closer and left no more room for any silence to squeeze between us. She hooked her arm around mine and rested her chin on my shoulder like she'd done countless times before. "That sounds wonderful."

"That way, I can properly introduce you as my girlfriend."

She leaned in to give me another soft kiss on the lips, one that lingered and pulled as much from me as the one before. A wide grin spread across her face. I loved how anytime I kissed her, that same smile curved her freshly kissed lips. The way she smiled at me like that had my insides on overdrive. I bit my lip, trying to hide the beam that wanted to take hold of my mouth.

Our summer was infinite again.

"So you'll watch the sky with me on Friday? Solidify this relationship with a night under the stars?"

Her smile grew, and even though she'd flashed me that beautiful smile countless times before, this one felt more special. It was all mine again. "I'll always watch the sky with you, Remi Brenner. Even when you're in it."

EPILOGUE

14 years later

"Babe. Can you see me?"

"Yes. I can see you," Harper said, her wide, beautiful smile taking over my computer screen. The connection was a little spotty, and she froze for a few seconds, but it gave me time to absorb all the beauty that came with it, the same face that I'd fallen in love with years ago. Now that I was two hundred and fifty-four miles away from her for the next five months, I found myself falling in love with her all over again.

She picked up her computer and walked through our kitchen out to our backyard. I missed the smell of her and our home and how the kitchen would have started collecting the smells of Harper's weekend baking. I could almost smell them from my sleeping quarters.

She lay on one of our lawn chairs, and the lights from inside the house illuminated her face. My sleeping quarters were the size of a shower stall, enough room for a sleeping bag to keep me warm, a few personal items, and two computers mounted to the wall. But having her face take over one of those computers was the best sight of all.

"The sunset was nice, wasn't it?" I asked.

Earlier, I'd caught one of the sixteen sunrises and sunsets the International Space Station experienced in a day from the Cupola, the dome of seven windows that had an amazing view of Earth.

Whenever I had downtime, I always made sure I visited the Cupola. I'd been up in the ISS for a month, and the view still wasn't old, especially when I saw North America peeking through the clouds, and my heart swelled thinking about my wife and my parents and stepparents down below. I had been able to sneak in an email to Harper, letting her know that she was in for a great sunset. In reality, I had no idea if that was true for Clear Lake, Texas, but it gave me a reason to email her. Emailing was basically texting on the ISS, and we emailed each other several times a day. I made sure she woke up to a good morning email with a picture of my view from the Cupola, and then I wished her good night on our daily evening video calls. I had another five months on the ISS, and despite loving every second of it, I still missed my wife. We hadn't been away from each other this long since college.

I was thankful for the advancement in technology over the years that allowed me to see her every night, and we timed our calls for when the ISS flew over North America. While her face took over my left computer screen, I was able to watch the map program on my right screen and the little dot that represented the ISS inching closer to Southeast Texas the longer we spoke.

"It was," Harper said. "Pink and orange clouds, and now the sky is clear, all ready for you to fly over. In the meantime, what did you have for dinner?"

It was always the first question she asked on our evenings calls because she still couldn't get over our freeze-dried food.

"Pizza and then strawberry shortcake for dessert with butter cookies, strawberries, and a little bit of milk. It was almost as good as the French-style strawberry shortcake we had in Paris. Remember that?"

It had been the summer right after I'd graduated from MIT. Harper had spent her last semester abroad in Paris, and since I had already graduated and had three months of freedom before I started my NASA internship in the fall, I'd gone with her. It had been the second-best summer we'd ever had. It was the first time we had lived together, and waking up and falling asleep next to her made me realize I wanted to spend the rest of my life with her.

We had tried all the French desserts in those three months, and Harper had attempted to make everything we tasted. I hadn't even cared that a lot of them were trial and error. My stomach had been so happy, even when Harper had declared her first ten batches of macarons failures. They weren't to me. Failing wasn't studying abroad in Paris like she'd wanted to do since she was a kid. Even if it took until her eleventh batch to get the macarons right, she had always been on the right path.

"Of course I remember that," Harper said. "All I wanted to eat was a French-style strawberry shortcake, and I was so upset that I ruined it. So you walked to the nearest bakery so I could still eat one."

"And while you ate the store-bought one, I ate yours, and it tasted perfectly fine to me. But it doesn't matter anymore because you have your own bakery now. I'm married to a baker who makes the *best* macarons. Ranked the best in Houston, even, so they said last year."

"I'm sorry to break the news to you, love, but none of that compares to my wife. She's an astronaut, you know?"

I feigned shock. "Is she really?"

Harper nodded. "She is. The youngest in her astronaut class too and currently up in the sky about to fly over me. I'm so proud. She's only a speck in the sky, but she's my favorite speck. The best speck. Far superior to Betelgeuse."

Somehow, Harper still had the power to make me swoon over and over again, like she had the first summer we'd met, like she'd continued to do every summer during college in Gaslight Shores, to the summer we'd spent in Paris, to the one after that when I'd proposed on Hunting Island, and instead of giving her a quartz necklace, that time, I gave her a rose quartz ring. Just like how she made me swoon every day since.

"Wait...I see it. Oh my God, I see you!"

I looked at my right monitor, and sure enough, we were right over Southeast Texas. Although I had no windows in my sleeping quarters, I didn't need one to watch the ecstatic smile claim her entire face. She had so many different types of smiles, but my favorite one was when she looked skyward and saw the ISS crawl across her view. It was so raw and beautiful, and I was the luckiest to have it dedicated to me.

"I wish I could tell you to slow down," she said. "I want to take you in for more than just four minutes. I miss you."

I clutched my quartz necklace, and with her eyes peeled above, she did the same. The necklaces I'd bought when I was eighteen still hung around both our necks with updated chains. We hadn't taken them off since we'd gotten back together that Thanksgiving. Our accessories had evolved over the course of our relationship, and now both of us wore rose quartz rings on our left fingers too, but we couldn't let go of our necklaces. Deep down, I'd known when I gave it to her that our summer would be infinite. It was when my life had clicked into place, when my heart had become rooted in Harper and Gaslight Shores. That was where we'd fallen in love, where we'd gotten engaged, where we'd had our wedding. Fourteen years later and two hundred and fifty-four miles in between, our summer continued to play out as I watched her eyes sparkling in the dim lighting, her eyes on the sky, on me, like they had been all throughout that first summer.

"I love you to Betelgeuse and back, babe. You know that?"

She pulled her gaze off the sky and back to her computer, and when she pressed her lips together in a closed mouth smile, crinkles in the corner of her eyes, she still found a way to make my stomach twirl. "I've known that since we were eighteen, but it still never gets old."

About the Author

Morgan Lee Miller started writing at the age of five in the suburbs of Cleveland, Ohio, where she entertained herself by composing her first few novels all by hand. She majored in journalism and creative writing at Grand Valley State University.

When she's not introverting and writing, Morgan works for an animal welfare nonprofit and tries to make the world a slightly better place. She previously worked for an LGBT rights organization.

She currently resides in Washington, DC, with her two feline children, whom she's unapologetically obsessed with.

Books Available from Bold Strokes Books

A Fairer Tomorrow by Kathleen Knowles. For Maddie Weeks and Gerry Stern, the Second World War brought them together, but the end of the war might rip them apart. (978-1-63555-874-6)

Holiday Hearts by Diana Day-Admire and Lyn Cole. Opposites attract during Christmastime chaos in Kansas City. (978-1-63679-128-9)

Changing Majors by Ana Hartnett Reichardt. Beyond a love, beyond a coming-out, Bailey Sullivan discovers what lies beyond the shame and self-doubt imposed on her by traditional Southern ideals. (978-1-63679-081-7)

Fresh Grave in Grand Canyon by Lee Patton. The age-old Grand Canyon becomes more and more ominous as a group of volunteers fight to survive alone in nature and uncover a murderer among them. (978-1-63679-047-3)

Highland Whirl by Anna Larner. Opposites attract in the Scottish Highlands, when feisty Alice Campbell falls for city-girl-about-town Roxanne Barns. (978-1-63555-892-0)

Humbug by Amanda Radley. With the corporate Christmas party in jeopardy, CEO Rosalind Caldwell hires Christmas Girl Ellie Pearce as her personal assistant. The only problem is, Ellie isn't a PA, has never planned a party, and develops a ridiculous crush on her totally intimidating new boss. (978-1-63555-965-1)

On the Rocks by Georgia Beers. Schoolteacher Vanessa Martini makes no apologies for her dating checklist, and newly single mom Grace Chapman ticks all Vanessa's Do Not Date boxes. Of course, they're never going to fall in love. (978-1-63555-989-7)

Song of Serenity by Brey Willows. Arguing with the muse of music and justice is complicated, falling in love with her even more so. (978-1-63679-015-2)

The Christmas Proposal by Lisa Moreau. Stranded together in a Christmas village on a snowy mountain, Grace and Bridget face their past and question their dreams for the future. (978-1-63555-648-3)

The Infinite Summer by Morgan Lee Miller. While spending the summer with her dad in a small beach town, Remi Brenner falls for Harper Hebert and accidentally finds herself tangled up in an intense restaurant rivalry between her famous stepmom and her first love. (978-1-63555-969-9)

Wisdom by Jesse J. Thoma. When Sophia and Reggie are chosen for the governor's new community design team and tasked with tackling substance abuse and mental health issues, battle lines are drawn even as sparks fly. (978-1-63555-886-9)

A Convenient Arrangement by Aurora Rey and Jaime Clevenger. Cuffing season has come for lesbians, and for Jess Archer and Cody Dawson, their convenient arrangement becomes anything but. (978-1-63555-818-0)

An Alaskan Wedding by Nance Sparks. The last thing either Andrea or Riley expects is to bump into the one who broke her heart fifteen years ago, but when they meet at the welcome party, their feelings come rushing back. (978-1-63679-053-4)

Beulah Lodge by Cathy Dunnell. It's 1874, and newly engaged Ruth Mallowes is set on marriage and life as a missionary…until she falls in love with the housemaid at Beulah Lodge. (978-1-63679-007-7)

Gia's Gems by Toni Logan. When Lindsey Speyer discovers that popular travel columnist Gia Williams is a complete fake and threatens to expose her, blackmail has never been so sexy. (978-1-63555-917-0)

Holiday Wishes & Mistletoe Kisses by M. Ullrich. Four holidays, four couples, four chances to make their wishes come true. (978-1-63555-760-2)

Love By Proxy by Dena Blake. Tess has a secret crush on her best friend, Sophie, so the last thing she wants is to help Sophie fall in love with someone else, but how can she stand in the way of her happiness? (978-1-63555-973-6)

Loyalty, Love, & Vermouth by Eric Peterson. A comic valentine to a gay man's family of choice, including the ones with cold noses and four paws. (978-1-63555-997-2)

Marry Me by Melissa Brayden. Allison Hale attempts to plan the wedding of the century to a man who could save her family's business, if only she wasn't falling for her wedding planner, Megan Kinkaid. (978-1-63555-932-3)

Pathway to Love by Radclyffe. Courtney Valentine is looking for a woman exactly like Ben—smart, sexy, and not in the market for anything serious. All she has to do is convince Ben that sex-without-strings is the perfect pathway to pleasure. (978-1-63679-110-4)

Sweet Surprise by Jenny Frame. Flora and Mac never thought they'd ever see each other again, but when Mac opens up her barber shop right next to Flora's sweet shop, their connection comes roaring back. (978-1-63679-001-5)

The Edge of Yesterday by CJ Birch. Easton Gray is sent from the future to save humanity from technological disaster. When she's forced to target the woman she's falling in love with, can Easton do what's needed to save humanity? (978-1-63679-025-1)

The Scout and the Scoundrel by Barbara Ann Wright. With unexpected danger surrounding them, Zara and Roni are stuck between duty and survival, with little room for exploring their feelings, especially love. (978-1-63555-978-1)

Bury Me in Shadows by Greg Herren. College student Jake Chapman is forced to spend the summer at his dying grandmother's home and soon finds danger from long-buried family secrets. (978-1-63555-993-4)

Can't Leave Love by Kimberly Cooper Griffin. Sophia and Pru have no intention of falling in love, but sometimes love happens when and where you least expect it. (978-1-636790041-1)

Free Fall at Angel Creek by Julie Tizard. Detective Dee Rawlings and aircraft accident investigator Dr. River Dawson use conflicting methods to find answers when a plane goes missing, while overcoming surprising threats, and discovering an unlikely chance at love. (978-1-63555-884-5)

Love's Compromise by Cass Sellars. For Piper Holthaus and Brook Myers, will professional dreams and past baggage stop two hearts from realizing they are meant for each other? (978-1-63555-942-2)

Not All a Dream by Sophia Kell Hagin. Hester has lost the woman she loved and the world has descended into relentless dark and cold. But giving up will have to wait when she stumbles upon people who help her survive. (978-1-63679-067-1)

Protecting the Lady by Amanda Radley. If Eve Webb had known she'd be protecting royalty, she'd never have taken the job as bodyguard, but as the threat to Lady Katherine's life draws closer, she'll do whatever it takes to save her, and may just lose her heart in the process. (978-1-63679-003-9)

The Secrets of Willowra by Kadyan. A family saga of three women, their homestead called Willowra in the Australian outback, and the secrets that link them all. (978-1-63679-064-0)

Trial by Fire by Carsen Taite. When prosecutor Lennox Roy and public defender Wren Bishop become fierce adversaries in a headline-grabbing arson case, their attraction ignites a passion that leads them both to question their assumptions about the law, the truth, and each other. (978-1-63555-860-9)

Turbulent Waves by Ali Vali. Kai Merlin and Vivien Palmer plan their future together as hostile forces make their own plans to destroy what they have, as well as all those they love. (978-1-63679-011-4)

Unbreakable by Cari Hunter. When Dr. Grace Kendal is forced at gunpoint to help an injured woman, she is dragged into a nightmare where nothing is quite as it seems, and their lives aren't the only ones on the line. (978-1-63555-961-3)

Veterinary Surgeon by Nancy Wheelton. When dangerous drugs are stolen from the veterinary clinic, Mitch investigates and Kay becomes a suspect. As pride and professions clash, love seems impossible. (978-1-63679-043-5)

A Different Man by Andrew L. Huerta. This diverse collection of stories chronicling the challenges of gay life at various ages shines a light on the progress made and the progress still to come. (978-1-63555-977-4)

All That Remains by Sheri Lewis Wohl. Johnnie and Shantel might have to risk their lives—and their love—to stop a werewolf intent on killing. (978-1-63555-949-1)

Beginner's Bet by Fiona Riley. Phenom luxury Realtor Ellison Gamble has everything, except a family to share it with, so when a mix-up brings youthful Katie Crawford into her life, she bets the house on love. (978-1-63555-733-6)

Dangerous Without You by Lexus Grey. Throughout their senior year in high school, Aspen, Remington, Denna, and Raleigh face challenges in life and romance that they never expect. (978-1-63555-947-7)

Desiring More by Raven Sky. In this collection of steamy stories, a rich variety of lovers find themselves desiring more, more from a lover, more from themselves, and more from life. (978-1-63679-037-4)

Jordan's Kiss by Nanisi Barrett D'Arnuck. After losing everything in a fire, Jordan Phelps joins a small lounge band and meets pianist Morgan Sparks, who lights another blaze, this time in Jordan's heart. (978-1-63555-980-4)

Late City Summer by Jeanette Bears. Forced together for her wedding, Emily Stanton and Kate Alessi navigate their lingering passion for one another against the backdrop of New York City and World War II, and a summer romance they left behind. (978-1-63555-968-2)

Love and Lotus Blossoms by Anne Shade. On her path to self-acceptance and true passion, Janesse will risk everything—and possibly everyone—she loves. (978-1-63555-985-9)

Love in the Limelight by Ashley Moore. Marion Hargreaves, the finest actress of her generation, and Jessica Carmichael, the world's biggest pop star, rediscover each other twenty years after an ill-fated affair. (978-1-63679-051-0)

Suspecting Her by Mary P. Burns. Complications ensue when Erin O'Connor falls for top real estate saleswoman Catherine Williams while investigating racism in the real estate industry; the fallout could end their chance at happiness. (978-1-63555-960-6)

Two Winters by Lauren Emily Whalen. A modern YA retelling of Shakespeare's *The Winter's Tale* about birth, death, Catholic school, improv comedy, and the healing nature of time. (978-1-63679-019-0)

Busy Ain't the Half of It by Frederick Smith and Chaz Lamar Cruz. Elijah and Justin seek happily-ever-afters in LA, but are they too busy to notice happiness when it's there? (978-1-63555-944-6)

Calumet by Ali Vali. Jaxon Lavigne and Iris Long had a forbidden small-town romance that didn't last, and the consequences of that love will be uncovered fifteen years later at their high school reunion. (978-1-63555-900-2)

Her Countess to Cherish by Jane Walsh. London Society's material girl realizes there is more to life than diamonds when she falls in love with a non-binary bluestocking. (978-1-63555-902-6)

Hot Days, Heated Nights by Renee Roman. When Cole and Lee meet, instant attraction quickly flares into uncontrollable passion, but their connection might be short lived as Lee's identity is tied to her life in the city. (978-1-63555-888-3)

Never Be the Same by MA Binfield. Casey meets Olivia and sparks fly in this opposites attract romance that proves love can be found in the unlikeliest places. (978-1-63555-938-5)

Quiet Village by Eden Darry. Something not quite human is stalking Collie and her niece, and she'll be forced to work with undercover reporter Emily Lassiter if they want to get out of Hyam alive. (978-1-63555-898-2)

Shaken or Stirred by Georgia Beers. Bar owner Julia Martini and home health aide Savannah McNally attempt to weather the storms brought on by a mysterious blogger trashing the bar, family feuds they knew nothing about, and way too much advice from way too many relatives. (978-1-63555-928-6)

The Fiend in the Fog by Jess Faraday. Can four people on different trajectories work together to save the vulnerable residents of East London from the terrifying fiend in the fog before it's too late? (978-1-63555-514-1)

The Marriage Masquerade by Toni Logan. A no strings attached marriage scheme to inherit a Maui B&B uncovers unexpected attractions and a dark family secret. (978-1-63555-914-9)